A DUKE'S DELIGHT

As the waltz began, Avanoll tightened his hold, shortening the distance between them to a still proper but more intimate degree, and his nostrils caught the light flowery scent of her newly washed hair. Tansy had never been in such close proximity to a man before and was finding the experience quite heady.

With Tansy's form gently but firmly in his control, he swept them into a series of turns that billowed out her muslin skirts and brought a smile of pure enjoyment to her face. Round and round the floor they glided, their eyes locked together as their bodies moved as if in silent communion.

It had been several seconds before the dancers noticed the lack of musical accompaniment. Once awareness set in they halted suddenly in the center of the floor and Tansy reluctantly made to move away, but Avanoll's grip tightened and he drew her still closer. She could see the question in his blue eyes as his head slowly moved towards her. . . .

Avon Books are available at special quantity discounts for bulk purchases for sales promotions, premiums, fund raising or educational use. Special books, or book excerpts, can also be created to fit specific needs.

For details write or telephone the office of the Director of Special Markets, Avon Books, Dept. FP, 1790 Broadway, New York, New York 10019, 212-399-1357. *IN CANADA:* Director of Special Sales, Avon Books of Canada, Suite 210, 2061 McCowan Rd., Scarborough, Ontario M1S 3Y6, 416-293-9404.

THE TENACIOUS MISS TAMERLANE

KASEY MICHAELS

AVON
PUBLISHERS OF BARD, CAMELOT, DISCUS AND FLARE BOOKS

THE TENACIOUS MISS TAMERLANE is an original publication of Avon Books. This work has never before appeared in book form.

AVON BOOKS
A division of
The Hearst Corporation
1790 Broadway
New York, New York 10019

First Avon Printing, April 1982

AVON TRADEMARK REG. U. S. PAT. OFF. AND IN
OTHER COUNTRIES, MARCA REGISTRADA, HECHO EN
U. S. A.

Printed in the U.S.A.

WFH 10 9 8 7 6 5 4 3 2

To my mother,
who believed

Chapter One

IT WAS a typical day for late March, a bit chilly, but tolerable for travel if one had an adequate cloak and a closed conveyance. The female urging her ancient, broken-in-the-wind steed to abandon his plodding walk along the North Road for at least a half-hearted trot had neither. She was aware she was beating a dead horse—well, *nearly*—but the traveler was feeling decidedly chilly.

"Come on, old fella," she bullied the horse, "surely you can do better than this. For a blacksmith's rental, you make a sorry advertisement for his establishment. You represent your employer as well as your own kind, you know, yet I dare say I saw a tortoise flash past us some two miles back. Have you no pride?" Other than by a twitch of his left ear, there was no response from the un-proud beast.

"I should never have agreed to be governess for the Squire's brats," she told herself aloud for the hundredth time, "if I had not been so desperate. Tare an' 'ounds, I bet they send me off to a cold garret next to a drafty schoolroom, without so much as a crust of bread or dish of tea. Oh, I'm cold, I'm tired, I'm filthy, I'm hungry, and this blasted gig is giving me splinters enough to have me eating my mutton from the mantelpiece for the next fortnight."

Poor, poor Miss Tansy Tamerlane (for that was her name) was obviously not too well pleased with her current lot in life, as indeed she had every right not to be, for she had not been born to penury and service. In fact, six and twenty years before—when Tansy's premature, rather puny self had first been brought kicking and squalling into this world to become the only child of Sir Andrew Tamerlane and his scatterbrained wife, Phoebe—her arrival could only be termed "well cushioned."

When she not only refused to expire, as many babes breeched

7

too soon often did, but steadfastly grew in size and strength every day, her Mama—who one would think would do more for the only child of her bosom—cursed her with the absurd appellation of Tansy, which she had heard meant "tenacious" and "persistent." Sir Andrew tried to point out that it was only a short hop from tenacious to stubborn, but his wife would have none of it.

Tansy's life on a small country estate was much like that of any young girl born to genteel, moderately wealthy parents until her Mama obediently succumbed to a trifling summer cold when Tansy was just ten years old. Her education was evermore left in the hands of a parent who directed his grief into bouts of drink and gambling for high stakes, which is the same as to say Tansy's education—at least at ladylike pursuits—ended when Mama did.

The girl now traveling the North Road to her fourth place of employment in less than two years knew nothing of French or Italian—indeed, knew just enough of the King's own English to get by—and most of that was not fit for a proper lady. She could not play upon the pianoforte or harp, sew a fine seam, or sing so much as a note. These deficits, plus a strong tendency to speak her mind, had made for her abrupt departure from her last three posts as governess, and explained her readiness to accept employment bear-leading Squire Lindley's four milkpudding-faced offspring.

If only she had been born a man! Perhaps then she could have halted, rather than simply delayed (by means of stringent housekeeping), the inevitable erosion of the Tamerlane wealth that ended with Sir Andrew's creditors cutting up the estate piecemeal after his death. As it was, her only legacies were a superior riding ability, a cool hand and clear head while up behind a spirited pair, a mind crammed with the name of every Newmarket winner of any moment (as well as the leading fists, their matches, and opponents), the location of the best fishing waters within fifty miles of her former home, and even the right to claim the Tamerlane Precision Fishing Lure as her own invention. She could also load and fire handguns and fowling pieces better than most men and—when pushed into losing her none-too-serene temper—could spout oaths with the best of them.

On the other hand, Tansy could not dance at all (not a step), did not know how to curtsy to a lord, would undoubtedly use the wrong fork on a lobster (a delicacy she had never seen, let

8

alone tasted), and had never mastered the blush, the simper, or, alas, the giggle. It was no wonder, then, that she remained unmarried and, if not firmly on the shelf, definitely at her last prayers, as her hired horse slowly covered the remaining miles to the Squire's abode.

She gave another flick to the ribbons. "Get up there Dobbin— or Horace, or whatever your blasted name is," she urged once more. "There'll be a nice bag of oats for you at the end of the ride." It wouldn't do to tell him he'd probably only get straw, and that moldy and damp. Dobbin, or Horace, perked up his droopy ears this time and broke into his own version of a trot for a few yards, then lapsed once more into what seemed his *forte*— the slow plod.

According to the blacksmith's scanty directions, the turnoff for the Squire's should be just around the next bend of the road. After a day and a night on the Mail, the tired traveler was anxious to arrive, no matter how thin her welcome. She thanked her lucky stars (or at least the single one she thought even she was allotted) that there was little traffic at this dinner hour. Constant trips to the side of the road to let other travelers by would have quite deflated her spirits, as well as delayed her arrival to the wee hours of the morning.

Just as Tansy was buoying her flagging spirits with this bit of uplifting thought, a sporting curricle sprang up behind her as if conjured out of Merlin's magic hat.

"Hey you, woman," came the loud call. "Haul that rig and that piece of offal pulling it to one side and let your betters pass." A swift look over her shoulder told Tansy she was in immediate danger of overturning as a pair of showy greys edged out from behind her, threatening to pass at the very beginning of the bend.

Horace—or was it Dobbin?—either could not or would not move his old bones to one side fast enough, no matter how much (or because) he was insulted. His driver took the only alternative and hauled mightily on the reins. The horse obediently (and thankfully) came to a halt, allowing the other equipage to pull in directly in front of the gig. This move also allowed the curricle to narrowly avoid a collision with the Southbound Mail that appeared round the bend, stretching its sixteen-mile-an-hour steeds to their fullest on the suddenly overcrowded roadway.

The driver of the curricle sawed frantically on the reins as his high-strung pair took rightful exception to such cow-handed driving, and the off-wheel of the conveyance came abruptly in contact with a deep scar on the side of the road. In a twinkling the Mail was past, but the curricle was well and truly stuck.

Tansy was neither hysterical nor vaporish. "Good!" she stated simply. "If there is any justice in this world, all his spokes will have cracked. I shall never get this ancient beast moving again!" The nag, far from being hurt by the maligning words, began nibbling happily at a nearby bush with his few remaining teeth.

She took a moment to assess the occupants of the curricle, quickly inspecting and categorizing the driver as a ham-fisted young looby who was probably more used to squiring pretty bits around the Park, as befitted his showy but out-of-place curricle, and should leave any country driving to his coachman. She dismissed his reasons for being on this road as none of her business. Actually, Tansy didn't give two hoots about anything but moving on to her destination, on foot if necessary.

As the driver was fully occupied with his horses, she studied him again. Dobbin—or Horace—wouldn't move until he finished his snack anyway, she reasoned, and gave herself up to the contemplation of the driver, whose foppish dress and unproductive maneuvers with the reins only confirmed her opinion of his inability to either quiet his pair or extradite the curricle from the ditch. Her Papa would have horse-whipped him for mistreating his animals that way. So she would do also, but not being a man had its drawbacks. Tansy wouldn't even be on this cursed road if she were a man. "No, I'd be in the Fleet for Papa's debts," she chided herself before shouting, "Move your vehicle, sir! You are blocking my way!"

She got back a strangled curse for her pains as the man pulled viciously at his team's mouths in an effort to get them moving. Obviously not a Four Horse Club man she told herself dryly. Equally obvious was the fact that to leave the curricle where it stood on the curve of the road was courting disaster. She shrugged her shoulders. So what? It wasn't her problem.

But then the other occupant of the curricle, who had let out a single piercing scream (a screech, were it uttered by one of the lower classes), recovered her composure enough to ask baldly, "And now what, Godfrey? How do you propose to get us to Gretna now? Ashley will overtake us and All Will Be Lost! What a fine muddle this is! How could you be so stupid? *I* told you to hire a coach and driver. But did you listen? On, no. *You* did not. Why even a—"

"Oh, shut up," came the ungentlemanly reply that cut right

into his companion's speech, just as she was really getting into the spirit of the thing.

"Shut Up, is it, Godfrey!" It seemed the girl was not quite finished. "How *dare* you say such a thing to *me*, the sister of *a Duke?*" The girl also seemed to speak solely in exclamation points. "I begin to think our marriage is not such a good idea. Whoever heard of a *bridegroom* telling his *beloved* to *shut up!* No!" Her mind seemed made up. "Indeed, I will *not* marry you! I insist you unstick our wheel and turn this equipage about! I wish to return to London." Her voice had taken on tones of great, if somewhat high-pitched, dignity. "If you can manage to keep from landing us in any more ditches, we can be back to Grosvenor Square before dark."

Her *hauteur* was short-lived, for her betrothed was unimpressed. "Back to London is it, Emily? Not while there's breath left in my body. It's marriage you wanted, and it's marriage you'll by damn get." The leer on Godfrey's vacantly handsome face made him look like a sneering cherub.

"Oh!" said Lady Emily. And once again, *"Oh!"* Her pretty face crumpled for a moment, then brightened. Jumping lightly down from the curricle before her tarnished swain could pull her back, she ran up to the female sitting none too patiently in the gig. "You heard?" asked the younger girl without preamble.

Tansy nodded and took the opportunity to take a good look at the girl-woman called Lady Emily. She *was* a beauty. Her peaches-and-cream English complexion appeared all the more delicate, set as it was against startling deep blue eyes, while guinea-gold ringlets, looking soft as kitten fur, fuzzed closely around a small heart-shaped face. Her soft, pink mouth was slightly pouting but distracted nothing from the whole. Add to that a deep-blue traveling ensemble and matching bonnet, trimmed in warm sable fur that the female in the gig would have gladly traded her right arm for, and the picture Lady Emily presented was one of beauty, taste, and wealth. And youth. Extreme youth.

Suddenly Tansy felt older, dowdier, and even more sadly used than she had when her last employer informed her she was a complete failure at ladylike pursuits and would be better employed mucking out stables at a back country inn.

She felt one other emotion as she looked down at the young girl standing so regally in the dirty road. She felt protective— fiercely so. What harm is there in being kind, she thought. Besides, to leave now would be like turning one's back on a lost

11

infant. So convinced, she smiled gently at the girl. "I did indeed hear, Lady Emily. As your swain seems, er, *entrenched* with his own affairs at present, perhaps I can be of some assistance. If you will but come up here and hold the reins—whatever for I vow I'm not sure for Dobbin shall not wander off—I shall go retrieve what I am sure is your portmanteau from the back of the curricle. Perhaps then the two of us can continue down the road to my ultimate destination at Squire Lindley's, and you can send a message off to your, er, brother."

A single, huge tear found its way caressingly down one prettily flushed cheek as Lady Emily bobbed her head in enthusiastic consent. Her unlikely savior saw it and her protective feelings for Lady Emily mushroomed. Lady Emily wiped away the evidence of her prowess as a play actress and grinned impishly behind her hand as the female stomped off toward the curricle, and—suppressing the urge to clap her little hands in glee—contented herself with rocking back and forth on her high-heeled kid boots.

"Oh, yes, miss, *please,*" cried Lady Emily belatedly. "I should like that Above All Things!" As usual, she had found herself a champion and come out of a possibly fatal scandal with nary a scratch. Only an optimistic nature and a limited mentality could think so, while standing stranded in the middle of nowhere with an irate brother on her trail and night rapidly coming down. But then, what other person would have gone off on such a hey-go-mad start but a spoiled ninny-hammer like lovely Lady Emily?

She had still one teeny niggle-jot of sense in her largely vacant brain box that told her she had nearly done it this time. She had almost sunk herself beyond reproach but, once again, Fate had come to her aid—this time in the form of a tall, shabbily-dressed quiz who looked more like a governess than a knight in armor.

The female Galahad had, meanwhile, climbed stiffly down from the gig, resisted an ungenteel urge to rub at her stiff posterior, and advanced on the young man who was ruefully surveying his broken right wheel.

"Good day to you," Tansy began airily. "I am happy to tell you that Lady Emily has agreed to ride along with me to Squire Lindley's, which is just down the road. If you will please place her portmanteau in my gig, we shall be off. If you wish, you may join her there later. The Lady Emily intends sending a note to her brother, the Duke—directly she arrives at the Squire's, you understand. Or, if you wish, I could instead have a message sent to the nearest posting inn to have a vehicle brought to your aid and you may continue to your destination." She finished with a devilish grin that totally negated the picture of feminine innocence her words painted.

This rambling speech first baffled the gentleman, but one look at Tansy's satisfied smirk changed bafflement to anger. "She goes nowhere with you, my good woman," he retorted in crushing accents. "The lady is my affianced wife, and *I* and *I* alone am responsible for her protection."

"You are not!" came a shout from the gig. "I wouldn't cross the street with you, *Mr.* Harlow, *So There!*" Lady Emily remembered her pose of betrayed innocence then and re-frained—just in time—from poking her little pink tongue out at the so-recent great love of her life.

Mr. Harlow flushed deeply and bellowed back. "Emily, get down from there before—"

"Oh, cut line, you young booby. Don't you know when to call it a day? You've lost this prize, and out of your own mouth, no less. She'll not have you now if you was served up to her on a silver platter with an apple stuck in your jaws."

Godfrey wheeled at hearing this outlandish speech coming from a female mouth, and his own mouth dropped open in amazement.

Tansy was taking a chance addressing a gentleman so boldly while standing unprotected in the middle of an abandoned highway near twilight, but she had little fear of the masculine gender. Her native ability to quickly judge the character of her adversary had added further ginger to her words.

She was not disappointed. Mention of Emily's brother, the Duke, gave Mr. Harlow pause, and a slight shiver skipped down his spine like a stone skimmed across the calm waters of a stream. The wretched woman was right, damn her. Without a backward glance at Lady Emily, he alit from the curricle, unhitched his greys and mounted—with more haste than style— the nearest one. Only then did he turn in his seat and doff his curly-brimmed beaver to the two ladies.

He seemed to have regained his poise, if not his scruples— which could not have been very strong in the first place considering he was an admitted abductor of heiresses.

"Ta-ta, Emily, love," he called jauntily. "Give my regards to your *dear* brother. And you madam," he continued, looking down at his ex-love's champion, "I hear Cheltenham is tolerably well sprinkled with plump-in-the-purse cits who are at least one generation away from the smell of the shop. My thanks, good lady. Upon reflection on the *charms* of sweet Emily, I do believe you may have saved me from a sad end on the gallows. I probably would have murdered the chit within the month, were we really leg-shackled. Speaks like a Penny Dreadful, she does, and unceasingly. Her pretty face was to be some compensation. But then, it seems I remember that the most glorious of birds, the peacock, likewise sends up an awful screech each time it opens its beak."

"Farewell, Mr. Harlow," replied Tansy, who relented and gave a genuine smile of amusement at this brash young puppy. "Good luck to you. You are a very well set up young man, just flying a bit too high for safety—absconding with the sister of a Duke! Better set your sights on an only child next time—or better still, an orphan. Goodbye, Mr. Harlow."

The young man, down but far from out, blew an irreverent kiss to the eccentrically appealing woman standing in the middle of the North Road. Then he kicked at his horse's flanks and was off at once, bouncing down the road toward—he hoped and Tansy secretly seconded—a brighter future.

Chapter Two

TANSY WALKED back to the gig, her head shaking back and forth slightly and a chuckle escaping her lips. "A fine one you are," exclaimed Lady Emily with a definite pout. "It would almost seem as if *I* were the guilty party and Godfrey an innocent lamb. I was used, I tell you, *sadly used!*"

"Fiddlesticks," countered her companion without rancor. "You got just what you set out for—excitement—and a bit more than you bargained for, I'll wager. You never intended to wed that young scapegrace. Confess! You left an enlightening note, right where your unfortunate brother would see it and come charging posthaste to the rescue," Tansy concluded. And then, in a gentler voice, she inquired, "What's wrong, my dear? Are you sadly neglected by this brother of yours? Not in a material way, obviously, but does he sometimes need to be reminded you are no longer hidden in the nursery with your governess?"

That arrow hit home. Instead of condemning her unfeeling relatives, though—or even resorting to the already used ploy of tears produced-to-order—Lady Emily gave out with a delicious giggle. "Oh, you are so very quick! Aren't I beastly to have used poor Godfrey so shabbily?" she bubbled merrily.

"Utterly criminal I'd say," concurred Tansy. "But then, had I your face, title and money, I daresay I should be an even worse termagant than you could ever aspire to be. I have a decided talent for mischief, or so my poor harassed Papa used to say. It is such fun to be the center of all attention, is it not?"

"Oh, dear, it is a very good thing for me you are not my aunt. If Aunt Ce-Ce thought as you, I should never have any diversions."

"My dear Lady Emily, personal gratification aside, do you not think the time has passed for schoolroom pranks? You must be all of eighteen, and ready for your come-out. There comes a

15

time, sadly, when we must put away childish quirks and at least outwardly behave as Society dictates. Though we can certainly still *think* what we wish and occasionally—just to lend an air of intrigue to our countenance—indulge in the odd devilment." By now the portmanteau was safely in the back of the gig and Tansy had retaken her seat.

The younger girl's eyes fairly danced. "I am to be popped off, as Grandmama so vulgarly says, this Season. It is ever so exciting to think of, but all I have been doing for weeks on end, ever since I came to town, is standing for hours and hours being fitted for the ugliest gowns imaginable. It is all so very *fatiguing,* and I just had to do *something* or go *mad.* Aunt Ce-Ce has charge of my wardrobe, you see—Grandmama being too frail for such exertions—and Ce-Ce has the vilest taste. The *modiste* she favors is so hungry for our favors she agrees to every horrid ruffle and spouts ecstasies about the absolute *tons* of lace Ce-Ce thinks must smother everything I wear . . . And Ashley, the wretch, refuses to listen to my complaints at all!"

Lady Emily paused for breath, her emotions on this so-near-to-her-heart subject having brought a becoming flush to her cheeks.

"So when I met Godfrey at the library," she resumed, explaining a brand of logic that smacked of a mind that readily made five of two and two, "and again several times in the mornings at the park, I decided to, er, *use* him to remind Ashley of my existence. He does sometimes forget me for months on end, what with his clubs and hunting boxes, speeches in Parliament, and the managing of all the estates, and—oh!—and any other excuse he can find," she wailed, thus condemning the unimpeachable lifestyle of the Duke to the ranks of the pointlessly silly. "Ashley is my brother," she added somewhat unnecessarily.

Tansy was busy trying to get the gig moving again. "I don't think I follow you."

"Ashley—he's my brother," repeated Lady Emily.

"That, my dear nodcock, I comprehend," her new confidant replied dryly. "What I cannot fathom is why you have so little to say as to your style of dress, if we may pass over your brother's failings for the moment and fall back to the subject of flounces and *smothering* lace. The tedium of fittings, and the lack of social affairs for one who is not yet Out, I also understand—for I have worked for part of a Season for a Miss Buxley during her

16

come-out." A small smile appeared as she recalled her sudden departure from that particular position. "Please enlighten me as I try to raise Lazarus here from the dead so we can push off for the Squire's."

At that she yanked the dozing Dobbin—or Horace—to a semblance of attention and the old cob, his hooves fairly dragging with each step, set off at an even slower pace than before.

"The fact is," Lady Emily willingly explained, "my gowns are much the same as any now in the mode, I guess. There is just something, I cannot quite put my finger on it, but Something rather Overpowering about them. I feel quite dwarfed. There just seems to be so Much Gown and so Little Me! The only things I've liked at all are this outfit and one other, my riding habit. Grandmama picked both of them before informing Ashley that one more trip to Bond Street with 'that young prattlebox'— that's me," she admitted artlessly, "and she would surely be carried off by an apoplexy."

Tansy gave a chuckle and inwardly agreed with the old lady's opinion that young Lady Emily's roundabout method of speaking for five minutes to say what could have been said in less than half the time—and with less than half the drama—could be a bit wearing.

The turn to the right was in sight now, finally, and Tansy tried with little success to coax Dobbin from his straight and narrow path. Perhaps showing up on the Squire's doorstep with the sister of a Duke in tow would soften any censure on her late arrival, she thought with little hope.

Just then the thundering sounds of an approaching rider reached her ears and she turned on the plank seat for a view of what would probably be a prime bit of blood and bone. The turn forced yet another sharp bit of the seat through her thin gown and into her already tender posterior. "Damn," she swore soundly.

"Oh, drat, you are absolutely right," agreed Lady Emily, who had also swiveled about for a better look. "However did you know that is Ashley approaching?" she asked ingenuously.

"I didn't. I have just been impaled upon a splinter half the size of Cornwall, as nothing else as unpleasant comes to mind except the home of my last unlamented place of employment. As for your brother, we don't stand a prayer of outrunning him with old Fleetfoot in the shafts. If you were of a mind to bolt for cover, that might be a means of escape, although I think it would have gone easier for you to face him for the first time with the Squire to act as a restraint on his undoubtedly sorely-tried temper."

Lady Emily at once burst into noisy sobs (this time they were genuine) as her brother was riding like a man possessed, for once uncaring of his horseflesh. If she could have swooned without tumbling ignominiously into the road, she would have.

A confrontation with Ashley in these surroundings was sadly lacking the romance of standing out of harm's way while her brother vented his anger by loosening a few of Godfrey's front teeth. Nothing seemed to come right for poor Emily lately, nothing at all. She sniffled loudly and hiccupped.

"There, there, don't go blubbering," consoled her no-longer-so-capable-looking champion. "All will come right soon enough. Just let the poor man rant and rave until he's spent, then flash him those soulful blue eyes while you tearfully promise to be a pattern card of virtue forevermore. And don't let him see you crossing your fingers behind your back!"

Tansy gave out with an unnecessary "Whoa, boy," for the horse had already decided on a halt after spying some interesting-looking long grass left untouched through the winter, forcing the pursuing brother to control a plunging, dancing stallion reluctant to discontinue a fine gallop.

After easily controlling his horse, the rider cast his eyes coldly over the ill-assorted pair and their antiquated vehicle. After a cursory examination of his sister he riveted his cold stare on Tansy, noting the drab brownness of her garb, hair, and eyes. In his anger he overlooked the fine bone structure of her pleasantly arranged face. Tansy in her turn returned his gaze, noting the Duke's large, well-muscled frame, his dark-brown curls (now well-tumbled by his long ride), and the startling blue eyes that stood out so well in his sun-darkened face. "Emily," he fairly purred in his deep voice when at last—his eyes still on Tansy—he broke the tense silence. "I perceive I have found you unharmed. I can only hope I also find you unwed and, this I hope most fervently, *unbed!*"

Lady Emily blushed to advantage and did so now, although her companion never batted an eye at such plain speech. "Oh, yes, Ashley," the repentant sister assured him. "But I've had the most dreadful—ouch!" A well-placed elbow jabbed directly into the tender area below her ribs made Lady Emily break off with a gasp that turned discreetly into a cough and then, most intelligently, into silence. Her friend was right, for complaints from a captured truant could not fail to blacken to pitch the already dark scowl Ashley was aiming at his baby sister.

"Madam," the Duke—not failing to notice that less than discreet nudge—remarked, still with a velvety smoothness that went so ill with his dire expression, "I do not understand your presence at the scene any more than I can explain the absence of that young villain Harlow, but I do believe I have to thank you."

"You certainly do," came the equally velvet reply.

The Duke was surprised. He even allowed one well-defined brow to arch. "I beg your pardon?" he questioned, with the tone used by one just addressed by a drawing room chair.

"I merely agreed with you, your grace," was Tansy's direct reply. "You do have *me* to thank for your sister's rescue. However, you have only *yourself* to thank for her near ruin at the hands of a rake-hell fortune-hunter who, luckily for you, possessed all the foresight of a grasshopper. If Mr. Harlow were not a wet-behind-the-ears looby, your sister would be well and truly ruined by now."

"*I* am to blame, madam? I do not quite see your logic, or remember any invitation for commenting on *my* guardianship of *my* sister." The velvet now dripped icicles.

Another woman would have been sent searching in her reticule for her vinaigrette. But this definitely was a different sort of female. "My logic is simple," Tansy explained, as though speaking to a particularly backward child. "If you paid more attention to what is going on around you, you would know your sister to be bored to flinders and a lonely child into the bargain—not to mention green as grass and easy prey for any pretty face or agile tongue. I *dare* because, between your sister and yourself, the pair of you have delayed my arrival at my new post, erased any hope for the supper I had optimistically hoped to find there, and denied me the snug cot my bones ache for. I also *dare* because my eyes tell me that—although you doubtless think you cut a right dashing figure on horseback pelting pell-mell in the pursuit of an eloping sister—you neglected to provide transportation for said sister once you had performed your splendid feat of derring-do. I do not wish to push the point, but I daresay you made an error in judgement when you decided to opt for speed over common sense. A curricle or coach would have been more the thing. Now," she told him with a pained sigh, "it is left to poor Dobbin—or Horace, I doubt my lapse insults the beast—and me to transport your sister to the nearest posting inn. *That* is why I dare."

This sizzling set-down was wondrously admired, if prudently not applauded, by the incredulous Lady Emily who belatedly cringed at the thought of her brother's soon-to-be-expressed displeasure. What was obvious was that the brown lady in the gig was decidely warm, "madam" was.

In fact, it was not exaggerating to say Tansy was nearly overcome with righteous anger. How dare this high and mighty Duke condescend to her! Look down his nose at her!

Just a minute! Tansy halted herself in mid-tantrum. She looked more closely at the Duke. That nose. No. It couldn't be. "Are you by chance the Duke of Avanoll?" she asked suddenly—apropos, so thought the Duke, of nothing—and just as he was ready to deliver one of his famous scolds.

"I am," the Duke replied, surprised into answering this unwarranted question. It is true then, he observed to himself, what the old lady my grandmother says: breeding *will* out. Here I sit, calmly being railed at like a schoolboy remiss at his sums, when I should like nothing better than to take that obnoxious hellion over my knee and give her the thrashing her parents so obviously declined to dispense. Such forbearance on my part reflects quite noble breeding. Almost kinglike, he complimented himself. And why, putting all that aside, is this creature looking at me as if I have suddenly grown another head? "Is something amiss, madam, or have you come belatedly to your senses and in turn been struck dumb with shame over your outrageous behavior?"

Tansy waved this last statement aside with a slight motion of her hand. The hand then continued upward until it reached her forehead, where it rubbed wearily back and forth as she spoke once more. "Nathaniel has cocked up his toes then?" she said quietly, as if to herself.

But not quietly enough. "*I beg your pardon?*" The velvet ice became a howling blizzard.

"Oh, forgive me, I merely spoke my thoughts aloud," Tansy apologized. "Has he been dead long—the late Duke, that is?"

The Duke was still a bit nonplused and answered almost automatically. "A little over ten years." Then he had an idea that shook him to his socks. "But what, if I may be so bold, is that to the matter at hand?" He spoke more softly, almost gently. The woman was quite possibly deranged, an escapee from Bedlam.

He would have to report the woman at the next town. Why, at any moment the sick woman could turn violent and do bodily injury to his sister.

Tansy's head rose once more to look the Duke straight in the face. "I apologize for my outburst, your grace. My only excuse is that I am extremely fatigued. I have been traveling for two days and nights and the last of my funds disappeared at last night's inn on a meager dinner of bread and cheese. That must be why I did not recognize it at once."

"Recognize what, my dear young woman?" the Duke crooned warily. Now he was sure the woman was deranged. He made sly eye-shiftings and head-jerks in his vacantly smiling sister's direction, willing her to climb down from the gig. Lady Emily winked happily back at him, thinking herself part of some fine joke and her sins all forgiven. The Duke sighed. Emily was a pretty chit, he granted, but there wasn't a problem of over-crowding in her upper rooms.

Tansy spoke again. "Why, the nose, of course. How could I, of all people, have failed to immediately recognize the Benedict nose! It is my father's to the life. Horrid beaky thing, ain't it? Oh, excuse me. Of course you cannot know. You must think me daft—or worse. My name is Tamerlane. My great grandmother was a Benedict. Her daughter married a Tamerlane, and they produced my father who, in turn, produced me. Great grandmother Benedict was first cousin to your great grandfather. We are cousins," she ended unnecessarily.

"A bit distant, I must say," put in the Duke quellingly, exchanging the label of Bedlamite for the milder one of eccentric—but definitely quite reluctant to claim kinship with the girl.

"Distant enough to be almost nonexistent," she agreed cheerfully, "which is why I did not contact you upon my father's death two years ago. Or rather, why I did not contact your father. His was the last name entered in the family Bible. I did not know of your existence."

"Or I of yours, might I add," commented the Duke, still secretly feeling the niggling idea he was holding converse in the middle of the North Road at twilight with a madwoman. Well, perhaps not mad, but definitely ill-bred, he mentally decided.

Emily, who had taken in as much as her brain could without the benefit of constant repetition, added her bit to the bizarre conversation while clapping her kid-encased hands, "Oh, how famous! Ashley! Isn't it wonderful? We have a Brand New

Cousin. Well, not brand new, precisely. I imagine you have been around for some time." She halted abruptly, put her hand to her mouth and giggled. "Oh, that didn't come out just right, did it? I just mean you are new to *us*. And *I* have discovered you! Miss Tamerlane, you must come home with us to Grosvenor Square for a nice long visit, you Simply Must! I knew there was something special about you when you so masterfully put that hateful Godfrey to the right-about."

She grasped one of Miss Tamerlane's none-too-clean hands between her own two immaculately-gloved ones and turned rapturous china-blue eyes upon her brother. "I declare Ashley, it is *Fate!* Please say we can keep her, dear, *dear* Ashley," she pleaded—for all the world as if she were still a nursery tot begging to keep a scruffy, smelly, stray dog she had dragged home.

Chapter Three

THE DUKE OF AVANOLL was not ordinarily left at a loss for words. Indeed, many of his cronies would have gladly plunked down a hefty sum to be privileged to see this normally almost infuriatingly articulate man in his present state. He was utterly without a rejoinder. His mind, however, was tripping over itself in rapid thought—and not a single one of those thoughts appealed.

The gel was a positive quiz. Even seated as she was in the gig, he could see she would tower over every female he knew, although she would fall far short of his own greater-than-average height. Her clothes and hair were abominable, her speech perhaps unexceptional in a man but totally untenable in a lady of quality. She was rude, unmannered, and, in total, unacceptable to the Duke's mental picture of what any of his blood kin should be.

"I believe, Emily, my pet, that Miss Tamerlane said she was on her way to a new post," the Duke finally offered without any real hope he would be heeded.

"A *position!* Governess, no doubt. Ashley, how *can* you allow a Benedict to *hire* herself out like any Common Person?" Lady Emily fairly shrieked.

"If I may interject a moment?" Tansy began coolly. "First, I am barely a Benedict. I did not even get the nose—perhaps my one blessing. Secondly, I deeply resent being talked around and across as if I were a piece of goods on a store shelf. In my opinion—"

"Pish-tosh to your opinion, dear cousin," cut in Lady Emily. "You are like a lone ship in a storm-tossed sea, and none but your family should even be contemplated as a safe nesting place. Am I not correct, Ashley? We have A Duty, do we not?"

The duke opened his mouth, appeared about to speak, and

then folded his lips together in a thin line. He opened them once more and admitted his defeat. "Dear sister," he began, "your metaphor is mixed but, rest assured, your point has been made." He turned his eyes to Miss Tamerlane, manfully suppressing a wince, and added, "Miss Tamerlane, my home is at your disposal. It would give my sister and myself extreme, er, *pleasure* if you were to avail yourself of our hospitality for," he sighed, "as long as you wish."

"Your pleasure? Ha! In a cocked hat it is," Tansy returned with some heat. "You long for my presence the way your chef yearns for the sight of roaches in his pantry. Thank you for the gesture, all references to stormy seas and warm nests are greatly appreciated, but Tamerlanes do not sink to charity nor fly to nests lined with conscience-soothing featherdown reluctantly offered by almsgiving hypocrites who would rather wish me at the bottom of the ocean. One can drown so easily in the outpourings of pity, you know—besides finding so little warmth in the molting feathers that cloak all obligatory poor-relations."

When the import of these words was realized (at least in part) by Lady Emily, she started in again to snuffle. The Duke, who by rights should have felt the heavy mantle of familial obligation floating blissfully off his already burdened shoulders, was amazed to find himself irrationally incensed by this cavalier refusal of his largesse. Ignorant drab, he thought; heedless of the trap he was setting himself. Does she know she has just bailed out of one of the deepest gravy boats in all England? And how dare she flippantly snap her fingers at *me,* the head of the family and, worse yet, by her thoughtless cruelty reduce my poor baby sister, Emily, to tears?

Actually, poor Lady Emily, left to her own devices, would probably forget the girl in less time than it took to ride back to town. But who's to say she wouldn't take it into her head to pout, even go into a minor decline? Females could be touchy that way. Witness the dowager, for heavens sake!

"Fie, my good woman! Fie and foul!" the Duke blustered, as he had always supposed a head of family was called to do, for hadn't his pater always gotten his way by merely railing louder and longer than anyone else? "Look what you have done to my dear little sister." (Far be it from him to remark on any lowering blow to his own mighty Benedict pride.) "I did not believe a member of the gentle sex could be so cruel. To think you would so malign your kinswoman as harboring such self-serving

24

motives, when her golden pure heart was—and is still even after being forced to hear such calumnies—full of none but the milk of human kindness."

"Oh, give over, your grace," Tansy came back with a barely suppressed smile. "I cannot abide another muddled metaphor. You know as well as I that I regard this watering pot by my side as no less than the greatest of Samaritans. It is you I accuse of baser reasons for your half-hearted invitation to visit your establishment."

The Duke colored angrily. "If you think I have designs on your virtue, my good woman," and his voice was frosty as a winter morning, "let me cast your fears upon the winds." That should squash her, he congratulated himself.

But Tansy only laughed, a clear, bell-like tinkling laugh that got the Duke's hackles even more on edge, "I had hardly any fears of cousinly compromise, your grace," she retorted gaily. "My greatest fear is the belief you mean to make of me an ape leader-cum-warden to this young puss here, and so free yourself for your own selfish pursuits. Come now, *cousin,* make a clean breast of it. You see in me a golden opportunity to unload your frisky little filly into hands you think capable of holding her."

"Oh!" protested Lady Emily, much offended. "She is as bad as you, Ashley. As if I am either a feline or a horse! I have quite changed my mind. If *Miss Tamerlane* wants no part of us I think it unseemly to embarrass her or ourselves by begging."

Lady Emily did not know it, but her statement set the seal on the matter as far as his grace was concerned. Here indeed was just the chaperon he needed for his witless sister. Egad, that antidote would give even the most desperate fortune-hunter pause. The Duke felt a conspiratorial smile pass between himself and Miss Tamerlane. The lady obviously knew her own worth. To his amazement the exchanged smiles widened into shared grins, and the grins burst forth into laughter. Within moments the two adversaries were chortling with unholy glee.

Lady Emily, her histrionics totally ignored, lifted her face from her bone-dry handkerchief and looked from Tansy to her brother, dissolved over a joke she could not quite—thank heavens, or there would be the devil to pay—fathom. She refused to be shut out from any gaiety, and so half-heartedly chuckled along with them for a little while, until the effort of her forced laughter was overcome by the numbing cold penetrating her fashionable half-boots.

"Ashley," she pouted. "Ashley!" she cried again, whereupon the ridiculous laughter died raggedly away. "Are we to sit here all the afternoon? I begin to feel the chill."

His grace looked down at Miss Tamerlane, testing the tenuous rapport that had been established, and cocked one fine dark eyebrow. "Well, cousin?"

Tansy, finding herself the object of two sets of penetrating blue eyes, shrugged her shabby brown shoulders and surrendered to her—as Lady Emily termed it—*Fate*. She arched one sable-brown eyebrow in mimicry of his grace and said, "Lead on, MacDuff. We shall follow you with all deliberate speed. Which is to say we should make London by late December, I should think, if noble Dobbin's performance to date is to be used as a yardstick."

"We shall hire a vehicle in the village where you borrowed that sad beast—and I recollect his name as Horace, I believe. Perhaps you have insulted him. I have no wish to spend the next nine months completing a journey that should take no more than three hours. Turn his carcass if you can, cousin, and let us be off."

Tansy bowed to the inevitable. "Get going, Horace," she urged.

"Horace," the Duke moaned as the aged creature groaned himself into a laborious turn. "Why, in the name of all that's holy, would anyone—even a blacksmith—name a horse *Horace?*"

"Oh, not the blacksmith. I think that worthy dubbed our noble steed Dobbin," Tansy corrected as they inched their way back from whence they had come. "I renamed him Horace after a childhood pet of mine that also refused to heed my commands."

"A singularly intelligent creature, I would say. What was it? One of those repulsive little lap dogs with a pushed in phiz?"

"You insult me, sir. I would rather forego a pet than have one of those horrid little beasts about, forever yapping and becoming nervous all over the drawing room rugs. Perhaps owing to my own size I prefer large dogs. Large, romping, tongue-lolling, tail-wagging brutes who are invariably affectionate to a turn. Besides, Horace was not a dog. He was a goldfish." This last was delivered with a solemn face that could not conceal the twinkling of two russet-brown eyes.

His grace was not daunted. "And he did not heel? Poor specimen, I dare say."

Tansy agreed gravely. "Indeed, sir, you are so right. In the

26

end, I was forced to be content with the ordinary tricks: fetching a stick, catching a ball between his jaws, you know the sort, I'm sure."

This was too much, even for his grace. "Were you spanked often as a child, Miss Tamerlane?"

Speechless for a moment, Tansy merely shook her head.

"A pity. If you were mine I would have applied corporal punishment quite often, I believe."

"But then I believe I should have run off at a very young age if you were my parent," she returned triumphantly.

"And I would have had the housekeeper pack your portmanteau, and myself supplied a map to the Orient—not to mention enough of the ready to set you firmly on your way."

Tansy opened her mouth to retort and found she had for once been solidly trumped. "*Touché*," she said gaily and made a mock bow, sadly ungainly when done while sitting in a gig.

Lady Emily interposed at this time, reminding the foolishly giggling pair of idiots that she was chilled to the bone. Tansy urged the horse into a bone-crunching trot, leaving behind, and quite out of mind, the dining room of Squire Lindley's snug country house. The Squire's lady, still content in the delusion that her four squalling brats were to be taken off her hands by a penny-cheap governess, was at that moment gleefully biting into a fluffy, cream pastry.

Chapter Four

THE JOURNEY to Grosvenor Square was accomplished in four rather than three hours, due to Tansy's refusal to budge one inch from the posting inn until her gnawing hunger was put at ease. But as the crier was just calling out the hour of ten ("All's well and it's comin' on ta snow") the weary party ascended the imposing flight of steps to Avanoll's mansion.

Tansy could do little more than catch a glimpse of the imposing stucco exterior and delicate grille work lining the upper storeys before being almost shoved indoors, where her eyes were completely dazzled by the brilliant light emanating from the hundred candles that burned welcomingly in an immense crystal chandelier that seemed almost small in the huge foyer.

She roughly disengaged her elbow from the Duke's vice-like grip. "Unhand me, sir. If you are in such a pelter about being discovered with so poor a specimen as I entering your abode, I could have as easily trotted round to the tradesman's entrance. I have not been so roughly handled since the oldest son of my last employer sought to play slap-and-tickle in the herb garden."

"I'm surprised he had the nerve," his grace hissed. "And be still, you moron," he added, painfully aware of Dunstan the butler, three assorted footmen, and a housemaid—who had no business using the front stairs—looking (and listening) with great interest to every word that was being said. "It is not you but Emily I wished out of the light of that veritable beacon in front of the house. You would think the house was lighting the way for the long-awaited return of the prodigal! Tongues wag often enough in this snoop-nosed town without some dowager eyewitnessing Emily, who is not yet Out, stealing into the house after dusk."

As Tansy opened her mouth to apologize—not an easy thing

for her—he shut her off quickly by saying, "Let me get shed of these nosey-parkers, if I may, before we continue."

She bowed to his wisdom, not meekly, but merely acknowledging his request with a curt nod.

His grace dealt with the assembled servants quickly. A quelling glance to the footmen sent them scattering on suddenly-recalled errands belowstairs. The housemaid, praying fervently for the anonymity of a servant most masters never bothered to penetrate, had already fled of her own accord back the way she had come, and was already tripping down the dark back stairs.

Having satisfactorily disposed of the lower staff, his grace turned to address his butler. "Dunny," he commanded the stately grey-haired man, who had somehow come into the possession of three woolen capes—the last of which, being a particularly undistinguished brown article of indeterminate years, which he held at arm's-length and surveyed as if he were indeed clutching a particularly vile species of vermin, "Lady Emily desires a cold collation brought to her in her chambers. And have her maid sent to her immediately."

At this preemptory dismissal, Lady Emily pouted and made as if to protest, but was struck down in mid-whine by a look much like the one that had sent the footmen scurrying. With a toss of her fair curls and a halfhearted stamp of one small foot, she turned and began ascending the staircase. Midway she turned for one last entreaty.

"*Now,* miss, if you please," came a stern female voice, not to be denied. Lady Emily blinked, blushed, and knew herself bested by Tansy. She retired without another word.

"Well done," congratulated his grace.

Tansy turned from the sight of a bit too much maidenly ankle, exposed as Lady Emily flounced her way abovestairs, and addressed his grace. "Thank you. I have always found it best to begin as you plan to go on. Our roles are becoming established nicely, don't you think?"

"Quite," returned Avanoll, happily amazed. "But be warned: that was just the opening skirmish in what may well prove an epic battle. My dear sibling may not be very astute, but she is inventive and mischief is her middle name. Shall we adjourn to the drawing room and allow the footmen to resume their posts at the door? My undependable aunt is assuredly still out and about, regaling everyone she meets with the details of the debilitating disease that will probably keep her niece abed and secluded for several days."

29

"Was that your brainchild or hers?"

"Mine, more's the pity. She'll probably lay it on so thick and rare only a ninny will fail to scent a scandal. But we—and if I haven't thanked you I do so now—have shut the door on any rumor by fetching our fledgling home safe and dry. I suppose you think me cold-hearted or unbearably rude in not allowing you to retire along with my sister?" suggested his grace, as he motioned Tansy into a large room and directed her to a chair near the neat fire blazing in the hearth.

"On the contrary, sir. I find it entirely in character," replied Tansy as she ignored the gesture to stand in front of the fire, holding her chilled hands toward the heat. His grace, having half-descended into a facing chair, hastily rose once more so that he fairly bumped heads with his cousin.

He could see her discomfort and fatigue and his conscience twinged as he remembered her protestations of hunger and bone-deep weariness. But he felt deeply the need to get a few things settled before his aunt, who headed the increasingly long list of banes upon his suddenly blighted life, burst in on them and opened her proverb-spouting, epigram-quoting mouth. Five minutes with Aunt Lucinda would be sufficient to make even the redoubtable Miss Tamerlane lope off to parts unknown.

So instead of dismissing his cousin—who was making only a cursory effort to hide several wide yawns—he launched into a detailed description of her duties as concerned his sister.

As these duties seemed all directed toward the same end, Tansy cut in rudely, "I believe you have made yourself abundantly clear and can say no more without repeating yourself. I am correct, I believe, in surmising from your words, dressed up in fine linen as they are, that you merely mean I am to keep Lady Emily on a stout and short leash while giving her the impression she has been given her own head. I am to be an ape leader without, thank goodness, having to teach sums, globe-reading, water color sketching, or fine needlepoint. I daresay it sounds no easy task you have set me, but it is head and shoulders better than slaving over Squire Lindley's brats." She rose as if to quit the room but hesitated as Avanoll spoke again.

"You are correct as far as it goes, cousin, but there is more to it than that. Emily must be chaperoned at all times and that means you must be fitted out with, er," his eyes flitted unflatteringly over her present attire, "what I mean to say is that you will need a complete new wardrobe." As Tansy started to protest he cut into her objections with a stern voice. "Be sensible, Miss

Tamerlane. As our cousin it is only right we assist you if the cost of the thing is what has put you on your high ropes. Besides, to be frank, if that gown is any indication of your wardrobe—any argument you make to appear in Society in more of the same would be ludicrous."

Two high spots of color appeared on his cousin's cheeks, but she swallowed hard and bowed to the intelligence of his reasoning. Indeed, what she stood up in was more than representative of her wardrobe: it was the best thing in it. Her firm (some would say stubborn) chin came up and she asked if she could now retire. Any minute her stomach would set up a loud grumble and destroy her last shreds of dignity.

"I will detain you no longer than necessary, but there are one or two more items—"

"Yes, yes, I know. Your sister is a very open and confiding person." She held out her right hand and ticked off the items on her long, slim fingers as her cousin mentally added fine bone structure to the plus side of his list on the girl—a side heavily outweighed by the minus column. "One: your grandmother, the dowager Duchess. An intelligent old lady from what I could glean, who washed her hands of Lady Emily's come-out after their first foray to Bond Street. Two, and here I am not as clear: your aunt, the woman responsible for your sister's dislike of her wardrobe, and whose laxity, laziness, or gullibility, is no more a deterrent to Emily's high flights than a parlor table. *Now* may I please be excused, your grace?"

"If you would cease to interrupt me every time I open my mouth, we could bring this interview to an end in short order. I too have had a trying day," his grace pointed out uncharitably. "My grandmother, who as you say is a highly intelligent and rather sly old girl, resides for the moment in town, but has decided to return to Yorkshire by the end of the week. If you guard your manners and refrain from stable slang and boxing cant, we should scrape by with her with no problem. It is Aunt Lucinda, who I am forced to keep here for lack of any relative to ship her off to—none of my kin being so desperate for a live-in companion or so out of my favor as to have dear Lucinda foisted off on them—who presents the most delicate problem. She will be quite hipped to find herself replaced, you see."

Tansy cocked one well-defined brow. "A real clunker?"

The Duke allowed a small smile. "Widow of my cousin, Jerome Benedict. Old Jerry turned up his toes some six months ago, about a week after losing his last groat at the gaming tables.

It seemed logical at the time to have Lucinda companion Emily for the Season. She has been under my roof for the eternity of time that makes up the span since Jerry's funeral. I should have realized a simple loss of fortune wouldn't be enough to make my cousin cash it all in. Living with that widget, I'm surprised he lasted so long, but in the end I'm positive it was the enforced rustication with the woman that drove him to sticking his spoon in the wall. You see, she has this, let's see, how can I put this? You see, Aunt Lucinda harbors a predilection to, er, that is, she, um—"

Whatever the uncomfortable Duke was about to say was forestalled by unmistakable sounds of arrival in the foyer, and both pairs of eyes went at once to the door. Out of the corner of her mouth Tansy suggested teasingly, "Drinks a bit, Aunt Lucinda, does she?"

The corner of Avanoll's mouth lifted as he returned ruefully, "Would that she did. I'd keep her so well supplied she'd have no time left to pest me into following Jerry to my heavenly reward posthaste."

Tansy's visions of her cousin did not include a halo, but the image of him with horns, tail, and pitchfork caused her russet-brown eyes to dance in her head and a wicked grin to light her fine face with mischief.

So it was that the first sight Aunt Lucinda had of the young hoyden (or so was her first impression) she would later learn was to usurp her position as guardian to the innocent little lamb—just now regrettably misplaced—did not show the girl to advantage.

For the moment, however, the lady was not to be deterred from informing her honored relative and head of the family of her success at Lady Jersey's *soirée*—strange females in the house or nay.

Watery blue eyes disengaged contact with startled brown ones, and not by even so much as a nod did the former recognize the necessity of being presented to the disgustingly *high* female who was in the act of leaning down a bit to get a better sight of the tiny woman in voluminous crepe draperies.

The eyes slid to regard Avanoll, and when she was sure she had his attention she raised one pudgy beringed hand (half-covered by dripping lace) to her blonde, ringlet-festooned brow, sighed deeply, and tottered—weary from fighting the good fight—to the chair nearest the hearth (there were several closer to the near-swooning female, but these were not nearly so well padded).

Once comfortably seated, her three-tiered, ruffled skirts arranged decorously about her ankles, she announced in the tones of one badly used: "'It is easy to tell a lie, hard to tell but a lie.' Thomas Fuller."

Tansy sidled nearer the Duke and whispered, "I cannot doubt Emily and your aunt are not bosom beaus. *Two* tragedy queens in the same household? Insupportable! But tell me, who is this Fuller person?"

"A divine, from the seventeenth century, I believe," Avanoll informed her absently, then added, "kindly hold your tongue while I endeavor to sort this out."

With the air of one about to begin an oft-performed but never looked-for office, he approached his aunt, who was now fanning herself with a wisp of lace hankie.

"I take it, aunt, that you did set it about tonight that Emily is unwell." Although Avanoll was only bound to Lucinda as a cousin, he called her "Aunt" as a form of courtesy.

"'A liar is a bravo towards God and a coward towards men.' Lord Bacon," his aunt answered, nodding.

The Duke was heard to sigh. "You have my bravos, too, for what they are worth, Aunt. I take it, I dearly hope, that you have succeeded in convincing the harpies that Emily is the victim of a *temporary* indisposition. I would hate to think a plague notice will be nailed to our door in the morning in answer to your fervor."

Aunt Lucinda raised her eyes to the ceiling and bobbed her head, as if confirming with her Maker her belief that any blame to come out of this entire sordid affair would be placed firmly at her door—everyone forgetting the great strain on her nerves the Duke's instructions to spread a falsehood abroad would be to one of her sensibilities. "'Who spits against heaven,'" she warned the architect of the lie, "'it falls in his face.' Spanish Proverb."

Throughout this interchange Tansy had remained silent—though dumbfounded might have been a better description. But this last was too much. That absurd little woman, dressed like a wedding cake and reciting words of wisdom in her high, childish voice on one hand, and the Duke of Avanoll, overwhelmingly masculine in this dainty room and undeniably holding his temper only by an impressive display of rigid self-control, swam

33

before her mirthfully tearing eyes. Imagine, the Duke *spitting* up at heaven. Better still, imagine the inevitable result. Oh, her sides ached from trying to restrain chortles of laughter.

It was no use. She could not resist. Rising from her chair placed discreetly in the shadows she approached the adversaries—one glaring, the other simpering—to add her bit to the farce. She directed her words to the Duke: "'Let not thine hand be stretched out to receive and shut when thou shouldst repay.' Ecclesiasticus."

Aunt Lucinda's abused look vanished in a twinkling as she beamed up at her champion, who wasn't after all, *that* very tall. For if one was in need of a savior, she should be of more impressive figure than anyone of just average height.

As Tansy candidly returned the funny little woman's scrutiny, the Duke tried to make amends for insulting his aunt's well-meant attempt at subterfuge only to be interrupted—quite thankfully, if the truth be known, for he dearly hated apologizing to anyone, least of all an irksome widget like his aunt—when said widget pronounced in suitably awestruck tones: "'She appeared a true goddess in her wrath.' Virgil."

The unlikely goddess gave a slight curtsy and replied, "Not a goddess, I am sure, and I am at the moment anything but wrathful, but thank you for the compliment, dear lady."

"Yes, well," his grace interposed before this show of mutual admiration got out of hand, with questions still mainly unanswered. "Briefly, Aunt, briefly, *succinctly,* and to the point if you please, tell me if your mission tonight ended in success or failure. In short, is my sister's reputation intact?"

His aunt bristled slightly but condescended to reiterate: "'When I'm not thank'd enough, I've done my duty, and I've done no more.' Fielding."

As Tansy hid an appreciative smile at this sharp-as-a-saber-thrust retort, Avanoll strove for more clarification. "You kept it simple, I hope. And I will not have to explain away Emily's amazing recovery from, say, cholera, in the next few days?"

The insulted lady sprang up from her comfortable chair, tipped back her be-curled head the better to see this Doubting Thomas who refused to take her words (or a selection of other people's words) as the truth. "'It is not every question that deserves an answer.' Publilius Syrus." With that, she picked up her voluminous skirts with the delicate repugnance often shown when forced to step around a slimy puddle, and made to quit the room.

"If you would but wait a moment, dear Aunt, I would like to express my thanks for your kind action this evening," the Duke cajoled.

The lady sniffed. "'In fine, nothing is said now that has not been said before.' Terence."

"But you will forgive me before you rush off?"

By this time his aunt had reached the doorway. "'Pardon one offense and you encourage the commission of more.' Syrus," she said. Her stern visage and pudgy, waggling finger presented a grand imitation of a Prophet of Doom, forecasting dire consequences if she were to soften her attitude.

Avanoll bit out a short, pithy epithet before the peal of his cousin's unleashed mirth brought him back to an awareness of his surroundings. "Aunt," he called out, taking a step toward the door, "You have not been introduced to—oh, damn and blast, why do I bother?" he ended as the last row of flounce disappeared up the staircase.

He approached his cousin and opened his mouth for, unbelievably, yet another apology, but Tansy forestalled him by saying, "If it is of any consolation, your grace, you have my deepest sympathy. I'm astonished you haven't forsworn your title and flown off to the wilds of India in search of some peace. However," she continued, pausing to stifle yet another yawn, "if there are no more of our eccentric relations yet to climb out of the woodwork tonight, I would appreciate being shown to my bed."

At that moment Dunstan, the Benedicts' long-standing (and long-suffering) butler, knocked and entered at the Duke's call. "The young lady's chamber is ready, sir, and a small repast already by the fire." Dunstan then bowed and left the room, Tansy in his wake.

"Wait, Miss Tamerlane. If you are to remain here there are some rules of common courtesy that must be adhered to, even if my theatrically inclined aunt chose to ignore them in order to enact a dramatic exit. I cannot countenance another such as she without slipping my wits entirely." Avanoll locked his hands behind his back and paced importantly about the carpet, his cousin's eyes boring into the back of his jacket. "As it is never too early or too late to learn, we shall now have lesson number one. *I* am a Duke, but *you* are not a Duchess. *You* do not dismiss *me* or leave a room I am inhabiting without first gaining my permission. You beg my pardon to retire."

"Oh, bother," his cousin groaned. "Wasn't once enough? All

35

right," she decided after swallowing down hard on her rising temper, and dropped into a curtsy that would have been tolerable had she not caught her hem in her jean boot, necessitating the putting out of one hand to steady herself against a footstool. She rose awkwardly and began in a monotone. "I am mightily fatigued, your grace, and humbly beg your kind permission to . . . "

"Damme, Miss Tamerlane, don't be impertinent or . . . "

". . . retire to my bedchamber where I shall . . ." she persisted, singsong.

"Enough!"

". . . immediately ring for hot water in which to soak my tired, aching feet. Standing on ceremony, I find, gives me a royal pain!" she finished doggedly before allowing a self-satisfied smirk—no amount of indulgence could term it a smile—and quitting the room.

The Duke sank into his chair, dumbfounded. Did he still harbor enough vitality to rant and rave or should he take the coward's route out and allow himself to be amused? He decided on the latter. Between smiles and frowns he thought back over the events since his acquaintance with his new cousin and their bizarre conversations. He chuckled and unwittingly repeated a few of her statements aloud. The chuckles grew into a half-hearted laugh, and the laugh into a near fit of hilarity which he would later attribute to his exhausted state.

A housemaid passing by overheard Avanoll's laughter, peeked in to see her master the sole occupant of the room, and scurried off to the kitchens to wonder aloud that it was a rare treat to see his grace half-foxed and all silly-willy like plain folks.

Dunstan heard, sighed deeply, and ordered another decanter of port for the drawing room, sure to find the one he put there earlier sadly depleted, before coldly reminding the housemaid it was not her place to make sport of her betters.

The Duke's valet, Farnley, who had sneaked down to the kitchens in the hopes of begging some bonemeal for a charm he was making to ward off warts, shrugged his shoulders and offered a silent plea he would not be called upon to undress his grace—a very huge man—in an unconscious state. Offering a further entreaty skyward that his grace would not slop wine on his waistcoat, he repaired to his master's chambers to lay out some night clothes.

He was very surprised once there to meet a sober Duke, with not a sign of the drink that had supposedly sent him into a fit of the giggles while all alone in the drawing room. Farnley raised his eyes to the heavens, apologized that his prayers had been unnecessary, but thanked the gods anyway—just to keep them happy in case he ever had further need of them.

If that Miss Tamerlane Dunstan had told him about caused his grace's strange behavior, and if it was true she was to be living with them all in London for the Season (such news travels fast belowstairs), Farnley felt he would be making many calls on the deities in the coming months.

Chapter Five

THE MAIN drawing room of Avanoll House was a huge chamber, its confines done in the classical manner—with festoons of draperies at each long window, light paneled walls embossed with wooden bouquets of flowers caught up with rams' heads and raised bundles of husks banded about with knots of ribbon. Its ceiling was a Cipriani work of art, consisting as it did of small armies of nymphs, goddesses, and assorted amorini cavorting within their intricate arabesque borders.

The furnishings were for the most part compatible with their background, Hepplewhite's work being most frequently represented. The only flaws to offend the discerning eye were to be found in the existence (in a far-off, shadowy corner) of two of Thomas Sheraton's mistakes in judgement—which Aunt Lucinda foisted off on her relatives as being "sentimental treasures" left to her by her late husband and vowed never to be allowed far from her sight.

The "treasures"—or chairs, as they could loosely be termed—were sufficiently alike as to be considered a pair, yet dissimilar enough to inflict not one but two separate insults to anyone of any discernment.

The first (for although painful to describe, the effort to do so exhibits the magnanimity of the Duke's indulgence) was composed of a griffin's head, neck, and wings, united by a crosspiece of wood, on top of which was draped a length of fabric that was tossed over to the back and tacked down. The front was made up of a dog's shaggy, maned head and legs, joined together with a reeded nail.

For the second creation, substitute two camel heads and two of their legs combined with two lions' heads and two leonine forepaws, add the same draperies, and the picture is complete.

When asked his opinion of the chairs, Ashley termed them

painful. Emily pronounced them vulgar. But the dowager, exercising the license that comes with age, did not mince words. "Anyone who would profess a liking for those monstrosities is either crazy or blind—or both. I'd as soon plant my rump on a cold stone floor than risk losing it entirely to one of those mangy beasts."

So it was that the persons assembled were for the most part congregated in one end of the large room, Lady Emily fidgeting and complaining from her perch on the edge of a heart-backed japanned chair, his grace absently gazing at the dancing flames in the grate of the Adam fireplace, the mantel of which was serving for the moment to hold up his leaning body, and the dowager Duchess herself lounging against the back of a fan-backed sofa. A good twenty feet downwind (as the dowager termed it), Aunt Lucinda hopped back and forth between the two Sheraton chairs so as to not favor either one overmuch with her attentions.

Just as the Brachet clock (a Thomas Johnson creation hung all over with boughs, leaves, steeples, and even a vacant-faced owl balancing on one spikey, gold limb—the entirety perched on an ornate wall shelf sporting the tragedy-steeped phizz of some anonymous Greek sage) struck eleven, Dunstan pushed open the double doors from the foyer and announced, "Miss Tansy Tamerlane, your graces, my lady," and Miss Tamerlane walked reluctantly into the room.

"Tansy," his grace gasped. "My God, no wonder you dragged your feet in revealing that preposterous handle."

And then he laughed. Miss Tamerlane, no faint-hearted baby and with her green years far behind her, was not crushed by this blatant display of mirth at her own expense. She drew herself up to her not inconsequential height, crossed the room with firm—if unfashionably lengthy—strides to stop not two feet away from her tormentor, and looked him up and down with an expression of mild distaste. "I agree, my name is not on a par with those appellations taken from Nature, the Bible, or some great literary work. But I fail to see the reason for such unbridled humor from a man who must carry the handle of Ashley. Personally, it puts me in mind of the messy, sooty pile found in the grate after a fire."

The Duke's laughter ceased abruptly and his face took on a fierce scowl. Lady Emily tittered behind the safety of a concealing hand. Aunt Lucinda missed the exchange entirely and decided her chairs would consider her time spent with them sufficient and hastened to a more advantageous seat. The dowager, that formidable dragon who still, when the mood struck her, ruled her family with an iron hand, choked on the sherry she had been sipping and then exclaimed roundly, "Oh, I do like this gel! Tansy, my dear, come sit beside me and we shall begin to get acquainted. I understand the connection with the Benedicts is tenuous, but valid just the same. Indeed," the thin, hatchet-faced woman observed as her keen eyes took a quick mental inventory of the rather dowdy young woman before her, "if I harbored any fears of an imposter trying to foist herself off on us they have been quickly laid to rest. You are, in build as well as manner, a pattern copy of your great-grandmother Benedict, whose likeness hangs in the long gallery in Avanoll Hall. Ashley, surely you see the likeness?"

Ashley probed his memory until he recollected the portrait his grandmother had in mind. "But, Grandmama, the girl in that painting was most handsome and, er, I mean, perhaps there is some slight resemblance. Both being tall and brown-haired," he ended lamely.

Emily chose this time to make her presence known by pointing out her brother's near *faux-pas*. "Shame on you brother, for speaking so thoughtlessly! How did you ever last in the Diplomatic Office during the war without raising the backs of at least a hundred dignitaries?"

Aunt Lucinda broke in before Avanoll could answer his sister. "'Nature has given us two ears, two eyes, and but one tongue, to the end we should hear and see more than we speak.' Socrates."

"Whom are you admonishing with that little tidbit, Aunt—Emily or me?" Avanoll asked.

"'Children and fooles cannot lye.' Heywood," his aunt returned doggedly.

"There is no question into which category you fall, Lucinda," the dowager sniffed. "You are nothing but an educated parrot, mouthing words and never ideas. Do be quiet before I throw a shawl over your cage to shut you up."

Miss Tamerlane, or Tansy as she had admitted to being named, was beginning to feel quite at home with both this odd little group and their assorted personality quirks.

Suddenly the dowager's attention returned to the girl now sitting beside her. She asked Tansy for her full name, pointing out that perhaps it wouldn't sound so much like the heroine in a Penny Dreadful.

"Tansy Marie Antoinette Tamerlane! Good God, were your parents foxed at the time?"

Tansy smiled and took the outburst in good form. "Mama had a failing for things French, though I doubt she would have so blessed me if she knew how tragically it all ended for that poor lady. Mama was very superstitious, you know. To her such a name would now mean I shall come to a sad end. Then again, as I think on it, perhaps she would not have been too unduly upset. I fear she never quite forgave me for coming along and disrupting her organized little life of tatting, tattling, and tittering with her neighbors. Rather like Nero fiddling while Rome burned, considering the never-ending coils my Papa was forever blundering into whenever left to his own devices."

The dowager listened with interest and then observed that perhaps multiple names were not the answer. After all, look at poor Emmaline-Lucille Pratt. All a double name did for her was to give her one more word to stumble over. "She stammers, you know," the Duchess told them. "Thank heavens I wasn't cursed with palming that one off. Getting Emmaline-Lucille hitched-up would be the coup of the Season."

The Duke was not at all interested in Emmaline-Lucille Pratt. To be honest, he wasn't very much more interested in Tansy Tamerlane.

All he wanted to do this morning was to establish Tansy as Emily's new keeper, bid a fond but not unpleased farewell to the dowager, and get on about more serious business.

"First things first, I think, cousin. If you would give me the direction of this Squire you spoke of I will write to him concerning your inability to assume your post. He will undoubtedly be concerned for your welfare."

Tansy gave a short laugh. "I doubt he'll be dragging the river for my body in his anxiety, your grace. But I shall write him myself and save you the trouble."

"'It is better to learn late than never.' Publilius Syrus," Aunt Lucinda pointed out.

"Then there is hope for you yet, Lucinda," the Duchess drawled, causing Lucinda's brow to pucker as she tried and failed to understand the dowager's subtlety.

"Enough," the Duke interrupted. "After yesterday's near disaster, I have found it prudent to entrust my sister's care to our new cousin in an effort to keep Emily from singlehandedly destroying the Benedict name in the coming months of the Season."

His aunt, rather miffed at her displacement, quoted, "'When the steede is stolne, shut the stable durre.' Heywood."

"Nonsense!" Tansy scoffed as Emily sputtered angrily, but luckily not completely comprehending the insult, "The little filly here was not stolen, or even lost. She was merely temporarily misplaced. Besides, no harm's been done, and we can even hope Emily has learned something from the episode." This last was said with a stern look in the truant's direction.

"'Pardon one offense and you encourage the commission of many.' P. Syrus," the suddenly strict ex-companion prophesied, causing Ashley to wonder where he had heard those words before.

All this was just too much for Lady Emily's tender sensibilities, and she bolted out of her chair in protest. "I think you are all perfectly horrid! Why don't you just lock me upstairs in my room and leave me to wither and die!" she shrieked, and ran sobbing from the room, her concerned aunt hard on her heels.

The remaining occupants were not so easily impressed. While Tansy smiled and shook her head and Avanoll uttered an exasperated oath, the dowager summed it all up nicely by wiping her hands on each other and saying, "Well, that routed them both quite nicely, don't you think? Now we can get down to cases."

"I beg your pardon, Grandmama?" Avanoll queried. "It was my impression your townhouse was in Holland covers and you were leaving today for Avanoll Hall. Surely you don't wish to be detained by our problems with Emily, seeing as how she wears on you so."

"That was before I met this girl here. Suddenly I feel quite rejuvenated and I have decided to stay in Town. There is no need to fill more servant bellies at town prices if you are in residence here, so I shall stay here. Have my chamber prepared, Ashley," she instructed imperiously, then added, "And take that vacant look off your face. If you just apply yourself a bit I'm sure you'll realize which chamber I require."

"I do, madam," his grace agreed, "but since that is now *my* chamber I believe the red suite will have to do, even if it is not exactly to your taste."

"Hummph! Hardly, grandson, hardly. I cannot imagine what imp of perverseness induced your mother to rig out an entire room in red. Such a color is only fit for whores and wild Russians."

"Madam!" the Duke protested, only to find he was being

ignored. The dowager had asked Tansy's assistance in rising from the sofa and was even now leaving the room on her arm, chattering nineteen to the dozen about morning gowns and rout parties and all the "jolly times" they would all be having shortly.

Avanoll groaned and sank into a nearby chair. Not only had he not rid himself of the silly prattlings of his aunt, but he had been burdened even further by the addition of both an irascible dowager and an impossibly *outré* cousin.

Why, oh why hadn't he had the good sense to be born an orphan?

Chapter Six

AS TANSY wandered around her pleasantly-decorated bed chamber, enjoying her first bit of solitude in nearly a fortnight, her mind traveled back over just a few of the many exciting happenings since her arrival at Avanoll House. She traced a vague pattern in the light layer of dust on her desk as she moved to gaze out over the Square.

Naturally, her first thoughts were of her newly discovered relatives—the silly, lovable Emily, the even sillier and just as lovable Aunt Lucinda (Tansy could not bring herself to call the old lady Ce-Ce), the irascible and unpredictable Dowager, and, of course, the seldom seen head of the family, the Duke himself. Tansy was well pleased with them, eccentricities, quirks, and all, and felt at home to a peg with these characters who so resembled her dear, departed Papa.

She had to admit, though, that she was glad the dowager had at last called a halt to the endless stream of bodies that had been cluttering up the house these past two weeks. Dressmakers, milliners, silk merchants, linen drapers, corsetiers, even an Italian-spouting shoemaker, had all appeared within moments of the dowager's summons, to poke, measure, pin, and fit until Tansy thought she would go mad.

The only respites from hours of standing about like a wax doll while strange hands pushed and prodded at her were a few excursions to shops on Bond Street, where her befuddled mind tried to gather ribbons and laces that would match the multitude of gowns that were threatening to outgrow her over-taxed closet. After two tedious hours spent being measured for kid gloves, Tansy finally revolted. If she changed her clothes from the skin out twice a day for a month she would still not exhaust her supply of gowns. So she informed the dowager matter-offactly, and stoutly refused to accept so much as another pair of lace-edged pantalettes.

Emily's wardrobe had not been so much augmented as adjusted. Under the dowager's orders, yards of discarded flounces, long streamers of ornately-worked lace, and miles of satin ribbon collected in near waist-high mounds on the sewing room floor. Aunt Lucinda was horrified, naturally, but not too overset to keep herself from bundling up all this treasure and cornering one hapless seamstress who soon found herself stitching these same flounces, laces, and ribbons onto any bare stretch of fabric to be found on the gowns Mrs. Benedict had graciously allowed the dowager to order for her (and all added to the dowager's bill, needless to mention).

Even the old lady herself had condescended to supplementing her wardrobe with several sedately-colored gowns, all fashioned with matching turbans that she announced would make it clear *she* at least was not so silly as to be hanging out for a husband at her age. This was said with a mocking glance toward Lucinda, who blushed, flustered a bit, then simply smiled shyly.

The Duke allowed this invasion of his domicile in good grace, probably because he made it a point to be absent from the premises whenever possible. What he thought of the not inconsiderable stack of bills that found their way to his desk he did not say, and only once did he raise his voice in displeasure.

Shortly after the first of the gowns was delivered, Tansy happened to come upon his grace on the stairs. He looked at her, looked away, and then cast his eyes over her again, his expression showing he was not displeased with what he saw. That is, until his eyes clapped on the cap Tansy had tied about her head.

"Take that demmed ugly cap and throw it in the fire—and any others you might have stuffed away in your room!" he bellowed. "I refuse to allow you to shout to the world that you consider yourself on the shelf. Why do you think I allowed my Grandmama to accumulate that mountain of debt if it were not so I could at least harbor the hope some kind soul would find it in his heart to have pity on me and take you off my hands? Did you really think I would want you hanging around my neck for all eternity? Chaperon m'sister, yes, but cast out a few lures for yourself while you're about it, woman," he ended decisively, and was climbing up and away from her before she could formulate any reply.

Tansy had entertained thoughts of defying the Duke, but could not bring herself to disobey the man who had literally paid for the clothes on her back. Besides, the stiffly-starched things itched abominably, and made her feel like a twenty-six-year-old baby rigged out for an airing in the park.

She gave the caps to Comfort, Emily's abigail, to dispose of as she pleased. From what little she knew of the maid, she was willing to wager the chit had hawked them on the corner for a pretty penny, for never before had Tansy encountered such a wily creature as Comfort.

A rather sad smile passed across Tansy's face as she recalled her own manipulation at Comfort's hands. The dowager had insisted Tansy, who had fended for herself since she was eight, must be provided with a personal abigail, and Comfort was Jill-on-the-spot with a quick solution. Why, wasn't it only last week that her own darling cousin Pansy had mentioned she was thinking of looking for another post, since her employer had been taking a bit too much notice of his young servant (not to mention his taking an actual pinch or two when the opportunity presented itself).

It was the perfect solution! Pansy could be installed within the space of a day, and Comfort could instruct her if there were any lapses in her education as to the duties of a personal abigail. Tansy soon learned Pansy had need of Comfort's guidance, as that organizing young woman had neglected to say that Pansy's main duties in her last employment consisted of scrubbing out kitchen pots and peeling vegetables for the cook.

The dowager was all for sending Pansy off and looking elsewhere, but once again Tansy's protective nature surfaced. She insisted the undersized, constantly whimpering girl was just what she had in mind. By now Pansy had settled down to her own version of a routine: scorching fine lawn nightgowns and then crying, dropping buckets full of soapy bathwater on the carpet and crying, closing all the dozens of tiny buttons on Tansy's gowns with fumbling fingers before discovering she had missed one tiny button halfway down and crying, etc., and so forth.

Another young woman would have been upset, and rightly so, but Tansy just sighed, handed Pansy a handkerchief, and sent her off to the kitchens where Pansy would sit peeling potatoes for hours in a high degree of good humor.

Comfort was surprised when Miss Tansy's wrath did not

come raining down upon her head on the matter of Pansy, but she was outraged when the companion warned her against allying herself with Miss Emily by abetting her in any more secret assignations or in the delivering of any more illicit *billets-doux* from young men willing to reward her monetarily for her cooperation.

Comfort was not so totty-headed as to think her part in Miss Emily's little escapades were untraceable, but she did not enjoy the dressing down a mere paid companion (poor relation or not) delivered one little bit. She did not believe for one minute that Miss Emily would come to any harm in the hoax she played with Mr. Harlow—surely everyone must know that—and besides, if she and Leo were to ever have enough put by to get hitched, there was no other way to make extra money than by letting all those young swells reward her for her help. What harm was there in a bunch of drippy lovey-dovey poems, anyway?

But Tansy's musings that morning did not go so far as to believe she had gained an enemy in Comfort.

That enemy was not alone in her feelings. Farnley, the Duke's valet, had made it plain he considered Tansy a harbinger of bad luck, but his mad dashes to avoid crossing her path and his ridiculous gestures meant to ward off the "evil eye" merely amused her.

A slight rumbling in her stomach caused Tansy to leave off her reminiscences and made her bold enough to descend to the kitchens to see what bit of food she could possibly coax out of Cook before luncheon. After all, hadn't she earned a bit of special treatment for allowing Cook such generous use of Pansy's finest talents?

Tansy had already met Cook on her original tour of the house, but her good impression of the woman was not matched by her opinion of the food served at the Duke's table. Quite often the beef was stringy, the fowl tough, and the vegetables—though heavily disguised with flavorful sauces—did not always taste quite fresh. Yet, since no one else had seen fit to complain, and heaven knew she was no gourmet, Tansy kept her thoughts to herself.

Once seated at the huge, well-scrubbed table in the center of the kitchen and munching greedily on a raspberry tart, however, Tansy's eyes could not help but notice the seeming scarcity of foodstuffs usually to be found in abundance in such an affluent household.

"Hasn't anyone been to the market today?" she asked Pansy, who was concentrating on digging an eye out of a potato while causing as little waste as possible.

Pansy finished her task and smiled smugly at her achievement before casting her eyes around the room and through the opened doors that revealed the pantry and meat locker. "Yes'm, Miss Tansy. Sally went to market at first light. Everything's here, just like always."

Upon hearing this piece of information, Tansy decided a closer investigation was called for, and set forth at once to make what soon became an extensive inventory-taking of foodstuffs, cleaning supplies, candles, linens, and fuel. She even climbed to the top of the house, where she inspected the furnishings in the servants' quarters. When she was finished she returned to the morning room at the back of the house and gave the bell-rope a mighty pull.

"Send Mrs. Brown to me at once," she ordered the footman who answered her call.

"Mrs. Brown, ma'am? There's no Mrs. Brown what lives 'ere," the footman answered in confusion.

Tansy's foot was tapping now. "The housekeeper, you goose. I want the housekeeper."

A light went on in the footman's vacant eyes. "Oh, you'd be meaning Mrs. *Green,* then, Miss," he corrected.

"Green, brown, purple, I don't give a bloody damn what color she is! You just get her thieving arse to anchor in here in less than three minutes, or I may start giving you the drubbing I have planned for her!"

To say the least, the very least, Miss Tansy Tamerlane was upset. The footman stumbled wildly for the door, but still heard the irate woman's parting order. "And tell her to bring the household books with her if she values her skin!"

Tansy spent the next few minutes stomping up and down the morning room in a high flight of agitation, until a loud voice cut into her thoughts by demanding stridently, "Just what is the meaning of this outrage?"

Tansy halted in mid-stomp and whirled upon the speaker, her eyes raking the tall, raw-boned figure of the housekeeper. Mrs. Green was standing, hands on hips, just inside the door, her severe black gown gathered in at the waist by a wide belt from which hung a multitude of keys. Her iron-grey hair surrounded her sallow-skinned face by way of a coronet of thick braids, and although she was no taller than Tansy she outweighed her by at least three stone—making of herself all in all a very imposing (threatening?) picture.

Tansy was not impressed. After allowing her gaze to travel slowly up and down the person of Mrs. Green she said, keeping a tight rein on her temper, "You will oblige me, madam, by sitting down and shutting up. What I have to say will take only a few minutes, and then—if you dare—you may try to explain yourself."

Tansy then launched into a pithy description of the findings of her morning's investigation, and as each new fact was presented Mrs. Green's complexion came one shade closer to mimicking her name. Condensing nicely, it was not too long a time (although it seemed an age to the housekeeper) before Tansy ended her speech by declaring her next targets of investigation were to be the huge clothbound books now reposing on Mrs. Green's trembling knees.

At her first opportunity, Mrs. Green sprang to her own defense by trying to lay all blame on the outrageous prices that were the bane of every housekeeper since the war ended.

"Don't try to cozen me with that outrageous faradiddle," Tansy warned.

Mrs. Green decided to take another tack. "I admit, the place could do with a bit of a wash and a brushup, and Lord knows how hard I try to drum some sense of duty into those lazy housemaids . . ."

"Stubble it!" Tansy cut her off contemptuously, her anger causing her to revert to the language learned at her father's knee. "Don't embarrass either of us with any more of your outrageous lies. Allow me to advise you that your position in this household is terminated. *Immediately.* So why don't you just nip off upstairs and pack your bags? I want you out of this house within the hour." Tansy made to turn away but then turned back to add one more note. "And please, don't hold onto any hopes of taking along a recommendation. Unless you are applying for employment as a thief: for that I feel sure you are most fully qualified."

Suddenly Mrs. Green remembered something. This Tamerlane hussy was nothing but a poor relation, with no authority to fire anyone. "You are not in charge here, missy," she pointed out nastily. "I'll just wait for the Duke, and then we'll see who's to be set out on the street."

Tansy smiled—a wicked, wicked smile. "You are correct, madam, I have no authority to dismiss you. Instead, why don't you look upon my order as being more in the nature of a suggestion. You see, my authority in the matter is not the issue here. What is more to the point are those books now reposing so innocently on the sofa over there. Do you really wish the Duke to examine them while you are still around to answer any questions his grace might raise?"

Mrs. Green was packed and gone—well within the time span Tansy suggested—and as she and Dunstan watched the departing hackney carry her away from Grosvenor Square the butler apologized for not being aware of the goings on beneath his aristocratically humped nose. "My only excuse is that I am only in town for the few weeks the Duke is in residence. As I much prefer Avanoll Hall, my attention to this house has suffered accordingly."

"It's of no matter, Dunstan," Tansy assured him. "I just hope I can manage to hold the household together until such time as we can find another housekeeper. The Duke and dowager must not feel the pinch of our shorthandedness. Can I count on your assistance, dear Dunstan?"

The butler drew himself up to his full imposing height and gave his solemn assurances that everyone, himself included, would be more than happy to do anything they could to help the young miss. "It seems the servants were none too fond of Mrs. Green, and they've already taken to talking of you as their savior. And, Miss Tansy, if I may be so bold," he added softly, "the family all call me Dunny. I would be honored if you would deign to so honor me."

Chapter Seven

BY TEA-TIME of that same day, the remaining females had been apprised of the morning's upheaval, and the dowager was clucking over the obvious inequities between the house-keeper's books and the actual expenditures for the household.

"You were too easy on her, Tansy, my pet. Too easy by half. The wretch belongs in Newgate. And Ashley, that *blockhead*, should be locked up for stupidity, for however he could have overlooked such gross mismanagement I cannot fathom. Having a charming wastrel for a father may not have been a pleasure for you, Tansy, but since his laxity pitchforked you into handling the running of his estate, he has indirectly done us a great service."

This praise was all well and good, but Tansy was wise to enjoy it while she could—for even at that moment Farnley was upstairs bending his master's ear with his own version of the story while his grace dressed for dinner.

"If you will but recall, your grace," Farnley pointed out smugly, easing his master into his evening coat once his tale was through, "I did try to warn you about the young lady. I knew she was bad luck for us the minute I clapped eyes on her. All the signs were wrong that day. If you but tie this hag-stone on your door key, it will go a long way toward heading off any more disasters. At night, I can hang it from your bed-head and nothing evil can harm you at night either. Please, sir."

"I'll hang you on the bed-head if you don't shut up, Farnley. You're as nervy as an old spinster who thinks there's murderers lurking under her bed." The Duke walked over to his dressing table and, picking up a small knife, began to pare his nails.

Farnley, who had been momentarily diverted while retrieving the Duke's riding jacket from the chair upon which its wearer had carelessly tossed it, suddenly realized what his master was about and cried out in alarm—nearly causing Avanoll to give himself a nasty cut.

"What the blazes?" the Duke barked.

His valet scurried over to the dressing table, carefully picked up all the nail-parings, and cradled them in his hand. "You must not trim your nails on a Friday, your grace, as I have told you so many times," Farnley admonished. "You will have ill-luck for certain. I'll save these pieces up until Monday and then scatter them over the back garden."

"Damned untidy, if you ask me, and damned silly. Farnley, you must stop all this superstitious nonsense, as it would grieve me deeply to have to let you go. But you *are* a bit queer, you know, and sometimes most unsettling. Now excuse me while I make my way downstairs to discover for myself just what exactly transpired this morning to send Mrs. Green bolting from this house, without so much as asking for her last quarter's wages."

To say that dinner that evening was not a resounding success would be dressing up in fine linen a domestic disaster too discouraging to recount step by depressing step. A crushing set-down from his grandparent, touching on the responsibilities of the head of any household in monitoring the goings-on under his own roof—delivered before Avanoll had so much as had recourse to a single glass of port—was compounded by his sister's undisguised glee in his discomfort and the rendering of a vague warning from his aunt that went: "'Anyone can hold the helm when the sea is calm.' Syrus."

The Duke could not dispute his Grandmama's words, and dismissed his sister and his aunt as unworthy of his sarcasm. The only target left to him, besides himself, was his cousin—that infuriating termagant who was just then sitting with a deceptively demure expression hiding what he knew could only be an overweening feeling of superiority.

"So," he suggested as he walked over to stand leering down at his cousin, "you are well on the way to worming yourself into convincing everyone that you are an indispensable part of this household. I didn't know you were so concerned with either my domestic routine or my purse. Or is it that you are simply a nosey busybody who delights in sticking her fingers into everyone else's pie?"

Tansy's brown eyes flashed fire. "That was a sinister remark," she responded boldly.

"'There are some who bear a grudge even to those that do them good.' Pilpay," came an unmistakable, trilling voice from across the room—a voice his grace ignored as best he could while he asked his acting housekeeper the menu for the evening.

Tansy's smile fairly dazzled him as she informed him brightly, "Baked river eel in parsley sauce, if it please your grace."

Once the figurines on the mantelpiece stopped shaking (due to the vibrations caused by the angry slamming of the front door), the ladies repaired to the dining room to partake of an outstanding example of the heights of culinary excellence Cook was capable once supplied with quality foodstuffs.

In the wee hours of the morning, a trifle worse for wear, the Duke stumbled into the foyer and dropped his house key, the hag-stone attached to it making a terrible din in the quiet house. The butler peeped his head around the corner to see what was the matter, and his grace—putting one unsteady finger to his lips—whispered loudly, "Shh, Dunny, it's only your sweet laddie-boy, home at last."

"The name is *Dunstan,* your grace," the old family retainer pronounced crushingly, before leaving his master to negotiate the path to his bedchamber as best he could in his castaway state.

When the Duke could no longer shut out the glare of the mid-morning sun that had crept relentlessly across his bed the next morning until it sent skyrockets of pain into his eye sockets, he pushed himself up on one elbow and cast his eyes about his chamber. The mantel clock told him it was only ten o'clock— not too late an hour, considering his activities of the night before. Further investigation showed him what his shivering body already had guessed: there was no fire in the grate, and, stranger yet, no cup of chocolate stood on his bedside table, no fresh clothes hung from the clothes-tree visible through the open dressing room door, and Farnley was nowhere in sight. Odd, indeed.

He leaned over, a move that sent cymbals crashing through his head, and pulled the bell rope. Farnley did not appear. When three more vicious tugs produced not one servant, he opened his mouth and gave a mighty bellow. "Farnley!" he called once, then clapped his hands to his head to still the bells that had set up a discordant clanging between his ears.

Finally, convinced help was not forthcoming, he searched out his maroon brocade dressing gown and spied out his slippers beneath the bed, but in the end he chose to forego the slippers as bending over to retrieve them proved too painful a project.

Eventually he groped his way unsteadily to the dining room—for by now his stomach was playing him up—following the sounds of voices in hopes someone would take pity on him and give him something to make his mouth taste less like a stable floor.

Once propped against the door frame he could make out the figures of the dowager, Emily, his aunt, Dunstan, and his accursed cousin, all seated around a dining table piled high with what must have been every piece of silver in the house.

His sister saw him first. "Oh, Ashley," she giggled, "you look Perfectly Awful!"

"I don't recall requesting your opinion, puss, and I am not here to amuse you. Where is my breakfast?"

"Oh," Tansy said sweetly, "we didn't expect you down before noon. I'm afraid there is nothing to be had right now." She replaced the lid on a silver bowl with a slightly heavy hand, and hid a smile when Avanoll grimaced in pain.

"What in blazes is going on in here anyway?" he asked.

The dowager informed him that they were, as any ninny could see, polishing the silver. "I know that," his grace said, "but why aren't the servants doing it?"

"You can't trust servants to take care of such good things," Tansy told him.

"Why not? I always have before."

"Perhaps that explains all the dented silver we found pushed into the back of the server," Tansy suggested.

Lucinda held up a small tureen with a very obvious dent in one side. "'This dim-seen track-mark of an ancient crime.' Sophocles," she intoned solemnly.

Dunstan, taking pity on his master, who after all wasn't a bad sort, suggested he set up a place for him in the morning room, to which Tansy replied, "Don't be silly! Luncheon is in little more than an hour; the Duke won't wish to disturb Cook unduly. Besides, I doubt soft eggs and kippers would be good for his constitution right now."

"I can speak for myself," Avanoll said with some heat.

"So, speak," said Tansy, whereupon his grace reconsidered looking down on a plate of kippers and muttered that he'd wait for luncheon.

Just then Farnley, who had been noticeable only by his absence, appeared in the doorway holding a large glass filled with a most revolting-looking concoction. "I got all the things you asked for, Miss Tansy, and mixed them up just the way you said." Farnley, although no fan of Tansy's, was reluctant to cross her in any way, and his absence from his master's side that morning was explained as necessary so that he could go to the apothecary and gather the ingredients for a posset. It was one that had worked like a charm every time when her Papa was suffering the aftereffects of too much liquor.

"Are you certain you have everything in there?" Tansy asked with a malicious grin.

"Yes, ma'am," Farnley assured her. "Two owl's eggs, a clove of garlic, a half-glass of onion juice, a tablespoon of eel's blood, one day-old fish head, and some crushed parsley for color."

There was a loud moan from the opposite doorway, and the Duke bolted toward the stairs with one hand to his mouth. Lucinda turned to Emily and pointed out: "'Learn to see in another's calamity the ill which you should ignore.' Syrus."

"That's strange," Tansy observed mildly, "it always had the same effect on Papa, but he at least had to sniff it first. It's not meant to drink, you know. I imagine it would probably kill an ox."

A little less than an hour later—just as they were about finished with the silver—the Duke, now fully dressed, rejoined the company. "That posset of yours seems to have turned the trick, cousin. My head is still a bit more tender than I'd like, but my stomach is much improved."

The dowager pointed out that his head wouldn't be so tender if he had not behaved like a spoiled baby. "It wasn't my idea," her grandson excused himself. "I was driven to drink by circumstance. Normally, I am most moderate in everything I do."

"Circumstance my great Aunt Alice," the dowager sniffed. "Bull-headedness is more like it, if you ask me. Here you were with your housekeeper cheating you all hollow and you too stubborn to see that no housekeeper at all is better than a thieving housekeeper. No, instead of being grateful—"

"Grateful!" Avanoll broke in. "I am without a housekeeper, my valet abandons me on orders from my *cousin*,"—this last said with a sneer—"my servants punish me for my rightful display of anger by leaving me alone in my bedchamber to freeze or starve or both, and all this for a few shillings I'd never have missed anyway."

Tansy objected to this statement. "Those few shillings, from my best reckoning, add up to over three hundred pounds in the last two years. Wellington could have fed his troops on less than Mrs. Green was skimming off the household budget."

Avanoll looked skeptical, but as Dunstan nodded his head in agreement his skepticism turned to reluctant belief. Perhaps if his head were not buzzing as if there were a thousand bees building a nest between his ears, he might even have found it in himself to be grateful. But it was, and he wasn't.

Instead, he climbed upon his hobby horse and started in to ride.

"Three hundred pounds, a thousand pounds—it don't make a pennysworth of difference to me as long as I can feed *my* belly at *my* table in *my* house at *my* convenience. What good is three hundred pounds if I'm to be made to suffer the country bumpkin housekeeping methods my cousin believes proper—even when applied to the establishment of a Duke?"

He knew his last thrust had hit home as Tansy visibly flinched at the words "country bumpkin." If but only for the sake of his pride (and his buzzing head), he would have gone on, had not the dowager come to her feet with an excruciatingly loud screech of her scraped-back chair.

"Grandson, I have listened to all the childish tantrums I intend to hear from you this morning," she announced sternly, reducing him with one sentence to the rank of naughty toddler. "Of all the selfish-minded, poor-spirited, rude, crude, and ungrateful wretches I have ever met, you, my buck, carry off the palm. Now, can I be assured of an end to this nonsense or must I first box your ears?"

Lucinda's fragile nerves were becoming terribly overset by all this shouting and she rose to retire from the fray, leaving behind her some typical words of wisdom (indeed, everyone would have felt sadly deprived if she hadn't). "'Of all animals, the boy is the most unmanageable.' Plato."

Once Lucinda's exit had broken some of the tension, and since he was secretly grateful the light-fingered Mrs. Green had been rousted, and because he had great respect for (and not a little justified fear of) his formidable grandparent, and in view of the hurt look in Tansy's eyes which was causing him a slight unfamiliar tender stirring in his chest, the Duke at once bowed to his cousin and uttered an apology. He then walked over and kissed the dowager on her overheated forehead and apologized once again.

Emily, who throughout the past few minutes had been

twisting her head back and forth between the speakers with an expression of unholy glee upon her pretty face, felt her top-lofty brother may have been set down a peg or two—but not quite enough.

"Ashley," she said artlessly, "do you not think a more fitting apology would be to take Cousin Tansy out for an airing in the Park this very afternoon? I know she has been simply pining to try out your new chestnuts. Why not hitch them to your phaeton—you know, the one that is so dreadfully high that it makes me quite faint with dizziness—and let Tansy take the reins?"

She turned from one startled face to the other and smiled an innocent cherubic smile. "Don't you think that would be a more fitting apology?"

Tansy never blushed in embarrassment; she only flushed in anger. She was flushing now. The dowager, however, seeing a chance to give Cupid a hand, quickly and quite firmly endorsed the plan. Mentally she made a note to scold her granddaughter later for her incidentally helpful but definitely maliciously meant suggestion.

Avanoll, not trusting his voice, grated his teeth together audibly (sending up a thundering racket in his head), mutely agreed, then quit the room. The dowager Duchess, well satisfied with her morning's work, went off to closet herself away with Jane Austen's *Pride and Prejudice*.

Lady Emily, having polished one half of a saltcellar in all this time, laid down her polishing cloth and retired posthaste to the safety of her chamber—out of reach of her vengeful brother.

Dunstan, who had been busily trying to appear invisible while soaking up every word of this juicy family squabble, muttered something about securing more polish from the kitchens and scurried away to give a line-by-line report of the *contretemps* (complete with proper inflections and gestures) to his good friend Leo, the Duke's groom.

Farnley rushed out of the kitchen as soon as Dunstan appeared, quick to seek out his master and try to get back into his good graces—although he could not resist reminding his grace of his prior dire predictions of this being only the beginning of a most *dreadful* period in Avanoll history.

Tansy was left alone in the dining room, deciding whether to hold the Duke to such blatant blackmail as Emily forced on him or to be sweet and understanding and let him off the hook. After all, the poor man had enough on his plate without having to squire his "country bumpkin" beanpole of a cousin through the Park at five o'clock with all the *ton* looking on.

But then again, as she thought on it a bit more, he really had been insufferable. She pictured his face as it looked when the dowager was ringing that mighty peal over his head and laughed aloud in the quiet room. Served him right, the pompous ass! How dare he react so boorishly when her intentions were so honorable? Besides, she really was itching to get her hands on those horses of his!

She rose slowly and carelessly pushed an errant brown curl back from her forehead—leaving behind a grey smudge of polish that neatly balanced out the ones on her chin, nose, and cheek—and went off to make sure her driving ensemble was not in need of pressing. She'd show him a thing or two about driving, or her name wasn't Tansy Tamerlane!

Chapter Eight

AT A QUARTER to the hour of five, a dashing young lady in a deep gold pelisse and matching bonnet was perched expectantly on a gilt chair in the foyer of Avanoll House. Her entire attitude—from her stubbornly uptilted chin to a single visible, stylishly-shod foot, at the moment tapping a rapid tattoo against the tiled floor—bespoke an impatience to be up and gone. Her strategic positioning declared she was not to be outmaneuvered by a cowardly Duke bent on escape from his promise.

"Blast" she heard from the top of the stairs. She turned her head sharply, tilting her precariously perched bonnet even further over one eye, to observe the Duke—looking dashing in his three-caped drab-green driving coat, in the act of putting one gleaming Hessian boot on the top stair.

"Afraid I'd renege, cousin?" he asked acidly as he descended to the foyer and took his gloves and curly-brimmed beaver from Dunstan's outstretched hands. "Never let it be said I was a white feather man who ran from battle, eh, Dunny? Ah," he breathed as if he had not erred on purpose, "I mean *Dunstan,* don't I? So sorry, old man, force of habit you know, since it was you, so you tell me, who used to be fond of bouncing me on your knee when I was but a babe. But, then, perhaps old ties were made to be broken and old friendships forgot. Tut, tut!" He held up one large hand to cut off the apology Dunstan had shown no intention of making. "Though you have cut me to the quick by deserting me to go over to," he shot a quick look at Tansy, "the *enemy,* I am determined to hide my pain and carry on with the National stiff upper lip. It is expected, you know."

"Oh, give over, Ashley. Can't you see you are not impressing Dunny one mite? Besides, your sorrow is all a hum so you can delay our outing, and as I hear the horses now I suggest you do

59

not leave them standing in the breeze any longer." Tansy then dismissed the Duke with a slight smile and turned to the butler. "Dunny, please remind Cook that dinner is for eight of the clock, and that although I approved the menu it was with the understanding the third remove be deleted."

As Tansy turned for the door the Duke's voice rang out in devilish glee, "Oh, Dunstan, I am afraid I had a short lapse of memory. It seems I have invited four guests to dine with us—gentlemen I met at White's this afternoon who were lamenting the lack of a dinner engagement. As I could not bear to think my friends at loose ends, I—foolishly forgetting I have no house-keeper now that Miss Tamerlane has seen fit to dispose of the woman *I* had employed—begged them to take their mutton with me tonight." His grace, suddenly feeling better than he had all day, turned for the door and encountered Tansy's wickedly dancing eyes.

"Dunny," she trilled, "have two places removed from the table, if you would please. It seems I have overestimated his grace's circle of friends. He has only four willing to play cat's paw for him, it seems." Tansy cocked her head toward the door. "Your grace—the horses are waiting. Shall we go?"

The Duke stormed angrily through the door and down the steps ahead of his cousin, determined to leave her standing in his dust as he sprung his pair away from her. But by the time he reached the phaeton his sense of humor took over. Infuriating wretch, he thought. Meddling, bothersome, clever, intelligent minx! Tansy saw his shoulders start to shake and then heard the clear baritone melody of his laugh.

He about-faced and held out his hand, saying, "Cousin, you have bested me on all suits, but never let it be said a Benedict was a poor loser. Allow me to help you up and, if you don't mind, as the horses are fresh I will hold the reins until we are in the Park. Then I shall turn them over to you to see if you handle them as prettily as you just handled me."

Looking back at the door and catching the smile on Dunstan's face, he pressed his luck even further. "Dunny," he called, "please tell Farnley to lay out my blue for this evening. I wish to look my best at my cousin's table."

"Yes, your grace," Dunstan replied, forgiving the once bounced and tickled baby with relief. "At once, sir!"

Avanoll had little trouble handling the fresh horses in the afternoon traffic, and in a few minutes they were turning into the Park. There they joined the press of curricles, phaetons, landaus, barouches, and tilburys—and their modishly-dressed occupants—all busy seeing and being seen by the rest of the *ton* as they bowed and nodded and occasionally condescended to stop and pass a few moments in conversation (successfully jamming all traffic in both directions and guaranteeing them the notice of their fellow promenaders—at least the ones not busy trying to keep their showy, temperamental cattle in check).

The social politics of all this head-jerking and hand-waving was totally lost on Tansy. She knew only that her skill in handling the ribbons would be limited to not allowing the horses to fall asleep in the shafts as they waited for a ridiculous old creature in orchid to stop waggling her bonnet's ostrich feathers all over the aging *roué* who was nearly tumbling from his mount into her more than ample lap in an effort to decipher her long and garbled attempt at girlish flirtation.

Avanoll could feel Tansy's tenseness across the short distance between them and almost—but not quite—wished to hear her sure-to-be pithy remarks on the orchid lady. Wordlessly he slipped the reins into her hands and she took them quite naturally, with no trace of nervousness. Just impatience.

Suddenly the air was split by three resounding sneezes as the ostrich plumes and the *roué*'s nose collided one too many times. Tansy's clear laugh rang out, to his grace's way of thinking, twice as piercingly as a Highlander's battle cry. The orchid lady looked pointedly toward the phaeton with murder in her eyes—but quickly adjusted her features to resemble indulgent understanding of the youthful high spirits so prevalent these days when she saw the miscreant's companion.

Without a backward look to her companion—whose face was now buried in a voluminous handkerchief—she motioned her driver forward, then stopped him when abreast of juicier quarry.

"Why, your grace, at first I thought I beheld an apparition. It is simply an *age* since last you graced us with your presence so early in the Season. Indeed, the Season is not yet officially here, is it, although one couldn't tell that by the turnout today, could one? I declare, half the two thousand, at least, must be in the park today."

Throughout the delivery of this speech the lady's watery-pale orchid eyes (an answer to the unasked question of why an aging female of little beauty and a rather muddy complexion would deck herself head to toe in pale orchid) darted back and forth between his grace and Tansy. Doubtless she was mentally trotting out and discarding reasons why this unspectacular looking and, if not on the shelf, definitely at her last prayers female should be the first of her sex to be seen handling an Avanoll pair since the dowager Duchess retired her whip twenty years before.

Since the Duke seemed ready to give her only a small smile and a nod before rudely dismissing his dear departed Mama's oldest and dearest friend—well, perhaps that was stretching a point, but they did have their come-outs the same Season, and her with her youngest still to get off her hands after three unfruitful Seasons, drat the chit—the lady blithely discarded the niceties and asked the name of the charming miss who had the pleasure of his grace's company.

"How remiss of me, Lady Stanley. It seems in my absence from town my manners have gone a-begging," he replied without any hint of gentlemanly remorse. Then he very quickly effected introductions and nudged Tansy's foot with the toe of his boot in an effort to get her moving.

Tansy was only too happy to oblige and raised her hands, only to be stopped by Lady Stanley's incredulous, "Your *cousin?* Why the only Tamerlane I know of was Sir Andrew Tamerlane, and that man couldn't *possibly* be related to you."

"Whyever not, Lady Stanley?" purred Tansy in a tone Avanoll already knew only too well.

But before his grace could wade in and smooth the waters, Lady Stanley sealed her fate by blurting out, "Why, really, my dear child, you must know Sir Andrew was a worthless ninny-brain who gambled and drank himself underground two years or so back—ending a singularly worthless and unproductive life. His wife, bless her soul, a sweet young thing several years my jun–er, *senior,* died of a broken heart, I heard—thanks to that wretch of a man."

Avanoll looked wildly about him for a hole in which to hide before the rockets started exploding around his head. As Tansy drew herself up to a commanding height—no mean feat, considering she was seated—his grace thought: here we go, cant expressions, stable language and all. Why didn't he leave well enough alone and let Emily elope with that young dandy? How easily he could have avoided all this mess!

But when Tansy spoke it was quietly and with great dignity. "My *mother,* Lady Stanley, expired from a putrid cold the summer I was eight. Her only regret in dying was that she must leave her beloved husband *Sir Andrew Tamerlane,* my *father.* His sorrow may have led him to indulge quite earnestly in vices only dabbled at during his grasstime, and it may have hastened his blessed release from an unhappy life to a reunion in heaven with his beloved wife."

Avanoll was impressed. This was a crushing set-down, delivered with the expertise of a seasoned London matron. But his mouth dropped to half cock as Tansy finished her speech thusly:

"And my father's life was not, as you say, worthless, for he taught me many things. For one, he always impressed upon me never to behave so commonly as to malign needlessly the dead or attack those, living or dead, unable to defend themselves. Which is much the same case in this instance, don't you agree?"

As Lady Stanley's face took on an unbecoming shade of puce that clashed badly with her plumes, Tansy delivered the *coup de grâce.* "And Mama, thinking of my future no doubt, told me on her deathbed—with all the veracity of any deathbed utterance—never, *ever* to wear any color that would make my rather brown complexion look like dirty ditch-water after the mail coach has passed through it." The tenacious chin thrust out triumphantly as she added, "Looking at you, Lady Stanley, I can at last understand her concern. Good day."

Tansy whipped up her horses and neatly slid by Lady Stanley's landau, which could not move until her driver recovered from his fit of silent laughter. She had gone only a few paces when a voice called out, "Ashley, you sly dog, stop at once."

The Duke heard the voice and felt his stomach shatter into a million pieces before settling somewhere near his toes. "Brummell!" he whispered hoarsely. "We're in the basket now."

George Brummell, best known as the Beau, approached the phaeton, his grinning face making it obvious he had heard every word of Tansy's impassioned speech.

Ashley whispered quickly to his cousin, "Keep your mouth shut and we may get out of this yet. So far you have amused Beau—God only knows why—but one wrong word and you may as well try to spin gold from straw than present your face in public again." Much louder he said, "Good afternoon to you, Beau. You are a pleasant surprise."

In the middle of answering the Beau's question as to the identity of his companion, Avanoll suddenly felt himself pitchforked into a bizarre play—or farce, as he later termed it.

His cousin was sitting sedately beside him: basking in the afterglow of her triumph over Lady Stanley, her hands folded in her lap, her eyes scanning the horizon almost as if the presence of the one man in England who had the power to make or break her socially was at the least a person of little interest or at the worst a crushing bore. For this his grace was almost thankful. Indeed, nothing could be more fatal than for Tansy to act the tongue-tied miss—or worse, open her mouth and let out another cant expression. The Beau might consider a slip in the heat of anger amusing but two slips would brand her common or brazen.

One moment the Duke was counting his chickens, the next he sat with figurative egg all over his face. For Tansy's idle glance had suddenly locked onto something in the near distance that made her entire body stiffen. Before the Duke could do anything to check her, she had turned and executed a neat vault from her loftly perch to the gravel path. It was a graceful descent, all things considered, and showed both a strength of limb and degree of courage most misses would take pains to conceal. But it was not, alas, a completely clean jump.

Tansy's underslip, a frothy confection of snowy muslin and lace—and one of her favorite possessions, considering the rough quality of her undergarments these past few years—had somehow caught itself on the hub of the right wheel, raising the entirety of her skirts to an alarming height.

With a pang of regret, but not a moment's hesitation, she gave a violent tug on her skirts and was rewarded by a resounding *r-r-i-i-p*, not to mention immediate freedom.

Needless to state, the Duke's phaeton instantly became a traveling show for those of the *ton* who seemed mysteriously congregated in this one particular area of the Park. As her first speech upon jumping center stage, Tansy shouted loud and clear, "Don't just sit there staring like a dolt with your jaw at half-mast, Ashley. Follow me!"

Avanoll, with some memory of his army days and blind obedience and all that sort of thing coming to the fore, reacted almost against his will. He threw the reins to his groom, Leo, then hopped down from his seat and took off at a fast trot after Tansy's retreating figure. He paused for a second, however, taking time for a second look at those previously revealed and very shapely ankles that—with her skirts lifted for less encumbered movement—Tansy was again parading before all the bucks who also chased after her, quizzing glasses firmly stuck to their eyes.

Chapter Nine

WHEN TANSY reached the banks of the Serpentine, an innocuous-looking target for such violent attack, she stopped and began berating an innocent-appearing servant who was so cowed by her tirade that he seemed to shrink closer to the ground with every word.

As he neared the mismatched pair (it was rather like Gentleman Jackson taking on a chimney sweep), the Duke was muttering under his breath, "Reward the girl, they said. Take her for a ride in the Park they said. Reward her? Ha! I'll wring her troublesome neck first!" He raised his eyes to heaven and implored, "Oh, please, Lord. Get us out of this coil and I'll make it up to You. I'll," and here he did display the greatest English stiff-upper-lip imaginable, "I'll forego brandy and, yes—cigars, for a fortnight. No, an entire month. I swear it."

This last was said a bit louder, possibly because of the great emotion the proposed sacrifice brought to bear. But whatever the reason, his audience—rapidly approaching a multitude—was to be forever grateful.

Tansy too heard the Duke's promises, but her heart was not moved. "Fustian, Ashley," she declared baldly. "Quickly now, hold onto this rascal's ear so he can't lope off while I rescue the poor thing. Not that the fellow will probably move in any event, for if ever I saw such a slowtop I cannot remember it." She took one step and then added, more kindly, "Perhaps he is a mute?"

Then, as the astounded Duke stood impatiently by, unable to do more than hold onto the servant's sleeve—he looked like a groom by his livery—and stare bug-eyed as his cousin and her brand-new clothing from Madame Bertin, no less, plunged feet-first into the lake.

There were gasps, then giggles from the ladies present, snickers, and a few hearty guffaws from the gentlemen. Tansy quickly waded out into the lake until the water lapped gently against her hips and then, with a cry of "*Huzzah*," she reached one hand out to snare a burlap sack just sinking beneath the surface.

She quickly raised the sack above her head, where it danced and wiggled and poured down a copious waterfall that darkened Tansy's upstretched sleeve, cascaded over her upraised face, and made a limp rat's tail of the once-proud peacock feather in her bonnet.

"I say," came a cultured drawl from over Avanoll's shoulder, "rather, er, unique, ain't she? Don't you own a tub, Avanoll?"

Avanoll was formulating some sort of reply for the Beau but was saved—a move first blessed, then thoroughly damned—by Tansy's plea to wade in and get her out because her "blasted skirts" were tangling her legs and one jean half-boot was sunk in some sort of hole.

"Beau," the Duke asked urbanely, figuring he may as well be hung for a sheep as a lamb, "be a sport and hold onto this fellow for me while I assist my cousin."

Beau raised his glass, assessed Tansy's predicament without the fluttering of an eyelash, and turned to the servant. "Be a good fellow and play a little game for me. Pretend I am Lord Elgin and you are a statue. There's a good man. Don't move now, your arms might topple off, you know." Turning his head to Avanoll he said, "Ashley, old man, you may go do the pretty now. I have all in train here. By the by though, *sport*, were your ancestors prone to inbreeding?"

"What?" Avanoll asked before realizing what Beau was inferring. "We have our share of eccentrics, sir, but I cannot blame Tansy on any first-cousin marriage. My conclusion is that she was dropped on her head as an infant," he told him. "Repeatedly."

"Either that, friend, or she's the only sane one and we're all Bedlamites. Whatever is she about?"

Ashley shrugged, turned to meet his fate, and at the same time consigned his twice-worn Hessians to a watery grave. Shortly two figures stood on the grassy bank, surrounded by an audience gathered with bated breath to witness the *grande finale*.

Lady Stanley—front and center as usual when there was any gossip to be found, violet plumes vibrating wildly as she nodded her head vigorously—was busily informing all and sundry of the identity of the outlandish chit with the burlap bag clutched tightly to her bosom. Oh, she would dine out for a month on this story!

Tansy, oblivious to all the commotion she had caused, or just not giving two pins what anyone thought of her, dropped to her knees and tugged on the twine securing the top of the sack. "Ashley," she ordered as her hands encountered yet another wet knot, "Give me your penknife."

His grace knelt on the grass beside her, putting paid to what was left of his buckskins deftly sliced through the knotted twine, then reached inside the sack. When he brought forth his hands they were filled with a wet, reddish-brown tangle of fur that yipped once, then turned a small head and thanked his rescuer by biting down firmly on the Duke's thumb.

Avanoll yelped and dropped the dog—at least he supposed it was a dog—whereupon Tansy grabbed it up. The dog, for that is what it was, immediately began licking Tansy's face, beating his water-logged tail back and forth in a frenzied expression of ecstasy that effectively wetted any part of the Duke that had managed up to this point to remain dry.

Throughout it all the Beau, who had not been so diverted since roasting Alvanley when his lordship blissfully asked his blessing on a puce and yellow striped waistcoat, remained mute. But he felt it was time he took center stage for a bit. The action, he chuckled to himself, had become a bit "drippy."

Brummell addressed his speech to the petrified servant. "Now then, fellow, you obviously have done, or tried to do, this dastardly deed on orders from your master. Who, we horrified animal loving Christians desire to know, just *who* is the scoundrel who would countenance—nay, *instigate*—such a dastardly deed?"

"Yes, indeed," piped up Tansy as she pushed the pup's nose away from her ear. "Even in his present state I can see this is a superior animal, perhaps a setter."

"Yes, yes, make him tell us," came several cries from the audience.

"I can answer that," came yet another voice from the group. "That's Jillson's livery the fellow sports."

The groom, frightened nearly witless as the formerly amused onlookers showed signs of turning into an extremely hostile group, and with all of them directing their fury at him, quickly blurted out that the pup was the only one of a litter still surviving—a litter born when by chance one of his master's prize setters mated with a stray. Jillson wished the animal destroyed because he wanted no reminder of the bitch's consort with the lower orders. Since the groom was cutting through the Park on his way to see his sweetheart, who worked in the kitchens of a certain peer near the Stanhope Gate, he felt the Serpentine a fitting repository for the little beast.

Naturally the groom was not so articulate in his rendering of the events, but his laborious and muddled rendition was translated for the crowd by Brummell.

Mutterings were heard throughout the crowd, words like "cad" and "villain" being a few of the most oft-repeated.

Avanoll was too stunned by the events of the day to give himself over to much profound thinking, but this much was clear. By clever questioning and frowns and head-shakes denoting grim distaste and displeasure, the Beau had made Jillson the goat. Indeed, the Duke himself was definitely feeling quite uncharitable toward the fellow just now, and with any luck at all Tansy could emerge—unbelievable as it might seem—the heroine in the piece.

Mentally banishing his after-dinner enjoyments for a character-building month (thank goodness April had but thirty days), the Duke rose to his not inconsiderable height and announced, "I believe we here present, indeed all England, owe this brave young lady a debt of gratitude for the heroic and humane service she has performed here today."

The Beau, always quixotic (and in debt to the tune of many hundreds of pounds to the Duke after one particularly plaguey run of luck at White's which the Duke had kindly overlooked these past six weeks and more), sensed the crowd could go either way concerning the chit and decided to have a little fun. The herd would follow him, as it always did—mindless animals that they were, he thought—for his opinion of his fellows' brain power was not high.

"What's your cousin's name, Avanoll?" the Beau asked quietly, just as the Duke was really getting the bit between his teeth. After Avanoll answered he thanked him and told him to hold his tongue and watch a master work.

"I concur with his grace," he began in a loud, clear voice. "With no concern for her safety, with strong presence of mind and purity of purpose, Miss Tamerlane here, er, *plunged* into the fray and rescued one of God's sinless creatures." He puffed out his chest, postured himself elegantly with one hand on his heart, and then boomed, "And a *dog*, no less! *Man*'s best friend. Today, however, today *man* chose to callously destroy this

68

innocent creature of nature. It took a young woman, a lady I place on a par with Boadicea, to see her duty and snatch this wretched animal from the watery jaws of death while the *gentlemen* among us did nothing."

He stopped for breath and passed his eyes over the crowd. Women wept openly into fine cambric handkerchiefs, and even a smattering of the gentlemen present appeared a trifle misty.

The Beau walked stage-left to where Tansy sat gazing up at her extoller with a bemused look on her damp face. The peacock feather drooped across her nose and she blew it upwards, only to have it hit the Beau in the eye as he bowed low before her.

Undaunted, he raised Tansy to her feet and turned to face his awe-struck audience. "Ladies and gentlemen. May I present to you all Miss Tansy Tamerlane, daughter of Sir Andrew Tamerlane and cousin of the Duke of Avanoll, whose distinguished guest she is to be for the Season." He lifted her hand above her head, much like the victor in a fistfight and exclaimed, "Let us hear three cheers for our heroine of the lake, our very own *tenacious* Miss Tamerlane!"

"Hear, hear!" rang out the crowd. "Good show. Hip, hip, hooray!" And then, "Speech, speech!"

The Duke's slightly lightened heart plummeted to his soggy toes as his cousin made every sign of complying with this last request. She bent down and scooped the shivering puppy into her arms and held him above her head, where he yipped merrily and lolled his pink tongue from side to side. "A cheer for Horatio, who has scored a stunning victory at sea!" she blurted in a very Boadicea-like way, endearing herself forever in the hearts of her audience. Even Lady Stanley condescended to applaud softly, knowing it the height of folly to buck the tide on this particular issue.

And to the Duke's amazement, the cheers rang out again. Before they could die down and more notice be taken of their heroine's hoydenish appearance, Avanoll sidled up to the Beau. "You have my everlasting gratitude, sir. Consider all debts paid in full," he said earnestly.

Without losing his handsome smile the Beau returned, "We're lucky to be away with our skins intact, but then the *hoi-polloi* (included in this sweeping classification were, to the Duke's quick deduction, three earls, a viscount and a marquess) is so lamentably gullible. Even gulling them becomes a bore. I would advise you to beat a hasty retreat now, however, and please, as soon as your clothes dry sufficiently, *burn* them. You and the little rescuer, I must make bold to say, smell dreadfully like a swamp. I myself already am reconciled to destroying every stitch now upon my person and sitting in a bath for at least three hours. Never before have I felt so entirely grubby. I shall be late to Carlton House, but there is no help for it. I do hope you appreciate the effort, Ashley. I could have destroyed that girl, you know."

"I know, Beau," Avanoll allowed, passing over the blatant lie of a dinner invitation to Carlton House when Beau and Prinney hadn't been on speaking terms for over a year, "and I repeat my thanks. Add a new rig-out to your wardrobe and send the bills to me."

"Yes, yes, of course, dear fellow," the Beau said as he raised a scented handkerchief to his delicate nostrils, so urgent his need to be shed of the Duke that he overlooked his immaculate attire being called a rig-out, of all things. "Be off with you now." As Avanoll turned to go the Beau ventured, "I wonder, Avanoll. Do we cut Jillson next time we meet, just to lend credence to our little drama?"

The Duke gave a short laugh. "I doubt the need. By tea time today the story will be all over the city, only it will be *three* dogs, all prime specimens, and Jillson will have been discovered skulking near the scene of the crime with at least one pitiable carcass at his feet and blood on his hands. No, I wager he will find it convenient to rusticate for a few weeks. Although I have no doubt Society will bear up well in his absence, as he always was a bit of a queer touch anyway. You and I both know it won't be long until another scandal will be found to dull the memory of his infamous deed."

"Would you care to wager another suit of clothes your dear cousin is involved in the next scandal, too?" the Beau teased.

The smile vanished from Avanoll's face. "I never bet on sure things," he bit out, and strode purposefully over to Tansy—and made to pull her unceremoniously away from four or five young bloods vying for her attention, to the extent of dirtying their lily-white hands applying affectionate pats on Horatio's toad-eating head.

Once Tansy was again seated beside him the Duke yanked the reins from Leo's hands, causing the man's broadly grinning face to rearrange itself into a suitably solemn, commiserating expression.

Tansy, however, was heady with her success and totally oblivious to the fact that the man riding next to her was ready to do murder. She chattered on about how terribly *natural* and *unaffected* Society people were, and how she had been so silly to have reservations about her eventual acceptance into their circle. She may even have been allowed to cling to this bit of *naiveté*, as the Duke was too overset to push a single sound past his lips, if not for Horatio.

It seems the animal had taken umbrage at the Duke's presence once he espied it, and immediately became quite vocal in his anxiety to have the offending person take himself off.

"Isn't that cute, cousin?" Tansy laughed delightedly. "Horatio recognizes you and associates you with his dunk in the lake. I really believe the poor misguided darling would nip you if I were but to loosen my grip a bit."

That tore it. His grace was cold, wet, humiliated, his thumb was throbbing, and he was probably in the early stages of pneumonia. Suddenly the words came quite easily, if they were only a touch difficult to understand—a pardonable offense when one is speaking through clenched jaws.

"Well, isn't Horatio *darling* just too, too amusing, Miss Tamerlane? But I must caution you not to loose your grip as I have already lost mine—on my sanity. I see no other reason I can sit here and listen to you babbling inanely on about your social *coup*, as if it were not the second worst disaster in history. You were only saved from stares, insults, and possibly even your very own straight waistcoat for your ride to Bedlam, by *my* quick thinking."

Tansy was finally forced to take the time to look at her cousin, and herself, and was prone to admit they did make a rather odd pair— driving through London in sopping wet, uncomfortable, and slightly offensive-to-the-nose clothing—the duke appearing disheveled, but still very much the gentleman, and herself, looking as if she had been dunked in a well and then dragged through a hedge backwards. The sodden Horatio added nothing to their consequence.

The day's heroine was slightly deflated but unrepentant. "We saved a poor animal from an undeserved, cruel death. I think we were justified. Besides, Mr. Brummell liked it and you yourself say he is the last word on what is proper. At least I think he liked it," she ended lamely as a vein in the side of the Duke's neck began to throb wildly.

"That's precisely the problem, madam, you *don't* think. You act. Eons later, perhaps, if the Gods are kind, you think. And there is no 'we' about it, madam," Avanoll pointed out. "I freely give you all praise—and all blame. It never entered your head, I suppose, to apprise me of what you had seen and let me order Leo to effect the rescue? Oh, no," he sneered, "rational thought comes no more easily to you than to any other female."

He turned to glare at her, nearly letting go of the reins, so intense was his anger. "Dash it, woman, if it weren't for my timely intervention with that tarradiddle about Englishmen and dumb animals, Beau's equally quick perception of what I was about, and a mellow crowd, you may as well have strutted stark naked down Bond Street for all the blasted fool you made of yourself today. As it is now your name will be a byword in every club from White's to the Daffy, an occurrence not exactly sought after by well-bred young ladies, might I point out. But then . . . oh, forget it."

"But, then, I am not a well-bred young lady. That was what you were going to say, wasn't it?" Tansy dared him.

Leo made a sound in his throat and endeavored to make himself invisible as the glaring duo in front of him appeared about to come to cuffs.

Luckily, Avanoll House was just ahead, and further arguments were pushed aside in the pair's haste to get inside and rid themselves of their sodden clothes.

The Duke hopped lightly down from his seat, and whether or not he would have assisted his cousin was not to be guessed at for she had climbed down by herself—and was already standing rock-still on the flagway waiting for him to enter the house before her.

Dunstan never blinked at the odd sight that greeted him as he made his way to the foyer, although his private thoughts would have proved interesting. His grace was already stripping off his mud-stained driving gloves, the ones with the hole in the left thumb, while Miss Tamerlane stood to one side, an ominous puddle forming about her feet and a smelly lump of fur in her arms.

"Dunstan," imparted his grace in awful tones, "I will not be dining at home this evening after all. I feel it, er, *safer* for all concerned to remove my person from the bosom of my family for a space, until the combination of an orderly, well-run establishment and the company of emotionally stable companions such as I may find at my Club convince me the whole world has not run mad."

Having delivered himself of this crushing set-down he turned on his heel, planning to ascend to his rooms, but he was forestalled by Dunstan's placid reminder that he had invited guests to dine at Avanoll this same evening.

The Duke dismissed this bit of news with a wave of his hand, some faint bit of humor entering his cold eyes. "Oh, that was all a hum, Dunny. I only said it to give our new housekeeper a showcase for her talent, a chance to strut out her *expertise* and instruct us all in the proper way to handle a domestic crisis, so to speak."

This blatant insult was enough to rouse Tansy from her brown study, the sarcastic remarks touching off a chord of memory. "One moment, please, before you slosh off, your grace. Just what, sir—if I, a mere employee, may make so bold as to ask you to enlarge upon just one of the many pearls of wisdom that dribbled off your tongue a bit earlier—is the *premier disaster* in *The History of the World According to Avanoll?*" She then stuck out her chin, her haughty demeanor slightly undone by the issuance of a violent sneeze—a sneeze that prompted the belabored peacock feather to give up the ghost and waft drunkenly down to become the object of a farcical burial at sea in the puddle at Tansy's feet.

The Duke halted his progress on the third step, turned, raised a muddy quizzing glass to his eye, and regarded Tansy through it as if she were a particularly vile clump of refuse.

"*That*, my good woman, should be obvious even to you. The day you came into my life beats both the Great Fire and the Black Death by a far piece. You, madam, are in fact a walking disaster," he sneered, dropping his glass and exposing the resulting imprint of mud that etched a perfect circle around his eye and totally destroyed the few remaining shreds of his dignity.

Tansy was too upset to find any comfort in Avanoll's bizarre appearance, and could only watch silently as he disappeared toward his rooms—where Farnley was undoubtedly ready to greet him with a hot tub and a long string of "I told you so's."

But the little drama was not yet done. In the foyer Dunstan approached Tansy, a look of pity apparent on his kindly face. She averted her eyes, not quite hiding the tears that threatened to fall, and asked him if he would be so kind as to have someone in the kitchens bathe and feed Horatio while she repaired upstairs to "clean up this mess I have become."

So overcome by her heroic display of composure was Dunstan that he himself deigned to transport the damp puppy belowstairs—at arms length, of course. As Tansy reached the same stair his grace had employed as a dais from which to utter his cutting remarks, she turned and appealed meekly to Dunstan. "I know I am impulsive and don't take time to think things through, but am I really the monster his grace believes me to be?" she implored.

Dunstan halted in his tracks and strove to appear dignified while Horatio licked at his ear. "Indeed, no, Miss Tansy. You are a capital person, and so say all of us belowstairs."

This loyalty buoyed Tansy's spirits so much that she summoned up a brief smile and replied, "That is kind of all of you, Dunny. But I know I can be a bit of a trial sometimes. Even Papa, who loved me dearly whenever he could recollect my existence, admitted I was capable of getting tangled up in the most dreadful coils. I do not set out to get into trouble, Dunny, honestly I don't; things just seem to have a way of *happening* when I'm around. But his grace thinks—well, his grace is just the rudest, most arrogant, top-lofty beast in nature! I am thoroughly out of patience with him. He casts me as a Jonah, a jinx. Let me tell you, *he* has been no ray of sunbeams in *my* life either."

Tansy's voice grew stronger and her posture more erect as she spoke, until now she just possibly did resemble a Boadicea, albeit a soggy one. She gave a defiant toss of her head, her natural high spirits finding solace in a bout of unladylike ferocity, and began a militant march up the steps. Tossing over her shoulder one last burst of defiance, she announced, "I hope Ashley takes a cold and his nose runs and turns red and he has to hide himself away in his rooms for a fortnight. Then I shall send up nothing but invalid gruel and weak broth until he begs me to accept his apology. And what will I do, eh, Dunny? I shall snap my fingers in his face, *that's* what I shall do!"

And with her ego well satisfied, she went looking for Pansy and a hot tub.

74

Chapter Ten

FOR THE FIRST few days after what the servants at Avanoll House dubbed "The Big Fuss," everyone tiptoed about the great mansion in Grosvenor Square as if they were treading on eggshells.

With some very noticeable exceptions. Lady Emily, while outwardly demure and subdued, was often closeted with her maid, heads together. Such occurrences usually presaged one of Emily's mad schemes and would have warned enlightened observers that trouble loomed heavy in the future. But any likely observers had other things on their minds.

Aunt Lucinda, once informed of Tansy's latest disgrace, waxed eloquent on several topics, dealing mainly with ingratitude, knowing one's place, the perfidy of man's best friend, and the decline of Greece, the last of which seemed unrelated to the subject at hand, but it was a thought no one felt inclined to pursue.

Nothing was known of the reactions of the two principal participants in the fracas. Tansy refused to speak of the incident at all, and the only outward change to be seen was the increasing amount of time she spent secluded in her room—where Horatio was being given instruction in the behavior expected of canines who had so far twice mistaken the Duke's bedpost for a tree trunk and selected Aunt Lucinda's satin bedspread as a repository for his bones and other treasures.

Little, too, can be told about the Duke, a sorely used man who invariably found his cravats overstarched, his eggs underdone, and his bedroom fire either meager or damply smoking, or both. No need to ask who the servants judged guilty in the affair.

Sad to say, but true, Avanoll—a man judged quite unflappable in Parliament, termed intrepid in the hunt, and hailed as a noted wit in the company of his fellows—was at a loss when it came to dealing with women and servants. Indeed, he had ignored his staff and avoided feminine entanglements all his life.

He was neither prepared nor anxious for a showdown now, so in the end he took the line of least resistance. He absented himself from his own home as frequently as he could, and for as long as he dared. He was, when he thought deeply about it, ashamed of his cowardice. But he did not alter his course. He saw the constant ribbings his friends gave him about the exploit as fitting punishment for his faint-heartedness.

The dowager, who had lived longer and seen more than anyone else in the household, considered the brouhaha to be a huge comedy. Granted, Tansy had had a lucky escape, for she could have been socially destroyed. Granted, Ashley had some valid reasons for climbing on his high horse.

But the dowager felt her grandson's outraged sense of *ton* was not his only tender spot, and that he was also suffering from a bad case of nose-out-of-joint-edness. It was not that unpleasant to witness his discomfort. Truly, things were developing along quite interesting lines, so the aging intriguer thought, and she was content for the moment to sit back and watch the sport.

Yet, unbelievably, one member of the Duke's household—though ever mindful to keep birch twigs tucked in his hat band so as to ward off Tansy's Evil Eye—had been made almost jubilant by his master's latest tangle with Miss Tamerlane. Farnley, the Avanoll's live-in doomsday prophet, was almost disgustingly delighted by the materialization of the heavy run of bad luck he had predicted Tansy's presence would precipitate.

Hadn't the lady arrived on a Monday—a day everyone knows to mean danger if a person in the household sneezes twice before breakfast? And hadn't the Duke been too liberal peppering his eggs that very morning (so unusual a lapse for the master), so that two very loud and distinct sneezes were to be heard ringing through the breakfast room? Farnley knew the way of things, he did, and from the moment Miss Tamerlane had set foot in the door later that same day, he had been fearing the worst.

If only the Duke would agree to the wearing of the blue beads Farnley knew would protect the innocent from the Evil Eye! But, no, the Duke had merely laughed and tossed the beads into a corner. He wasn't laughing now, thought the valet. Perhaps if he put the beads where his master could see them he would have second thoughts on the matter.

Yet amulets and domestic *contretemps* not withstanding, time was marching on toward the opening of the Season—with still so much to be accomplished before the young women of Avanoll House were ready to make their debuts.

It was in partial remedy to this situation that the women of the household were hard at work in the dust-sheeted ballroom.

"No, no, no! My dear gel, you are not, I repeat, *not* to take such gargantuan strides. This is a waltz, the epitome of grace and beauty. You are to float in your partner's arms as a fairy drifts across a meadow of daisies." The dowager's voice dipped to a mannish lowness to emphasize her point. "You look like a farmer wading through his cow pasture and trying not to trod in anything."

As the dowager spoke, her granddaughter—who sat curled up daintily in a window seat—bit on her handkerchief in order to hold back her giggles while Tansy, flushed with frustration and feeling very little the fairy and very much like a knock-kneed pachyderm, threw down her dancing partner (a housemaid's rush broom) with a resounding slam.

"Try if you can to come to grips with the obvious, your grace," Tansy implored, stretching out her arms to her tutor-cum-tormentor, "I am a hopeless case. The country dances and the rest are all well and good—I rarely will come close enough to my partners to risk maiming them—but I am never going to master this blasted waltzing. I cannot even take to the floor with a broom, who I might add does not lead with much authority. Besides, I am to chaperon Emily, am I not? And chaperons do not waltz," she ended with conviction.

The dowager sighed and repeated her arguments for, she fervently hoped, the last time. "My dear Tansy, chaperons don't usually dance, I agree. But you are so young, and so well-known—although my grandson would say notorious," she added as an aside, "since you rescued that beastly mutt Horatio—that you are sure to be asked to stand up for the waltz any number of times. You are moderately proficient in the milder dances, but in the waltz you must be more than adequate. You must be flawless. A partner suddenly yelping in pain because you have blundered onto his instep is not a happening to be thought of as anything less than a capital sin. And," she added without a hope of being heeded, "ladies do *not* say 'blasted.'"

At the end of this homily the old lady signaled to Emily that it was time for some musical accompaniment to the spoken "one-two-three, one-two-three" cadence they had been calling out for the past half-hour, and Emily dutifully approached the spinet.

Tansy looked mutinous for a moment, then sighed and picked up Sir Humphrey—her fortunately footless partner. As Emily began playing, Tansy curtsied mockingly to the broom and commenced whirling about the Avanoll ballroom once more. "One-two-three," she said addressing the broom before launching into an example of the light conversational drivel she was told must accompany her steps.

"Yes, thank you, I am enjoying the Season above all things, one—two—three, how kind of you to ask," she breathed as she batted her eyelashes at the spikey shafts that made up her partner's head. As she completed one turn of the room and neared the dowager, she could resist no longer and pointed out impishly, "I wager you have the devil's own time finding a willing tailor, Sir Humphrey, one—two—three. Are we to see you at the opera tomorrow night, one—two—three? Those foreign howlers are such bores! They make it impossible to hold a decent conversation at times with their bellowing, one—two—three, but *everyone* attends, and what one cannot abjure one must endure, one—two—three, I always say."

Both the dowager and Emily burst into laughter, and once again the broom clattered loudly to the polished oak floor. This time the unfairly condemned Sir Humphrey was further insulted by a well-placed kick that sent him skidding through the open double doors and into the foyer, where he come to an ignominious halt against one glossy, black Hessian boot.

A few seconds later Sir Humphry re-entered the ballroom, this time held grudgingly in the grasp of his grace, the Duke. He advanced purposefully toward his cousin, who was now standing with arms akimbo in the middle of the floor, daring him to say something cutting. "Your broom, cousin," he offered solemnly. "I take it the naughty thing has offended you in some way? Did it make untoward advances on your virtue, or was it simply a case of mutual disenchantment? Perhaps you are unfair to the poor thing, judging it at fault when in truth you are not using it correctly." His lips twitched in barely concealed mirth as he dug the needle more firmly home. "I am convinced if you but put a leg over it the thing will oblige you by flying you anywhere you wish to go."

Emily looked vacant for a moment, then clapped her hands and cried gaily, "Oh, Tansy, Ashley is saying you are a witch! Isn't that right, Grandmama? I am right, aren't I?" she added as silence greeted her words.

The dowager shot daggers at her granddaughter and was

about to insist her grandson apologize when Tansy replied warmly, "You are correct, Emily. That is exactly what your brother implied. And he is quite correct. Indeed, I *am* a witch. As you can all see, I have already turned a Duke into a toad. Some other witch before my time made some inroads on making him a boor and a bully, so I fear I cannot take all the credit. But since my parlor tricks so amuse you, Emily, stay around a bit and I'll see if I can capture the Duke's true character and transform him into a poisonous toad*stool*. At least then we shan't have to listen to him croak."

"Bested you, grandson," her grace pointed out with a chuckle. "Care to try again? Emily do be quiet. I swear you cackle like a hen laying a three-pound egg." She directed her next words back to the man now balefully glaring at his cousin, who was balefully glaring back. "Ashley, your services are required here for approximately one hour," she announced in a tone that brooked no argument.

The Duke gave Tansy one last searing look and turned to his grandparent. "I am terribly afraid I must disoblige you, madam. I am due at Cribb's in a few minutes," he inserted without much hope of being excused.

"Splendid. You can do much the same here as you would there. The footwork doesn't vary all that much, and you can toss verbal punches instead of real ones. Not to say you'll come off any less bruised. Our Tansy is a proper right'un, you know, when it comes to sparring and, leave er, wisty castors."

The Duke was at a loss. "I do not wish to play dancemaster to any lead-footed miss who cannot even caper about with inanimate objects without accident, Grandmama. And," he added darkly, "I must question your sources on the knowledge of fisticuffs and boxing cant."

The dowager explained happily, "Tansy has witnessed a mill or two in her earlier years, and has kindly explained all sorts of things—like uppercutting and boneboxes and the like." The Duke's eyes rolled in mock horror. "What we require now is a dancing partner for Tansy," the dowager continued. "It is impossible to capture the correct mood and rhythm with a broomstick."

Any amusement the Duke experienced at his grandmother's inelegant interest in boxing evaporated in the heat of his indignation. "I repeat, I'll be damned if I'll dance with her," he exploded angrily. "Every time I come within ten feet of the chit, disaster strikes."

"And I'll be damned if I'd let him within twenty feet of me!" Tansy retorted hotly. The two returned to glaring at each other.

"The children are squabbling again, Grandmama," Emily supplied facetiously. "Shall we send them to bed without their porridge?"

"Stow it, brat," her brother warned her. "You are not too old to be spanked." Emily promptly burst into tears.

"Don't include an innocent infant in our quarrel," Tansy threatened. "She has always looked to you, her so *tonnish*, perfect brother, for guidance in how to go on. She only follows your sterling example."

"That will be enough, from *all* of you," the dowager pronounced coldly when it appeared the scene before her was about to degenerate into violence. "Tansy, you are to master waltzing and you are to master it today. If Dunstan knew the steps we would not have to make use of Ashley, who is only a mediocre dancer in any case."

Avanoll's head jerked up at this calumny.

"Ashley, as your grandmother and a frail old woman sorely tried in her declining years and worthy of better than she is receiving, *and* as a woman fully capable of making your life a veritable hell if she so chooses, I must insist you resign yourself to partnering your cousin. Emily, you may accompany them when you have done with those crocodile tears. They may work on Lucinda, but they'll cut no wheedle with me."

Emily moved to the spinet and stood there. "Well," coaxed the dowager, "sit down."

"Oh, did you want me to play?" Emily questioned blankly.

"No, I just thought you could see better from there. I am going to hum the tune in German."

Emily giggled. "Grandmama, you are so droll!"

The dowager shook her head. "That gel is such a ninny," she told the room in general. "I truly believe my late daughter-in-law played my son false. No son of mine could have sired such an air-head."

Lady Emily, who cast herself as a blameless innocent in a harsh world, born into a family of vile-tongued creatures whose blood contained not one drop of sensibility, patted carefully at the two tears she had produced on demand and began pounding out a technically correct tune in a belligerent military march tempo.

The two combatants—dancers—eyed each other warily and assumed their battle—waltzing—stations. Tansy laid her hand lightly in Avanoll's outstretched palm and gingerly placed her other hand on his broad, unpadded shoulder. Avanoll closed his hand just enough to keep their arms angled correctly and grasped her surprisingly small waist in a wary hold.

They started slowly, feeling each other out as fighters in the ring, Tansy mentally monitoring her steps and the Duke slowly counting to ten to cool his temper. From her chair halfway across the room the dowager admonished them to stop looking like they were dancing their way to Tyburn and the gibbet, and further directed her grandson to give Tansy some practice in the art of pleasant conversation while dancing.

Actually, Avanoll found himself not as adverse to partnering his cousin as his countenance implied. After a few false steps she seemed to find the correct rhythm, and in point of fact was as light on her feet as the petite Emily. This after he had expected her to try and lead *him* around the floor. He tightened his hold, shortening the distance between them to a still proper but more intimate degree, and his nostrils caught the light flowery scent of her newly-washed hair. He wouldn't delude himself into think- ing he was enjoying himself, but it was becoming increasingly difficult to maintain his earlier anger. "I see no problem in your form, cousin. Perhaps the old dragon was just pushing you too hard."

Tansy had never been in such close proximity to a man before and was finding the experience quite heady. She had no wish to antagonize Avanoll again and cut short her enjoyment. She didn't answer for a moment or two, and then thanked him prettily for his appraisal of her expertise—which she disclaimed credit for, suggesting the adeptness of her current partner over Sir Humphrey.

Puzzled, the Duke asked who this Sir Humphrey could be. Again her answer was slightly delayed, and then she informed him with a grin, " You were not properly introduced, I know, but he quite threw himself at your feet a few minutes ago, begging sanctuary."

Avanoll tossed back his head and laughed, then asked why she was delaying her answers. "Perhaps civility to me comes hard, and your words must first be carefully screened in your mind," he suggested.

For the first time he was treated to the sight of a very flattering blush on his cousin's face. "I could not reply in the middle of my counting. I answered you as soon as I reached three. You wouldn't want me to tread on your toes, would you?"

Again the Duke's laughter rang out, and the dowager and Emily exchanged sly looks. See, their eyes said, if we but persevere they will cry friends yet. At least that was the extent of Emily's hopes. Her grace's aspirations went considerably higher, but there was no need to rush her fences. There was plenty of time for mother nature and herself to work their combined wiles. If not, a well-engineered compromise or two should do the trick. I'd lock 'em up together in the conservatory for a sen'night to force a marriage, she told herself smugly, if I didn't believe they'd pelt each other to flinders with the oranges.

Emily put a gentler, more romantic tone into her playing as her mood improved, and the dancers matched her by whirling and swaying with increasing confidence. The Duke's hand tightened on Tansy's waist and she responded unwittingly by holding more firmly to his ungloved hand. As they neared the far end of the dance floor the Duke spoke again. "Are you still counting, my dear?"

Tansy's head snapped up at his use of this casual intimacy, and she blushed again as she assured him she had stopped counting some time ago.

"Good," he answered with an accompanying wink. "Then what say we give the old girl a little exhibition?" With Tansy's form gently but firmly in his control, he swept them into a series of turns that billowed out her muslin skirts and brought a smile of pure enjoyment to her face. Round and round the floor they glided, their eyes locked together as their bodies moved as if in silent communion.

The dowager signaled to her granddaughter and the two rose and stole silently from the room. Once outside the old lady shook her head at Emily. "Close your gaping mouth before a moth finds its home in your molars, and hie your precious self out of the path of destiny."

"Whatever do you mean?" Emily gasped.

The dowager sighed and gave the girl a none-too-gentle shove toward the stairs. The dowager then went off to the morning room, where she raised her eyes heavenward and addressed her departed husband. "Dearest, pray your grandson is not so stiff and proper as to pass up a golden opportunity like this. Or worse yet, so dull-witted as not to recognize it as such. Ah, but then he couldn't be your offspring and be such a slowtop, could he, my dear?" She gave a sly wink, then, unbelievably, the old lady's cheeks blushed a faint pink at a long-forgotten, sweet memory.

She recovered herself quickly, cast her eyes about to be sure she had not been overheard, and returned to the foyer, quietly closing the double doors to the ballroom as she went. Horatio sidled up to her and she tersely commanded him to "sit," which he did; and to "stay," which he had every intention of doing— even if it meant missing his dinner, since his beloved mistress was still behind those closed doors; and lastly, to "guard," which he did not quite understand, but then two out of three wasn't really so bad for a pup as young as he.

Almost before the dowager was out of sight, Horatio, head comfortably settled on his outstretched paws, was sound asleep, dreaming of his mistress' ecstasy-producing talent of scratching that one unreachable spot behind his left ear.

Chapter Eleven

IT HAD BEEN several seconds before the dancers still inside the ballroom noticed the lack of musical accompaniment. Once awareness set in they halted suddenly in the center of the floor and Tansy reluctantly made to move away, but Avanoll's grip tightened and he drew her still closer. She could see the question in his blue eyes as his head slowly moved toward her. (Somewhere his grandfather was smiling.)

Avanoll halted in his move for a moment, giving Tansy time to back away, but she was too startled to take heed of his chivalry. Her eyelids briefly widened, then fluttered and closed as his lips covered hers in a soft, tentative kiss.

All too soon he lifted his head to stare at her as if he had suddenly discovered a stranger in his arms. He released her only to bring his hands up to cup her face and whisper, "I must be mad!" then kiss her again, this time not at all tentatively.

At first Tansy was stunned, but then a sudden weakness invaded her limbs and she clutched at Avanoll's lapels to keep herself from falling. She heard his muttered exclamation and silently agreed: they must both be quite mad. His second kiss succeeded in banishing this and all thought but one: the conclusion that being kissed knocked anything else she had ever experienced all to sticks. A convulsive shiver ran down her spine, and she could feel an answering tremor in Avanoll's body as her hands encountered his muscular, silk-clad chest.

Then, suddenly, it was over, and she was roughly pushed backwards and would have fallen but for her convulsive clutching of the Duke's lapels.

Avanoll's countenance was a study in conflicting emotions as he ran his eyes over Tansy's features: her mouth, moist and trembling; her cheeks, slightly flushed; her eyes, misty and a bit dazzled-looking. Tansy, in her turn, could see the disbelief, indignation, and what a more experienced woman would recognize as a rising desire, registering on his face in their turn.

Indignation finally won. He raised his hands and brusquely disengaged hers from his coat. "I shall have a hard time explaining my crushed appearance to Farnley," he said stiffly, if a bit shakily. "I am at a loss to understand my total lapse in propriety. I can only say I regret it, and beg humbly for your forgiveness."

Tansy was shaken to her core and felt an overweening desire to burst into loud, raucous tears. To prevent such a humiliating occurrence she took refuge in anger.

"I do not know how you arrived at your conclusion, but I have the distinct impression you believe me the instigator of this touching little scene. As I would have had to stand on tiptoe and forcibly yank you down to my level by your ears in order to so compromise your honor, however, I fail to see any such guilt resting with me. Furthermore, I seriously doubt I could have lured you into my arms, as Emily has only had time for one short lesson in flirting and that to do with making calves-eyes at gentlemen overtop a fluttering fan."

As a slow, red flush rose in his grace's cheeks, she added in a terrible voice, "Uppermost, I greatly resent your weak-kneed apology. You speak of, er, our—er, it—as if it were a distasteful interlude best erased from your memory. Well, I am not of the same mind for, frankly, I enjoyed it more than a little bit! I shall regard it as my first lesson in romance—given, no doubt, by a master." As the Duke tried to get a word in, she further informed him, "And do not fear I shall cry rope to your grandmother and force you to wed me, perish the very thought," at last her voice showed signs of cracking under the press of her injured feelings, "for I shouldn't have you if you were served up to me on a platter of gold with—with a dressed duck hang—hanging from your mouth!"

Avanoll reached out and grabbed Tansy's shoulders, wishing only to shake her into listening to reason. Why did this infernal female always take his words and twist them around to make him sound either a cold, callous brute or a mindless, blithering idiot?

He didn't mean he *regretted* kissing her, dammit, in fact, it ranked as quite the most enjoyable kiss in his memory. He only wanted to save her embarrassment when she had time to recall that she had, instead of resisting or even fainting, as any female might, in actual fact, kissed him back with unschooled but extremely unmaidenly ardor. He knew she was past hearing his explanation but gave it a try anyway.

"You are quite wrong, Tansy, my dear," he contented himself with saying, as Tansy's tirade seemed spent. "I far from regret our, er, recent closer acquaintance. I quite enjoyed it, actually," he informed her in an only slightly amused voice. Tansy's wavering smile allowed him to think he was forgiven.

Deeper pondering of this incident would come easier at his Club, with a glass or two of port to hand. For now he contented himself by simply dipping his head quickly and kissing the tip of her nose before making for the door, leaving a bemused Tansy staring at his retreating back—one hand absently touching her lips.

Avanoll turned at the door and—in celebration of his startling discovery of a new and vastly intriguing side of his cousin, not to mention his superior handling of a sticky situation the girl could have mushroomed into an ugly tale of compromise if not for his quick talking—jauntily saluted her.

Be good to give the girl a little romance to dream about, he congratulated himself. The incident wouldn't be repeated, for that could lead to problems, but now that she had had a taste of womanhood, perhaps she would join Emily in her husband-hunting and he would be rid of her. Strangely, that thought destroyed some of his good mood, but he refused to let it ruin his day.

As he made to turn away again Tansy suddenly called out his name but he merely smiled, letting her know that although romantic dalliance had its place, it was time now for other pursuits. He shook his head in the negative and wagged a finger at her that meant "Naughty puss, I must be off," and turned once more for the door, "the hero making his exit," and with one step turned his hoped-for dramatic exit into a circus stunt as he tripped over Horatio and went sprawling head-first onto the black and white tiles of the foyer.

As he fell, one outstretched hand struck up a passing acquaintance with a bust of Homer perched atop a pedestal, and both objects immediately joined him in making a closer acquaintance with the rapidly-rising floor. After the resounding crash—which deprived that noted poet of one of his finely sculpted marble ears and the tip of his majestic nose—there was a brief, succinct utterance describing, in a high degree of color, the Duke's conclusion as to Horatio's base character and an unnecessary pointing out of his mother's sex.

Naturally, Horatio took exception to this vulgar abuse, not to mention the insult of a booted toe being stubbed mightily into his slumbering form. He immediately took up a menacing stance at the head of his fallen foe, and with barks and growls and bared teeth gave back as good as he had got.

The Duke, picturing his face in peril of being disfigured in much the same way as the head slowly rocking to and fro nearby—be it by way of canine teeth rather than a hard floor—made haste to remove his head (indeed his entire body) from said canine's proximity. But upon attempting to rise a stabbing pain in his right ankle brought yet another string of unmentionable words past his lips, and he had to content himself with an ignominious slithering retreat across the tiles on his hindquarters to put any distance between himself and his attacker.

By this time Tansy was kneeling at his side and trying desperately to hold the enraged Horatio in check. "Oh, my dear Ashley," she inquired breathlessly, "are you all right? I did try to warn you."

He favored her with a speaking glance and spat, "Am I all right, she asks? I go flying to the floor, landing heavily I might add, am nearly concussed by an avalanche of marble, suffer what will surely prove to be no less than a broken ankle, am threatened by a mad dog, and she asks if I'm all right. Oh, I'm just fine, Miss Tamerlane, right as a trivet," he informed her sarcastically. "Ah, you smile. How wonderful. I live only to please you, you know. Perhaps you wish me to feed my hand to your vicious brute here as a reward for nearly killing me—but not the left one, I implore you, for it is only just healed from my last encounter with the bloody beast."

"'Pride goeth before destruction, and an haughty spirit before a fall.' Proverbs," came a voice from behind and above the fallen hero.

Avanoll ignored the voice. He had more than enough on his plate without encouraging Lucinda to expound more fully on this last uncalled for and grossly undeserved observation on a probable reason for his having been so badly used.

Aside from his aunt, the noise of the accident had roused nearly all the family and staff so that by the time of the Duke's little speech the dowager, Emily, Dunstan, Farnley, three footmen, two chambermaids, and a tweeny who had yet to learn better, had all converged on the foyer to make up a not insignificant audience.

"Dunstan," Tansy ordered, "kindly remove Horatio before

the master goes into a taking. Have Leo rub some liniment into his back where he was kicked, and perhaps Cook will give him a nice bone to soothe his feelings."

Turning to the Duke she queried politely, "Perhaps a soupbone to gnaw on will help your disposition as well, your grace, or would you rather a vinaigrette or some feathers burnt under your nose? I do fear you are suffering from shock and hysterics."

A titter running through the onlookers brought a thunderous look from the Duke, and the servants quickly melted away.

What an unusual household! thought the tweeny, fresh from the country. First they come home all wet and evil-smelling, and then they roll about on the floor talking about soup bones. Queer in the attic, she surmised, and wished she could write so she could tell her mum of the frightful goings on in London Town.

The dowager stood looking down at the pair on the floor, glaring hotly at each other with angry words fairly bursting to be uttered, and her hopes came down a peg or two. Surely any progress made by their seeming enjoyment of each other during the waltz had evaporated, thanks once again to that mangy, ill-favored cur Tansy set so much store by.

Actually, the dowager was only half right. Both Avanoll and Tansy were on their high ropes about their conflicting opinions on the worth of Horatio's presence on this Earth, but neither could entirely dismiss from their minds the events preceding Avanoll's latest mishap. Tansy felt pity, and not a little guilt, as she tried vainly to assist her cousin to his feet. Her hand, as she grasped his, tingled, and her heart did a nasty flip-flop in her breast.

As Avanoll's larger hand closed around Tansy's, his fingers touched her wrist, and he could feel the increased tempo of her pulse. He felt a momentary gladness because her touch did much the same to him. But then sanity took over.

"Unhand me you—you nemesis! Your assistance is not needed, not now, and not ever," he blustered in self-defense. "Since your advent in my life, I have walked around with a thundercloud over my head and a stream of cold rain constantly running down the back of my neck. I haven't had a peaceful moment since we met. Unless I seek an early grave—or at the least, permanent disability—I intend to give you a very wide berth in the future. You may remain under my roof until Emily is bracketed, and then I will settle an allowance on you to keep you from endangering any other poor souls who would be so unfortunate as to employ you. But from now on, madam, we are as strangers. Kindly remove yourself from my presence whilst I endeavor to haul what is left of my body upstairs to my chamber."

And so Ashley waved away Tansy's helping hand and tried to rise, only to fall back down once more.

"'Not easily do they rise whose powers are hindered by straitened circumstances.' Juvenal," his aunt pointed out, causing her nephew to utter some few phrases of his own that the woman barely understood, let alone ventured to commit to memory. Which was extremely fortunate, as they were more earthy than profound.

It was a white-faced Tansy who wrung her hands helplessly as she watched the Duke crawl to the newel post, haul himself upright, and hop ungainly up the long staircase. Not even the dowager's attempt at mimicking Lucinda by calling out after her grandson, "'He that lies with the dogs, riseth with fleas.' Herbert," was able to lift her spirits for more than a moment.

Emily went to Tansy and started to speak, then thought better of it, simply kissed Tansy's cheek, and went quietly away. The dowager tried for some minutes to alternately joke, cajole, or lecture Tansy into a better humor, but in the end she too simply patted Tansy's ashen cheek. Then she was off to instruct Dunstan to summon the doctor to look at his grace's ankle.

Lucinda walked over and gave it her best shot: "'There's no cause for despair.' Horace."

"Where have you been these last minutes, Aunt? On the moon? Of course there is cause for despair. I am in disgrace—*again*—and the Duke cannot stand the sight of me."

Lucinda kissed Tansy's cheek. "'To have been acceptable to the great is not the last of praises. It is not every man's lot to gain Corinth.' Horace," she said bracingly before wandering off to the library, there to reread her Horace and find out just who this man Corinth was for the poet to speak of him so highly.

All alone now in the foyer, Tansy hung her head in shame. Her disgrace had been too public, too profound, to leave her able to see even one silver lining in the dark clouds overhead. She deserved nothing more than to pack her portmanteau and slink off to a damp hole in the ground and expire, but she had only two pounds and sixpence to her name—and no references. She simply had no choice but to stay in this house: where the servants might worship her as a savior, where Emily and the dowager and even Aunt Lucinda might feel some slight affection for her, but the master of the house chose to pretend she didn't exist.

And what was worse—as if anything more could be added and still be borne!—was her revelation in the middle of Avanoll's scathing denunciation that he was the one person in the house who held the power to make her happy ever again. And he hated her, really hated her. Only a complete idiot could fail to realize that.

Well, she told herself philosophically, she had opened her heart to at least the beginnings of something that may have grown into love in the space of an afternoon. Surely it could take no more than a few days to restore herself to her previous heart-whole state.

Tansy squared her shoulders and marched purposefully up the stairs to her room. But before she reached the door her shoulders had slumped, and once the door closed behind her the proud chin quivered and the pent-up tears fell like silent rain.

Maybe she should give herself more time. Perhaps a fortnight, or a year, or a lifetime.

Chapter Twelve

AS IT TURNED out, Avanoll's ankle was not broken—merely sprained; a painful nuisance that his doctor warned him could eventually turn into a chronic weakness if he dared put any weight on the foot for at least a week.

His guilt-ridden cousin made sure Mrs. Birdwell, the new housekeeper, did not stint on the trays of tempting dishes that seemed to be traveling in an almost constant parade up the back staircase to the Duke's chambers. Tansy herself carefully cut a wide path around those same chambers, especially after Horatio somehow gained admittance to the bedroom and promptly leapt upon the Duke's bed (perhaps to offer a woofed apology) and landed squarely on Avanoll's swollen and sore ankle. A loud howl from the sadly abused man brought Aunt Lucinda on the run, and she entered the chamber just as Horatio—slightly upset by the incident, but not so much so as to not notice and claim for his own a succulent pork chop that was to be a part of the Duke's dinner—flashed past her and into the hall, his pilfered treasure protruding from his larcenous phiz.

"'The dog, to gain some private ends, went mad, and bit the man. The man recovered of the bite—the dog it was that died.' Goldsmith," she offered by way of comfort.

It wanted only this, the Duke thought, feeling himself sadly used. "He didn't bite me this time out, Aunt, though more's the pity if I could hold out the hope your fellow Goldsmith had a grain of truth in his little ditty. The cursed hound merely did his canine imitation of a whirling dervish on my injured ankle and then, low-life that he is, absconded with my supper," the Duke told her testily.

Aunt Lucinda tut-tutted and intoned severely, "'Recollect that the Almighty, who gave the dog to be companion of our

91

pleasures and our toils, hath invested him with a nature noble and incapable of deceit.' Sir Walter Scott."

Avanoll laughed ruefully. "And there you have your answer, my oh-so-wise aunt. Disabuse yourself of the notion that the Almighty had anything whatsoever to do with that particular 'gift.' No, *his* creator comes from a much warmer clime, I am sure."

His aunt looked puzzled for a moment. Then an affronted flush rose in her cheeks before she gathered up her heavily-ruffled, lime-green skirts and stalked from the room—her sensibilities highly insulted by her nephew's affrontery in speaking of heathens in her hearing. She was further boosted on her way by the sound of the hearty laughter brought on by the Duke's first real amusement in days.

On Monday afternoon two of the Duke's cronies passed a few hours with him, but instead of raising his sullen spirits, he seemed even more tense and restless after they had gone. Farnley, thinking his master to be still in pain, offered to send for his cousin Betty's second-born son Tom, who had been a footling (born feet-first), so that worthy could press his feet against the Duke's "affected part," thereby drawing off the "evil humors" within.

When that suggestion was met by a rather blank stare and the information that the prospect of touching toes with the estimable Tom left his grace totally unmoved, he dared give voice to his second slightly less documented cure: wrapping the ankle round with the body of an eel (he did not specify the condition of this eel as either dead or alive). Although Farnley could swear to the powers of eels for curing warts and drunkenness, he had never been given the opportunity to use one in this sort of case—as Tom had always been more than kind in lending his gifted appendages to any sprain to occur in the family these two decades past.

"Eels, eels, eels!" the Duke bellowed. "One more word about eels and I'll loop one of the slimy things around your scrawny neck and tie it in a bow under your chin! Get you gone, Farnley, I warn you, as I am experiencing an almost uncontrollable desire to murder you. Save yourself, man, and flee while you can!"

After Farnley made his hasty departure, the Duke was left alone to swear long and terribly under his breath.

Emily was much too delicate to enter the sickroom (and too apt to say something stupid and so irritate the patient even more), and the dowager seemed to consider her grandson's outbursts in the nature of juvenile bids for attention—flatly refusing to pander to his whims. And since the household had run out of servants willing to be verbally abused (or even physically pelted with assorted cooked vegetables), it was left to Tansy to try to beard the growling tiger in his den.

This she did, quite simply, by refusing to rise to the bait of his sarcastic taunts or dire threats of physical violence to her person once he was quit of—and this last he said with great dramatic pathos—"this rack of pain."

Tansy did unbend then enough to express her regret once more for Horatio's part in his recent accident, although she couldn't resist qualifying her apology by reminding him that, had he not been too busy acting the departing Romeo to take heed of her warning, he could have avoided the whole mess.

"You do have a charming way of expressing remorse, cousin. But if your presence here is meant to be by way of making amends, let me tell you that the prospect of you cast in role of personal attendant, frankly, terrifies me."

Tansy lifted one fine, dark eyebrow and returned flatly, "Ashley, I fear you must fortify your mind to the likelihood that you and I will be in rather constant company for the duration of your recuperation, the servants all having lively senses of self-preservation and a bit reluctant to expose themselves to your temper. Besides, I feel I owe you some recompense, considering myself—if I am to be honest—just a teeny bit responsible for your fall."

Avanoll said in pretended amazement, "By Jupiter! Can it really be *concern* I see on your face? Concern, and—mayhap—even a smidgen of guilt? Heavens above, I do think if I had suffered some permanent injury in my fall you would have been plunged into complete despair."

"It would seem to me, *cousin*, that your allies are lying too thin on the ground for you to consider alienating one of the few remaining persons willing to take an interest in your welfare. Rather than getting your back up over events over and past, I would suggest you behave yourself—because I, for one, do not feel obliged to take any sauce from you. Frankly, I would just as lief spoon-feed a baited-bear as listen to any more of your childish tantrums. And I may just take it into my head to leave you with only your own nasty distemper for company."

Tansy didn't know it, but the sight of her in a temper—russet eyes sparkling, cheeks flushed prettily, and her uncommonly fine figure made even more appealing by the rapid rise and fall of her nicely-rounded bosom—had caused the Duke to discover that his cousin had been somehow transformed into an extremely handsome woman. So struck by her looks was the Duke that he surrendered without further argument. "I have been behaving like a bacon-brained idiot. Please accept my deepest apologies, Tansy."

Tansy nodded her agreement and quickly went about the business of straightening his rumpled bedcovers, picking up the newspapers and sporting magazines strewn all over the floor, and ended by draping his supper tray across his knees with the bribe that—on the condition he cleared his plate like a good little soldier—she would agree to provide him with the opportunity to brush up on the art of displaying good sportsmanship while she firmly trounced him in a few games of chess.

The challenge was just what the Duke needed. He proceeded to do justice to one of Cook's more tempting creations before demanding Tansy draw up the table nearby, with its inlaid chess board, and place out the chess pieces. Give him a chess lesson, would she? A temporary truce was one thing, but if she thought he was going to become her tame pet she had another thought coming!

The ensuing silence was broken only by the ticking of the mantel clock and the occasional settling of a log slipping in the grate, as Avanoll found himself hard put to hold his own with his resourceful cousin. While he fretted and pondered over his moves—and more than once had to wipe at his sweat-beaded brow with his handkerchief—Tansy passed the time reading the dowager's copy of Mrs. Radcliffe's *An Italian Romance*. When it was her turn to make a move she would lay her book down across her lap, congratulate the Duke on his clever strategy, and seconds later move her piece—usually collecting one of his pieces along the way—and then return to her novel.

By all that is right, Tansy should have lost every game. As it happened, however, of the five games they played she won four, two of them with ridiculous ease. Her cousin demanded a chance at revenge the following day, but Tansy demurred. "Chess has never really been my best game. It moves so slowly I find myself almost bored at times. Instead," she relented, "I will agree to a few rubbers of whist, or any other card game you might choose. I believe I am quite good at cards, actually," she added with naive honesty, and perhaps a bit of pride.

"You're on!" cried Avanoll, smiling quite evilly for a man

who was supposed to be an honorable peer of the realm. "Only tomorrow, to add a bit of spice to the games, I suggest we play for money."

Tansy frowned. "I have less than five pounds to my name, Ashley. I doubt you will think such a paltry sum worth the bother."

The Duke waved her protest away with one generous sweep of his arm. "I shall stake you to fifty pounds. If you are lucky, you may pay me back from your winnings. And if you lose, well, the fifty pounds was mine anyway, wasn't it?"

Tansy wasn't too sure of the ins and outs of that last statement, but one look at Ashley's face and its smug, superior smirk, and she fell in with his suggestion at once.

Next morning at ten, the two players faced each other across the cleared chess table that again stood between the bed and a pulled-up chair. Each had a stack of pound chips in front of them (Ashley's chips outnumbering Tansy's at a rate of six to one).

Luncheon for two was delivered to the room only to be returned to the kitchens hours later, cold and untouched. Just afternoon tea for the lady—and a goodly supply of burgundy for the gentleman—were received with any favor, as the day wound down into dusk and Farnley went about the room lighting candles to keep away the darkness.

The encounter ended much as it had begun, with the two adversaries still facing each other across the chess table. Only now the piles of brightly-colored chips were all sitting in front of only one player. And that lucky gamester was none other than Miss Tansy Tamerlane.

"Your trick, madam, and yet again, your game," Avanoll declared wondrously. "I'm all to pieces, unless you will accept my vouchers."

His opponent declined politely, stating that she did know it was rather unsporting to quit while ahead and deny him a chance to recoup his losses. She was quite done in, however, and could only agree to another match in the morning—this time naming piquet as another game of which she was particularly fond.

Avanoll nodded his agreement to this plan, but advised her to take all but one hundred pounds (fifty as a stake and his original advance) and invest it with the four percents as security. "As I recall, your father was quite a gamester," he then commented, "but I am equally certain he did not have your ungodly good luck with the cards."

"The word is *skill,* Ashley, not luck, and yes, you are unfortunately correct about my father. Poor Papa could never get the right of such games, and I can't recall losing to him after I was ten years old. I often wondered if the majority of our fortune found its way into the hands of others simply through Papa's never-ending search for a player more inept than himself. I really felt very sorry for him at times, but if I deliberately tried to let him win he'd become exceedingly put out, more enraged at being cosseted than he ever was at being bested by a mere female."

"Yes, well, that 'mere female' has just relieved me of approximately three hundred pounds, and *I* am known as an extremely competent player. It seems you have missed your calling, cousin. You should have set up your own discreet gaming rooms on the fringe of Mayfair just as soon as you found yourself without support. By now you'd own half of London."

The two parted that night on good terms, promising to meet at the same hour the next morning. But Avanoll's two friends were already closeted with him by the time Tansy arrived, so she retreated in order to give him time for a masculine gossip session. When she joined him after luncheon he expressed a wish to postpone their game, as he was feeling a bit depressed and was "no fit company" for anyone.

"That makes two visits from your so-called friends, and two descents into the sulks immediately on the heels of their departure. Next time they call I'll show them to the rightabout straightaway if they are so unthinking as to upset you in your condition," Tansy stated with some heat.

"No, no, Tansy, my dear," Avanoll put in quickly, as "my dear" Tansy's heart did a sudden disconcerting flip in her breast at both his words and his tender tone. "My friends would not purposely, or even thoughtlessly, distress me. I asked them to report to me. Sit down, my dear"—ah, another "my dear"—"and I shall give *you* a lesson today: a lesson in the perfidy of those creatures we so laughingly call the *human* race."

Tansy obediently took up her place at the side of Avanoll's bed, this time with no chess table to impede her proximity to the Duke's bedside, and he told her of the latest news his friends had brought.

"Have you ever read anything written by George Gordon Byron, or Baron Byron, if I were to use his title? Good. And did you enjoy his works?" At Tansy's fervent nod he smiled in agreement with her sentiments. "When George wrote his *Childe*

Harold's Pilgrimage in 1812, he awoke suddenly to find himself the most famous and praised literary lion of this young century. Society flung open its doors and this shy, lame, but oh-so-very-*beautiful*—for he could only be described as beautiful—young man was courted by everyone from the man in the street to the man who will someday wear the crown of England.

"Surely, even in your secluded village, his romantic exploits and his dangerous association with that titled jade, Caro Lamb, filtered down to your ears."

Tansy nodded again, afraid to speak and perhaps put an end to her cousin's confidences, and Avanoll went on.

"Finally, last year, Lady Melbourne talked poor George into marrying her niece, Annabella Milbanke, and a more mis-matched pair you cannot imagine.

"A child, Augusta, came of the union before Annabella left George. But instead of returning him to the personal peace he craved, she set out to do her best to slander George's name. Rumors that he was having an incestuous affair with his half-sister, also named Augusta—and now I see I shock you, my dear—began to be whispered about. Even George's poems were dissected by his detractors and purported to contain horrible double meanings of the most scandalous, scurrilous nature.

"George tried his best to carry on, but as I said, he is a shy person at heart, perhaps even a timid or even weak one. The pressure caused him to take on some rather bizarre affectations. He took to dosing himself heavily with laudanum, and he could not sleep in any but a lighted room with his pistols always close beside him."

Tansy made a sympathetic noise and Avanoll brought his gaze back from some spot in the middle distance to look at her.

"Oh, yes, Tansy. George is a bit of a queer fish. Even we who consider ourselves his friends cannot deny that. But, then, aren't such great talents allowed eccentricities and insights—some-times sublime, sometimes terrifying—we 'normal people' are spared by our lesser gifts?"

Avanoll laughed at a sudden memory. "While we were at Cambridge, George took exception to the rule disallowing pet dogs or cats. So he bought a trained bear, Lord only knows where, and kept him in his room. He said the rule did not specifically outlaw pet bears, but only dogs and cats.

"Anyway," he went on, sober once again, "George has slowly found himself on the fringes of Society, with only a pitiful few still willing to stand his friend. For a time we believed he might weather the storm, but then Claire Clairmont—some silly chit Percy Shelley dragged back here from abroad—loudly proclaimed that George seduced her and made her pregnant. My friends and I knew then it was all over for George in England, but we could not dissuade a few of his women friends from attempting a large party at Almack's last night with both George and his half-sister, Augusta, as guests. The other *honored* guests ignored Augusta most rudely. And then, when George arrived on the scene, the miserable bastards—excuse me, Tansy—fled from the room like rats deserting a sinking ship."

"How could they do such a thing to that great man?" Tansy cried in horror.

"They could not help themselves, I suppose," Ashley explained caustically. "It seems an unwritten law that at least once in every ten year span our so-fair, so-loyal English Society feels itself obligated to unite in a sordid conspiracy to pull down their one-time idols from the pedestals to which they themselves had previously raised them. I am ashamed to be a part of such a Society," he fairly shouted into the huge chamber, his words rebounding off the paneled walls and high ceiling before slowly ebbing away.

"Is there nothing you can do, Ashley?" Tansy spoke into the now ominously silent room.

He shook his head sadly. "There isn't a single thing anyone can do, my dear. There is nothing for it but for George to leave the country. My friends tell me he plans to take ship to the continent before the month is out, and that he swears he will never set foot on these shores again. I can't say as I blame him, but England, through her own fickleness, has lost a great talent. Perhaps the finest poet she will ever have."

"Well, I certainly wish I could do something to help. But if you cannot aid him, nobody can," Tansy sighed sadly.

As the room grew heavy with silence once more, Tansy rose from her chair and put it back in its place against the wall, then poured a goodly amount of burgundy into a crystal goblet before returning to her cousin's bedside to extend the drink as the only solace she could offer. Avanoll looked up as if suddenly becoming aware of Tansy's continued presence, and removed the goblet to place it on his bedside table. With his other hand he took hold of Tansy's wrist and pulled her down to sit beside him on the bed.

"If you cannot help our poor tarnished bard you might wish to give aid where you can," Ashley whispered huskily. "Come closer to me, sweetings, and comfort me with a healing kiss."

The impropriety of her position—alone in a man's bed-chamber, and indeed, sitting on that man's very bed—did not occur to Tansy. Slowly, as if in a dream, she lowered her lips to brush across Ashley's with a gossamer softness that his hand, now tangled in the loose tendrils curling at the nape of her neck, increased to a much more solid contact with just a slight downward exertion of pressure.

When the Duke's other hand encircled her waist, Tansy was propelled forward so that her entire upper body now rested against his broad chest. Somehow, she didn't exactly know how, her own arms crept around Ashley's neck to cradle his head in an unschooled but surprisingly pleasing manner.

She could feel the Duke's muscles rippling against her softness as his kiss deepened, and demanded and received an answering quiver of enjoyment from her own body. The embrace caused her to tremble in his arms like a butterfly he had once captured had beat its fragile wings against his cupped palms.

A long time later, slowly and most reluctantly, Avanoll called a halt to a situation only he knew was rapidly progressing beyond a point where he was still able to control his actions. Tansy was gently, but firmly, returned to her former sitting position.

"Ashley, I—" Tansy began at the same time Avanoll was saying, "Tansy, I—"

Whatever thoughts might have been uttered were lost forever as an abrupt knock was followed by the opening of the door, followed by Dunstan and his reproving *harrumph.*

"Pardon me, your grace," said Dunstan, "but this note was just delivered to the servant's entrance and as there is no name on it I felt it should be brought directly to you."

Avanoll took one last, long, frustrated look at Tansy's moist and inviting lips, then sighed deeply and held out his hand for the note.

Tansy discreetly, if somewhat belatedly, removed herself to stand at the large window, studiously gazing out onto the Square, totally oblivious to the colors and noise below.

The Duke had a difficult time deciphering the contents of the note, which seemed to be a hastily scribbled missive setting up a meeting the following morning in Green Park to "bring together two star-crossed lovers whose desires are surely destined to be fulfilled," if only they could have speech with one another.

In total, it was a silly piece of romantic drivel only a green babe could swallow as being anything but a shabby trick meant to lure the reader into waters well above her head—yet the words "as we have discussed" were also very easy to discern.

Whoever this "Red Rose" was who signed the note, he was sure he would be met, and the message was only a confirmation of a meeting already planned.

The Duke dismissed Dunstan with a curt nod, and his face slowly took on a dark expression as he read again the first line of the note which began, "To my faithful Tansy."

Tansy, unaware of this new development and its effect on her cousin's disposition, breathed a sigh of relief at Dunstan's departure and hurried back to Ashley's bedside—hands outstretched and sure to be drawn down into his embrace once again. She was brought up short when the stranger sitting in Ashley's bed (wearing a face that would turn the cream) pronounced coldly, "I have no further need of your company, *Miss* Tamerlane. You may go now." Thus dismissing her, he lay back and turned his head to the wall.

Now, Tansy was no weak-spirited miss who retreated at the first sign of trouble, her usual reaction to a problem being to take the bull by the horns and demand an explanation. But this was a new Tansy, a vulnerable Tansy, a girl horribly out of her depth and experiencing a pain so terrible it could have been the result of an actual physical blow.

Her hands dropped to her sides and, head bowed in utter disgrace, she walked as composedly as she could to the door before racing blindly down the corridor to bolt herself in her room and indulge herself in a good long cry.

At the same time, elsewhere in the great mansion in Grosvenor Square, Lady Emily squirmed nervously as Comfort—resigned to obeying Tansy's strictures and finding another way to raise the blunt needed for that cottage in the country than by taking bribes from her mistress's suitors—tried for the third time to adjust her ladyship's golden curls in an intricate new style.

Little did Comfort know that Emily's case of the fidgets stemmed from exasperation at Pansy, "that ignorant chit," and her whimpering explanation that the note Sir Harry Leadham had promised to send via Pansy had not yet arrived.

Pansy, with a P. Tansy, with a T. What a pity, and what a sad waste, that Avanoll had so slim a knowledge of his own servants! And what typical masculine folly, to allow his stiff-necked pride to overrule the promptings of his heretofore untouched heart.

Tansy was once again in his grace's bad books, this time for a reason she could not fathom one little bit.

Once again the Duke reverted to a snarling, growling beast, terrorizing all who dared come within roaring distance of his "cage." The servants added to his exasperation by becoming—overnight, or so it seemed to him—a pack of brainless ninnies who couldn't pass on one single message correctly, follow any given order through to its logical conclusion, or, in general, tend to his needs with any more competence than a cockroach.

When the Duke was at long last allowed up three days later, sighs of profound relief could be heard from all corners of the mansion as he departed, leaning heavily on a malacca cane, for his Club. In fact, if the truth be known, one particular member of the household (who had been concentrating on devising a perfect way to deliver to the man a crushing set-down without causing herself and her poor puppy to be thrown out into the streets) was even then hiding behind her curtains as the Duke crossed the square. Her face was contorted by a series of grimaces, scowls, and—just once—by the poking out of her pointed, pink tongue in the general direction of his grace's departing back.

Chapter Thirteen

THE FINAL two hectic weeks leading up to Emily's Come-Out Ball were so filled with activity that Tansy had little difficulty in avoiding Avanoll and his nasty moods. The dowager had the girl's head in a whirl, trying to teach her the endless intricacies of that nebulous thing called good *ton*—from the proper way to curtsy to a marquis to warnings about allowing any of her admirers to become too demonstrative in their affections. According to her grace, anything more intimate than a polite smile constituted a proposal of marriage.

Horatio had been on his best behavior, his only lapses being the soup bone Farnley found in his grace's favorite slippers and a nervous accident on Aunt Lucinda's satin bedspread when that lady had been so misguided as to waken the hound from his post-luncheon nap by aiming a hairbrush at his head.

Avanoll's bad temper had eased somewhat in this interim, but had not totally disappeared. Tansy was still all at sea as to the cause of his sudden withdrawal of friendship (her heart refused to give their association any other name).

And so it was that, on the night of the ball, four fashionably-bedecked ladies found themselves lined up like well-trained servants at the foot of the stairs in the foyer, waiting for the Duke to inspect their attire and pronounce them fit for the exalted company due in less than two hours.

Three of the ladies waited with bated breath and fluttering pulses, for even the dowager—who outwardly shunned such feminine vanities—looked forward to hearing her grandson's confirmation of her ensemble. The fourth lady, standing slightly in the shadows cast by the huge chandelier, was also waiting for the Duke, but she was not on the hunt for flowery speeches. Her chin was raised in an attitude that dared her cousin to say *anything* at all.

Finally the Duke descended the staircase to the tile floor, stopped, and ran his eyes up and down each of them, until he at last gave a one-sided smile before executing an elaborate bow. "My compliments, ladies. I shall be the envy of every man present tonight for my lovely family."

Four deeply-held breaths released in three gratified (and one exasperated) sighs. If the Duke believed he was to get off this easily, though, he was sadly mistaken. Almost before he had completed his bow, Emily raced to his side to appeal to her brother to be allowed to wear the Benedict emeralds—brooch, bracelets, ear-drops, ring, and tiara—instead of the simple strand of pearls now gracing her swan-like neck. "Too babyish, by half," she pouted prettily.

"'You need not hang up the ivy-branch over the wine that will sell,' Syrus," Aunt Lucinda pointed out, while rearranging the tiers of pink, patterned-lace flounces that wrapped round her plump frame from chin to toe before coming to rest upon the tiles some three feet behind her. She looked as if someone had rolled her up within a huge bolt of tulle and she was just now fighting her way out.

"Aunt is quite right, my pet," Tansy inserted before Emily's frown could ruin her previously angelic expression. "There is no need to paint the lily, as it were. You are 'slap up to the mark,' as my Papa used to say."

Aunt Lucinda nodded vigorously, nearly dislodging one of the half-dozen ostrich plumes riding precariously upon her curls. "'Of surpassing beauty and in the bloom of youth.' Terence."

The dowager chose this moment to draw her grandson's attention to her own attire. "Youth may manage very well unadorned, but what of this old lady? Will I suit?"

Avanoll ran his eyes once again over his majestically regal grandparent as she stood before him in full battle-dress, with a swatch of purple draperies wrapped round her, a king's ransom in diamonds sparkling about her neck, wrists and fingers, and her coronet sitting proudly upon her iron-grey head.

"You do me proud, madam," he returned. "But heed me," he unwisely added, "be careful not to overdo this evening. Do not be ashamed to retire early if you tire."

"I ain't in my dotage yet," the dowager replied heatedly, prepared to do battle.

"You were last month," her granddaughter ventured from a

safe distance. "I remember quite distinctly your saying you were too old and frail to endure another Season."

"That was last month, you impertinent minx. All I really needed was some new blood around here," her grace shot back. "And what a prime sight she looks tonight, I must say. You'll have to barricade the windows tomorrow, Ashley, to keep away the *beaux* our girls will have tumbling over themselves to pay their addresses."

Tansy, who had kept to the background as much as possible until now, moved forward to contradict her benefactor. "It won't be my hand the bucks will be battling over, your grace, thank you anyway. I am a far shot from a debutante if you remember, and as *dame de compagnie* do not entertain thoughts of romance—except as they pertain to Lady Emily."

"Oh, pooh," the dowager returned with a wink. "Ashley, tell the gel how the gentlemen pump you about your cousin."

Tansy's russet-brown eyes turned in astonishment when Avanoll concurred. "It is true, cousin. I can go nowhere without being harassed with inquiries about the fair Boadicea. It's enough to send a fellow to the dogs directly, if you'll pardon my weak humor," he ended with a reluctant grin.

In the two weeks since the accident to his ankle, Tansy and Horatio had behaved with almost saintly respectability, and he had unbent enough to begin to forgive—if not to forget—his cousin's lamentable lapses from grace. Tansy, nonplused by this piece of news, silently led the way in to supper.

During the quiet family meal that was taken in the smaller dining room, the Duke took time to subject his cousin to a covert, but most thorough, inspection. Her gown of soft green was neither plain nor overpowering, and it set off previously unnoticed auburn highlights in her long, brown hair, which had been brushed on the curling stick earlier and was now caught in a topknot from which a few tendrils had escaped in order to curl about her nape. Her unusual height, he had already noted, did not make her appear awkward, and she moved with a fluid grace that made her skirts whisper about her feet like sea-foam. She had learned her lessons well.

So what was wrong?

Suddenly his eyes lit up as he realized what was missing from the picture. "Cousin, have you no jewelry?" he asked baldly as the last dishes were being removed.

Tansy instantly drew back her shoulders and raised her firm chin. "I do not, your grace," she told him in a carefully controlled fury. "I came within Ames-Ace of a rather tacky ruby pendant once, but m'father's horse stumbled in the stretch and the stone remained safe in the tout's hip pocket—to be joined shortly by my silver teething ring, which Papa had put up against it."

"Good girl!" yelped the dowager, and dealt Lucinda one firm clap between the shoulder blades as the woman choked on the water she had been swallowing at the moment of Tansy's outburst. "That was well done, with full marks for spirit and honesty. And don't you go screwing on your Friday Face, Ashley, for you got that set-down as reward for your uncouth, uncalled-for prying. Does she own any jewelry? If she did, do you think she'd be wiping noses or bear-leading silly chits like our Emily here? Whatever my sins, I cannot believe I deserved such a muckworm as you as a grandson."

"Oh, gemini," Emily hooted, for once not on the receiving end of one of her grandmother's great scolds. Being called a silly chit was an everyday occurrence. "Box his ears, Grandmama! Muckworm! Oh, that is so good, Grandmama!"

"'And in one scene no more than three should speak.' Horace," admonished her aunt softly, with little hope Emily would either understand or heed the advice.

The Duke was more direct. "Stow it, brat. You're not too grown up for a little ear-boxing closer to home, you know."

The dowager was forced to rap her fork sharply on her water goblet to restore order. "Enough, I say. Our guests will be arriving shortly, and I would as lief they were left in the dark about this particular strain of insanity in the family that makes you two revert to childhood at the drop of a napkin.

"All right, Ashley," she said more softly as the room fell silent, "now that I am recovered from your lapse of manners I must admit I understand the object of your inquiry, even if I cannot commend your approach. Perhaps you can suggest a remedy?"

At once Ashley winked at his grandparent and quipped, "Exactly, and I believe you and I even have the same jewelry in mind."

With her own protests pushed aside as too trivial to be considered, it was only a matter of minutes before Tansy found herself in the library with the Duke, standing nervously by as he worked open the hidden panel in the huge mahogany buffet and withdrew a slender, velvet-covered box.

"If you will oblige me by turning around, cousin," the Duke said kindly, and Tansy's eyes caught sight of an unbelievably lovely strand of bright, aquamarine stones just before they descended to lie comfortably in the hollow between her breasts. But even this joy was overshadowed by the nervous flutterings of her pulse as Avanoll's fingers brushed her nape when he secured the diamond clasp. His fingers lingered even after the task was done, his thumbs rotating slowly as they raised goose-bumps along her spine.

Tansy knew she must move, and move quickly, to break the spell she felt enveloping her. But when she began to step away, Avanoll's grip pulled her back against his hard, lean frame. She could feel his warm, sweet breath on her neck moments before his lips descended to blaze a gossamer-light trail of kisses from her nape to the tip of her creamy shoulder.

"Oh, Tansy," Avanoll groaned hoarsely, before he turned her in his arms and captured her startled lips in a very different manner than he had ever done before. It was a gentler contact, almost reverent in its soft caress.

When he at last lifted his head he marveled at the change one small bauble of jewelry could make. The girl was more than tolerably fair, she was really quite lovely.

After she had quit the room, running from it with only an incoherent mumbling of thanks for the loan of his mother's necklace, the Duke stood puzzling the odd compulsion to take his cousin in his arms that seemed to be constantly overcoming his best intentions, as well as his native intelligence. The last thing his well-ordered life needed was an entanglement with his irksome cousin.

As the evening progressed, it became apparent that the Duke was not alone in his opinion that Tansy was in prime good looks, and the bewildered *dame de compagnie* found herself being whirled from partner to partner without a break until the musicians struck up a waltz. Of course, Lady Emily was forbidden the dance until the patronessess of Almack's gave their seal of approval—but even if this stricture did not apply to Tansy she had been warned not to insult the ladies by appearing to disregard their silent authority.

While she, Aunt Lucinda, and Emily sat on a comfortable striped sofa, taking a well-deserved rest, a young man Tansy judged to be about four-and-twenty approached, balancing three glasses of punch that threatened to spill over at any moment. Tansy was drawn to the handsome youth immediately, as she was always prejudiced toward the shy and uncertain. He was a strikingly handsome gentleman, she noted quickly, though not quite her type: tall, but slightly built, with bronze curls as silky and soft as Emily's, and cursed with an almost feminine pink-and-white complexion that—as one of the glasses tilted and the punch ran over to stain his lace cuff a bright crimson—showed a most lamentable tendency to blush.

"Hoo!" Emily chortled. "Did you ever see such a gudgeon, Tansy? I swear that Digby Eagleton is the most pathetic creature in Nature. The simple fool believes himself hopelessly in love with me, you know," she added in a highly audible whisper. "It is most embarrassing, really, the way he tags at my skirts like a mewling kitten."

A second punch glass twisted awkwardly in Digby's grasp, probably as a result of overhearing the love of his life speak so blightingly of his devotion, and with two out of three refreshments running down his sleeve he gave up the effort and withdrew before gaining his objective.

"'No one regards what is before his feet; we all gaze at the stars.' Quintus Ennius," Lucinda observed solemnly.

"At my feet is right, Aunt Ce-Ce. Digby clings like a limpet whenever he spies me. He is such a child! I wish he might find someone else to drool over, as I am mightily fatigued with both his romantic prattlings and his tortured sighs. Do you know he had the nerve, the absolute gall, to ask me to marry him? It was all I could do not to laugh in his face!"

Lucinda let go with her appraisal of the young gentleman. "'The flower of our young manhood.' Sophocles," she gushed girlishly.

Emily picked pettishly at her demure, white skirts and declared, "If you are so smitten, Aunt, you may have him. I give him to you, or Tansy here for that matter, as a gift!"

Tansy had listened to as much—nay, more—of this smug recital than she had wished to hear. "Keep up your foolishness, young lady, and you may just whistle a fine young man down the wind."

"Never!" Emily declared airily. "If ever I were so unladylike as to *whistle*, that dumb Digby would come to heel at once like a faithful hound—tongue lolling and tail wagging in ecstasy."

"Lord love a duck!" Tansy groaned contemptuously. "If ever there was a more unfeeling, self-centered, vain, ungrateful, and cruel — yes *cruel*," she repeated as Emily opened her rosebud lips in protest, "creature, Emily Benedict, I cannot imagine who she might be. I have not met Mr. Eagleton, and know nothing of him except for his misguided opinion of what constitutes a lady of breeding sufficient to doing her the honor of a proposal of marriage. But I tell you this: if he were a Tothill Fields link-boy he'd be too good for you.

"And don't try tears, my fine young actress," she hinted when Emily began a furious blinking of her china-blue eyes, "for it cuts no wheedle with me. I live for the day Mr. Eagleton finds a new place to fix his interest and snaps his fingers in your face like this." So saying, Tansy lifted her hand to Emily's nose and demonstrated with a loud *snap*.

Aunt Lucinda leaned across Emily to impart complacently, "'This and a great deal more I have had to put up with.' Terence."

"You have my deepest sympathy, Aunt Lucinda," Tansy said absently, for a plan was just then forming in her agile brain. From under her dark lashes she studied the hapless Digby until his beautiful face was thoroughly familiar and she could not help but recognize him when next she saw him. It was about time one top-lofty young puss was taken down a peg or two, and Tansy Tamerlane was just the one to do it!

Just then the musicians decided to take a short rest, and the dowager marched over to place herself down rather wearily in the remaining end seat. "How goes the ball, ladies? I never saw a room so stuffed with toadies. Emily, I think you are flinging yourself about just a bit too enthusiastically, my dear. Try for a little less spirit and a little more decorum, if you please."

Emily told her companions they were always trying to throw a damper on her fun and reminded them that it was, after all, *her* ball. She then escaped, before she could be scolded for her impertinence, with a dashing young hussar who approached to beg leave to lead her into the set now forming on the floor.

"Outrageous little baggage," the dowager remarked calmly to Emily's retreating skirts. "Tansy, did you see that fool Stanhope, the fourth Earl of Harrington if you wish to be precise, prancing about as yet?"

Tansy shook her head.

"Oh, my dear, you must keep your eyes peeled for him. He is really quite odd. It was bad enough when he began affecting that inane lisp, but now he has gone beyond the pale. Only imagine, he has *painted* on a beard!"

Aunt Lucinda clucked at the dowager's obvious enjoyment of the foibles of a peer. "'Society in shipwreck is a comfort to us all.' Syrus," she pointed out facetiously.

The dowager, the bit between her teeth now, agreed. "And

you'll never guess what Lady Clark told me about a *very* highly-placed personage who shall remain nameless. It seems he has an entire collection of snuff boxes with false lids. Under those lids, on the second covers that he shows about in public quite freely— thinking none are up to his tricks—are dirty pictures! Yes, naughty pictures—painted up in natural colors and drawn in fine detail—with a different scene for each lid.

"Tansy, I did not bother to measure my words, for I know you are no prudish miss after living with that rakehell father of yours. But if you cannot blush, at least have the decency to wipe that obnoxious grin off your face!"

"'What a time! What a civilization!' Cicero," Lucinda cried in horror.

"If I might change the subject, your grace," Tansy put in, "I would appreciate your opinion of one young Digby Eagleton."

"Digby Eagleton? Oh, yes. Fine family, the Eagletons, only son of his widowed mother, and with a good deal of money invested with the four percents, I believe. He's in line for a baronetcy too, once his uncle sticks his spoon in the wall, and that should be any time now. Why? Are you thinking of throwing your handkerchief in that direction?"

"I may be a bit raw around the edges, your grace, but I stop at cradle-robbing. No, Mr. Eagleton is head over ears in love with your cruel wretch of a granddaughter, and she won't give him so much as the time of day. I was just wondering if the poor tyke is worth the time it would take me to give him a few pointers on how best to handle the hard-hearted Emily."

The dowager laughed and twisted in her seat to give Tansy a broad wink. "You are a constant source of delight to me, my dear. Ashley did me a good turn when he brought you home, whether he will admit it or not."

"I'll admit to being Bonnie Prince Charlie if only my cousin will rescue me from another hour of squiring more uglies and wallflowers about the dance floor. The last one was so huge it was like hefting about a pack of meal to get her to move." The ladies looked up to catch the Duke in the act of wiping at his heated brow with a fine lawn handkerchief.

"As it is your responsibility to, as you say, squire all the uglies, I can only think you look upon me as part of your duty, with my only attraction being that I will agree to content myself with a sojourn to the refreshment table instead of insisting you stand up with me in the next set," Tansy returned with feigned hauteur.

Her heart had begun thumping painfully against her breast at the sound of his voice, but Tansy refused to let Ashley see he had the power to discomfit her. "Do not be afraid of plain speech, cousin, nor try to wrap up your words in clean linen."

"Clean linen, is it, cousin?" The Duke returned with a deceptively bland smile. "It is you who are skirting the real issue by deliberately misunderstanding me. If you do not wish my company, then just go about the business as is your custom: say something nasty and have an end to it. I have had enough pointless chatter this night to last me out my days."

Tansy capitulated with a smile. Surely Avanoll wouldn't have sought her out if he were feeling uncomfortable about their interlude in the library. Obviously the dowager was a bit behind the times and did not realize how much freer society had become since the days when a single kiss was enough to ruin a girl for life. Her cousin wouldn't so compromise her, she was certain, and she would just have to follow his lead and learn to dismiss his occasional embraces as simply temporary aberrations that meant little or nothing to him.

So thinking, she again smiled up at her cousin. Little knowing the tumult the sight of her laughing eyes and moist, full lips set off in his solid chest, she laughingly implored, "Do not rage at me, cousin. I would be honored to have your company at the refreshment table."

Once the pair had taken themselves off, Lucinda and the dowager cheerfully put their heads together as they perched happily on the over-stuffed cushions.

"'The quarrels of lovers are the renewal of love.' Terence," Lucinda assured the dowager brightly.

"If quarrels give birth to love, my dear woman, those two are besotted beyond redemption," her grace replied in a weary voice. "At times I wish to knock their heads together until they see what I saw clearly the moment the two of them began spitting fire at each other that first morning. A marriage made in heaven, I thought then, and I haven't changed my mind. I vow to you, Lucinda, if they haven't murdered each other in the meantime, I'll have them safely bracketed before this year is out!

"Lucinda, you flea-witted female, stop bobbing your head up and down like the village idiot! Your plumes are jabbing my eyes out. Mark my words, woman, once my two grandchildren are settled I'm going to direct whatever energies I have left to me into trying to make some sense out of you. Like Tansy, I have a weakness for hopeless cases."

The Duke somehow braved the crush around the refreshment

table, and emerged with two glasses of orgeat (which he loathed) before steering Tansy to an alcove beside the dance floor and commandeering a brocade love seat by directing his iciest stare at the young sprig who was, until then, progressing quite famously in his silken-tongued pursuit of Lord Chatsworth's youngest and least-homely offspring.

"Demmed Peep-O'Day boy," the Duke swore under his breath.

"How do you know?" Tansy asked, spreading her skirts wide over the seat in an effort to keep her cousin at a less heart-disturbing distance.

"My dear child," the Duke imparted with an air of world-weary wisdom, "*anyone* who chases after a Chatsworth chit has got to be either blind, beetle-headed, a climbing-cit, or a money hungry wastrel.

"Didn't you get a good look at that horror? And she's the best of a bad lot. If my pockets were to let there would be little I wouldn't do to line them again, but I draw the line at wedding a Chatsworth. That blank stare she favored you with was the most intelligent expression she's ever worn."

Tansy's bell-like laugh rang out in pure enjoyment. "I believe I should feel sorry for one of them, but for the life of me I cannot decide who's more to be pitied—the girl or her ardent swain."

Avanoll's answering smile became arrested on his face as he listened to the velvety peals of Tansy's laughter. "Do you know you have a most delightful laugh? M'sister squeals like a pig caught in a gate. In fact, I can't think of another woman whose laughter I can stand for more than a few moments, as they either giggle, or titter behind their fans, or cackle like hens in a barnyard. Why is your laughter so pleasant?"

Tansy strove for lightness as she could feel her none-too-recovered heart melting again toward this man. "I studied chuckling in Vienna under the great Professor Herbert Von Laughington, your grace," she replied, tongue-in-cheek.

Now Avanoll's laughter burst forth, full and rich and deep, and although Tansy was pleased with the sound she withheld comment and quickly steered the subject to less intimate areas.

"Who is that atrociously vulgar-looking man standing beside the orchestra? He speaks so loudly his voice nearly drowns out the music, and the words I've heard so far have been far from fit for mixed company.

"And his dress!" she went on. "I do not pretend to be all the crack, but that gentleman, fine though his clothes might once

111

have been, looks like he spent the afternoon riding to hounds."

Avanoll's eyes quickly picked out the man Tansy described. "That old *roué*, for your enlightenment, is Sir John Lade. He and his wife are both horse-mad, and he has taken to imitating a groom in both language and dress. His wife is, if it is possible, even more vulgar and crude than he, and I advise you to cut a wide path around the pair of them. Two years ago Sir John was locked up in the King's Bench for debt, but his luck turned and he was released. There is a rather amusing story about the man, if you wish to hear it."

Tansy did. Anything to keep Ashley at her side for a few more precious minutes.

"Well, it seems Sir John, a betting man, wagered the rather portly Lord Chalmondely he could carry him around the Steine twice on his back—no mean feat, as it is quite a distance. As Sir John is of a much smaller build, his lordship was more than willing to make a large wager against him.

"At last the day for the test came, and everyone and their Uncle William crowded about the Steine to watch the fun. The participants were there, the crowd was there, but Sir John just stood quietly inspecting his nails until Chalmondely asked him the reason for the delay."

"And what reason did Sir John give?" Tansy asked, thoroughly intrigued.

"'I am waiting,' said Sir John, 'for you to *strip*. I said I'd carry you, but I'll not carry an ounce of clothes. Come now, do not disappoint the ladies.'"

Avanoll was rewarded for his tale with Tansy's unaffected laughter. "And how did it all end, cousin?"

"Chalmondely forfeited, of course, and Sir John was the toast of Brighton for many a day afterwards, though of his lordship little was seen for some time," he informed her. He then frowned as Lord Dartly—who was fifty if he was a day, even if he was well-preserved—interrupted to lay claim to Tansy for the next dance.

For the next two hours Avanoll propped up the wall with one broad shoulder and looked like a thundercloud whenever Tansy took the floor with another partner. He hadn't thought to ask her to pencil in his name on her card, as it did not occur to him that she would be such a huge success.

When later he espied her at supper, surrounded by no less than three fawning admirers, he could not resist the temptation of approaching her table and reminding her in a strident whisper that she had a job to do and was not free to fritter away the hours with a bunch of flea-witted greenheads.

Tansy was brought up short by this lightning change of mood, and was prompted to snap back testily, "And how can I serve you, your grace?"

"I should not think you could serve me at all, madam, but if you could possibly find the time to locate your charge before she lands us all in the basket I am sure my grandmother would be most grateful."

With that, the Duke bowed shortly to the three gape-mouthed gentlemen who were clearly astonished by his cavalier treatment of Miss Tamerlane, and withdrew to the cardroom. Here he remained for the balance of the evening, to the delight of his opponents, who departed the ball quite a deal richer than when they had arrived. Avanoll did not even notice the extent of his losses. He was much too busy making serious inroads on the wine decanter Dunstan was ordered to keep full at his elbow.

Tansy spent her time chasing Emily out of dark corners and keeping an eye on the girl as she skipped about the dance floor with a seemingly unending supply of eager partners.

Finally Emily lodged a protest. "I have a good mind—" she began before an overwrought Tansy cut her off by saying,

"That is an extremely debatable point, young lady, and precisely why I shall remain as watchdog until the last guest departs."

And she did.

If a ball is judged enjoyable by the amount of food and spirits the guests consume and the lightness of the early morning sky as it looks down on the carriages bearing off the revelers, then Emily's Come-Out Ball was a resounding success.

As Dunstan closed the door on the last straggling couples, Lucinda leaned on the bannister before she turned and wearily mounted the stairs—for once, too fatigued to cap an event with a maxim.

Emily, still chattering and showing no signs of fatigue, thoughtfully helped the dowager up the steps, careful to keep clear of Lucinda's dragging flounces.

Only Dunstan and a few other sleepy servants were around to accept Tansy's thanks and to be reminded of the ball to be held in the servants' hall later this same day.

"I hope you set aside enough food from the Ball to make your evening enjoyable," Tansy said with a weary smile. "From the way everybody was eating you would have thought they'd been starving themselves for weeks to get ready for a Roman feast."

Dunstan assured her that there was more than enough for the staff, and thanked Tansy again for arranging the servants' ball. "It made a big hit belowstairs, if I may say so, Miss Tansy. Everyone speaks highly of your kindness."

"That's our *Miss* Tansy, all right, *kind* and *thoughtful* to everyone, everyone but the poor fool who puts a roof over her sainted head."

Tansy and the servants turned to look, open-mouthed, at Avanoll, who was at the moment swinging back and forth precariously as he gripped the drawing room doorknob with one hand and tipped wine into his mouth (and down onto his crumpled, twisted cravat) from the decanter held in his other hand.

"You're castaway!" Tansy accused hotly.

"You're damned right I am, *cousin,* and never did a man have more right to the solace only a good bottle like this can provide. Don't think I didn't see you tonight, hopping from man to man like a common strumpet. But do you spare a kind word for the simple-minded dolt who took you in, who feeds you, who puts the clothes on your back?"

The Duke's voice dropped and he whispered harshly, "That back—that lovely, snowy-white, kissable, soft back. *No!*" his voice rose again, "you do not think of that man! God," he groaned, "I think I'm going to be sick."

Tansy stood straight as a poker throughout the Duke's verbal assault, although her eyes were suspiciously bright.

"Good!" she shouted at his last words. "Good, good, *good!*" She advanced on him, fumbling with the catch on her necklace. "Here," she cried, flinging it into his face so that he dropped the decanter in reaction.

As he stood in the archway with the necklace clutched against his chest and his fine, clocked silk stockings dripping all over with wine, Tansy gave him a piece of advice.

"Make up your mind, Ashley, for I cannot stand this constant shifting of moods. Either you want me under your roof or you don't. In either case, in the future I would appreciate it if you would stay away from me."

Her full bottom lip trembled for a moment before she pointed her index finger into his chest and jabbed him ruthlessly to punctuate every word she spat out between her gritted teeth. "Just stay away, cousin, or I'll, er, I'll— *oh,* curse your stupid hide!—I'll break your bloody nose!"

Ashley Benedict stared in stunned silence (as did the servants) as Tansy whirled on her heel and catapulted up the stairs, hand pressed to her mouth, as if all the hounds of hell were after her. He turned to meet his butler's condemning countenance and tried feebly at a joke.

"I'll lay a monkey to a turnip I've got to call you Dunstan again, old friend."

The long-term servant was not called upon to answer, but just to pull open the front door hastily to allow his grace the dubious pleasure of casting up his accounts on the flagway adjoining Grosvenor Square.

"Good," Dunstan echoed Tansy's opinion softly. "Very, very good."

Chapter Fourteen

ASHLEY BENEDICT roused himself most reluctantly the morning following the ball, tried to raise his head, and was rewarded for this effort by the appearance of a stabbing pain that shot across his broad forehead. It faded to a dull, sickening throb only after he prudently buried his face in the scratchy bedspread beneath him. The discomfort of lying sideways atop his bed, his long legs dangling almost to the floor, combined with the distinct chill that pervaded the room, convinced him that a further attempt to rearrange his limbs into an upright position was worth the agony such a move entailed.

Slowly, and, oh, so carefully—he prized himself up and away from the dubious comfort of his massive bed, staggered over to lean heavily against his tall dresser, and contemplated his bleary-eyed visage in the tilt-mirror.

"Egad, can that drunken sot be me?" he groaned incredulously. He raised one hand and stroked his beard-shadowed chin. It was he, all right, but the memory of what horrendous happening had driven him to so abuse his constitution he was unable, for the moment, to recall.

Just then Farnley burst into the chamber from the dressing room, without preamble starting in to harangue his master with a complaint about "that she-devil" Miss Tamerlane, who refused to heed signs that were as plain as the nose on his grace's face, begging his pardon.

Tansy! Of course! Who else but that infuriating menace of a cousin had ever gotten so firmly under his skin that he was forced to resort to take refuge in the bottom of a bottle—or two or three.

"Drat you, Farnley, stow it! Can't you see I am in excruciating pain? Have you so little pity for a fellow human being that you would so callously add to my burdens by bringing me your petty problems?"

Farnley looked embarrassed for a moment, but after apologizing he made one more try at laying his side of the story before the Duke.

"Enough!" Avanoll barked, immediately raising his hands to his throbbing skull. "Prepare my bath and get some coffee up here. And you may shave me today, if you can collect your nerves sufficiently to refrain from slicing my throat."

Once dressed for his afternoon meeting with some friends at Tattersall's, Avanoll gingerly descended to the breakfast room where he found himself confronted with muddy coffee, underdone eggs, burned bacon, and cold toast. The servants were obviously, in their own subtle way, expressing once again just where their allegiance lay.

As his memory of the previous evening slowly filtered back to him he had to admit that—perhaps this one time, at least—he had behaved just a trifle badly. Furthermore, if he ever hoped to enjoy a decent meal under his own roof again he would either have to make it up with Tansy or replace the entire staff.

As it was less trouble to perform the former requirement, and because he really did feel a slight twinge of remorse for his boorishness, he abandoned his unappetizing meal and went to seek out his cousin, thereby making his first meal of the day a serving of "crow."

But the Duke was to be thwarted in his attempt to smooth the domestic waters, for when he entered the main drawing room it was to find the chamber filled almost to bursting with floral offerings from gentlemen guests from the night before. The furniture was likewise littered with fashionable young bucks, foppish dandies, ridiculously perfumed old men, and not a few matchmaking mamas who had chosen this morning as the perfect time to corral the comely young heiress into attending their upcoming entertainments.

Avanoll stood on the threshold for some moments and watched his young sister smugly preening herself, batting her sooty lashes at the circle of adoring males about her, and generally having a merry old time flirting with every male in sight. Aunt Lucinda, he next observed, sat perched in one of her beloved chairs, nervously fanning herself and trying to monitor the goings-on with all the fervor (if not the competence) of a proper chaperon.

Then Avanoll spied out Tansy standing off to one side of the room and was amazed to see that, on second glance, the near regiment of suitors was actually divided into two distinct groups. While Emily held court with a crowd of fortune-hunters and mama's-babies, Tansy was looking quite at her ease entertaining a half-dozen or so of his own cronies, as well as a respectable sprinkling of more mature gentlemen—all sportsmen of the first rank.

He overheard a snippet of a story Tansy was just then relating, concerning a particularly fine battle she had with a trophy-sized salmon whilst she and her Papa were in Scotland (a most unladylike topic for discussion), but missed the end of the tale, which was truly a pity for it seemed to have set her listeners off into ridiculously juvenile paroxysms of mirth.

In a twinkling, all the Duke's good intentions went a-flying and before turning on his heel and stomping off, he, quite rudely, called across the room for Miss Tamerlane to attend him in the library. Amid moans of regret and easily overheard expressions of outrage, Tansy excused herself from the company, evincing all the social correctness the dowager had drummed repeatedly into her head. It was only after she was out of sight of the drawing room that her stride became rather long, her footfalls disintegrated into purposeful stampings, and her smiling face took on the narrow-eyed aspects of a hawk on the hunt.

Horatio, who had been dutifully awaiting his mistress's emergence from a room strictly out of bounds to canine types (a truth brought home by repeated application of the dowager's cane to his tender hindquarters), joined her in the march to the library—where he quickly staked his claim to the rug before the cold fireplace, growled once at the Duke (as was his custom), and curled up for a pleasant snooze.

Tansy took note of Avanoll's strategically superior position—standing behind the wide mahogany desk and, refusing to sit down, thus placing her at a psychological disadvantage—belligerently took up her own position directly across the room, feet braced and slightly apart, arms akimbo, and her chin at a challenging tilt.

It was left to Avanoll to either shout down the length of the room or walk around the desk and narrow the gap between them. He knew he had been out-maneuvered, but there was little he could do. And as an imposing posturing with one arm draped on the mantel was impossible without exposing his ankles to

Horatio's razor-jaws, he did the only thing left to him. He advanced until he stood face to face with his cousin, a mere three feet separating them.

And then they stared at each other—or glared at each other, if meticulous honesty was truly to be served—neither wishing to speak first and so be put on the defensive. At last, possibly her sense of fair play owning up to the fact that by moving from behind the desk Avanoll had already made one concession, Tansy broke the tense silence by demanding:

"Well?"

The Duke came to himself with a start. In the midst of his anger he had somehow found himself overcome with the desire to take Tansy in his arms and kiss her quite ruthlessly. This realization only added fuel to his anger, and he immediately went on the offensive. "Just what do you mean, madam, upsetting my man this morning?" he sneered, grasping at the first straw to come to hand.

This bizarre query was definitely the last of a long agenda of possible bones of contention Tansy supposed Avanoll about to gnaw on this morning. In point of fact, Farnley did not even appear upon her mental list as a subject for debate. As a result, she was in turn speechless, confused, and—finally—downright angry.

"You mean to stand there and tell me," she demanded incredulously, "that you burst into the drawing room, made a perfect spectacle of yourself by bellowing like an enraged bull, and dragged me rudely away from our guests to discuss your superstitious twit of a valet?"

She flung her hands out in exasperation and shook her head in an expression of disbelief. "Ashley, either you're the greatest ignoramus in nature or you've temporarily slipped your wits after your disgusting descent into drunkenness last evening." Before Avanoll could search his senses, still oddly disturbed by thoughts of romance, for a rebuttal, Tansy continued, "As all you seem capable of since your first hysterical accusation is to stand rooted to the carpet like a wilting potted-palm, I imagine I will be forced to dignify your question with a suitable explanation."

Tansy then began to pace the floor as Avanoll looked on—feeling, if absolute truth was to be the rule of the day, exceedingly foolish. "The set-to—or *contretemps,* as the dowager would no doubt phrase it, though I see no need to wrap this particular farce up in clean linen—began earlier this morning, when I discovered your estimable servant to be the instigator of a near-riot in the kitchen.

"It seems one of the servants dropped a crystal wine goblet while clearing away last night's debris, and the thing shattered in a thousand pieces."

While Avanoll watched his cousin's agitated pacings, his brow becoming more creased as she recounted the morning's events, Tansy ceased her assault on the priceless Aubusson carpet and told him:

"When I arrived on the scene to discover the reason for the shrieks of alarm audible in the breakfast room, Farnley was being forcibly restrained from reaching the cabinet where the kitchen crockery is kept by the presence of three whimpering maids and an irate Cook, wielding a huge meat cleaver. Once order was restored, Cook explained that Farnley wished to break two more pieces of china—inexpensive items he termed expendable—so that the more costly china would be spared."

Now the Duke was completely at sea, and his baffled expression registered the fact. "Why break more china?" he asked bleakly.

Tansy laughed ruefully. "Surely, your grace, you have heard that all bad events come in threes. Farnley wished to fulfill the requirements necessary to end this particular run of bad luck with the least cost to you and your heirloom china. I," she ended rather smugly, "sent him away with a flea in his ear, and he obviously scurried straight to you to give vent to his injured feelings."

Avanoll had the good grace to look ashamed. "Farnley *is*, as you say, a bit superstitious," he explained feebly.

"Superstitious!" Tansy chortled. "The man's a lily-livered ninny with more hair than wit. My major complaint, if I might be allowed the same freedom Farnley has to talk behind another's back, is his influence upon my own ninnyhammer attendant, Pansy, who is so susceptible to his ravings."

"I understand your concern, cousin, but I fail to see any way, short of dismissing Farnley, that can serve to put a halt to it. If only we could find some personal weak point of his we could, er, *convince* Farnley to leave off filling the poor girl full of his nonsense."

Tansy gave an exasperated sigh. "His weak point is easy to spot, Ashley, as it sits directly above his neck. Would you suggest the Froggies' contraption, the guillotine?"

Avanoll chuckled at the joke, then noticed the air in the room was no longer fraught with tension. Crossing his fingers behind his back he launched into a belated apology, a note of bitter self-mockery in his voice. "I know I blotched my copybook last night and was in general behaving like the worst of boors. I have no explanation, unless it is to plead that I was a trifle up in the world at the time."

Tansy magnanimously accepted Avanoll's out and out drunkenness as being a *trifle* castaway and replied soothingly, "Please do not think me to be such a booby that I would be overly put out by what a man says whilst deep in his cups."

"Yes, well, I thank you, cousin. But I know I behaved like a regular hot-headed halfling, and for no reason other than my own perverseness."

Now Tansy giggled. "You were proper sloshed at that, your grace, I agree." And with that bit of plain speech, any remaining constraint floated magically away and the pair quit the room quite good friends once more—Tansy to return to her gentlemen callers, Avanoll to trot off to his engagement at Tatt's.

Once the last of their admirers had been reluctantly shifted back onto the flagway outside Avanoll House, the three ladies ascended the stairs to look in on the dowager, who had pleaded fatigue and remained in bed for a rest following the excitement of the ball.

"Get up, you slug-a-bed," Emily trilled, still heady with her triumph as she burst into her grandmother's chamber. "You will not believe the absolute success my ball has been."

"It's true, your grace," Tansy supplied more calmly. "The entire household has been knee-deep in posies and bucks all this morning long."

She approached the spare figure still reclining in the huge dome bed, almost lost amid the heavy wood head-and-tester deeply carved with clouds, suns, and cupids, and hung about with red velvet, richly fringed round with weighty gold tassels.

Tansy cast her eyes around the huge room, still steeped in shadow behind the firmly-drawn, red velvet draperies, and took in an intricately fitted-out Ince dressing table, a many-compartmented writing desk, a Chippendale commode and clothes-press, as well as a china case awe-inspiring in both size and decoration—and stuffed full of a motley assortment of painted glass birds and small forest animals. Finally her attention was drawn to a chaise-longue that could only have been the result of an early brainstorm of Sheraton's. Draped all over in rusty-red velvet cut in an overblown rose pattern, its frame was decorated in burnished gold and carved into contortions that defied description.

"Awful, ain't it?" her grace chuckled weakly. "The only thing good about this room is the dumbwaiter that leads right to the kitchens. My food arrives hot, even if the room itself robs me of my appetite."

As the dowager spoke, Tansy could not help but notice the huskiness in her voice and questioned the woman as to how she felt.

"I must admit I am not quite in plump currant. No doubt the hey-go-mad pace I set myself making ready for the ball has finally caught up with me. You ladies just stay back so that you don't catch anything from me, though it's just a little cough and a bit of a tender throat. Don't let me spoil your fun," she ended stoutly.

Tansy took no heed and walked straight up to the bed. "That's deuced agreeable of you, ma'am, but I think there is a trifle more amiss here than a simple tickle in your throat. If you don't mind, I'd like to feel your forehead, for your cheeks look a sight too pink and your eyes, though always twinkling, are a tad too bright to suit me."

"Stay away, I say!" the dowager croaked. "I'm not so feeble that I'll stand any sauce from you, gel. And ladies do not say *deuced*," she added automatically as Tansy's cool hand descended to touch the old lady's fevered brow.

"Aha, just as I thought. Trifling cold, indeed. You, madam, are burning with fever," Tansy declared. "We must get you something for it at once."

"'Better use medicines at the outset than at the last moment.' Syrus," Aunt Lucinda proffered helpfully, if somewhat pessimistically.

"Be quiet, you beetle-headed widget!" the dowager rasped while Tansy smothered a chuckle.

"Such a kickup," Emily pouted, seeing her moment in the limelight rapidly being replaced by the household's overreaction to her grandparent's piddling indisposition. "Grandmama has lived long enough to recognize whether or not she is really sick."

Aunt Lucinda seemed in prime form today and quickly countered by quoting, "'Age carries all things, even the mind, away.' Virgil."

"Now, now your grace," Tansy soothed, while pressing the indignant old lady's thin shoulders back down on the pillows. "Aunt Lucinda means well."

"Oh, she's a well-intentioned enough *old tabby.*" This last was said with a quelling stare in Aunt Lucinda's direction. "But if I am in fact to be confined to this grotesque abomination of a room for any length of time, like a molting pigeon cooped up until I am fit to be seen, I must insist you keep the *dear* puss the deuce out of my sight and hearing."

"Mustn't say *deuce,* Grandmama," Emily tittered impishly, gaining herself a pithy set-down in the process.

By mid-afternoon, the doctor had been called in to pronounce the dowager the victim of a severe bout of influenza. He prescribed rhubarb and calomel for her headache and cough, as well as an assortment of vile-tasting possets and embrocations guaranteed to encourage his patient into full recovery if only to halt the doses of the stuff.

Aunt Lucinda was in succeeding days wont to shake her head over the myriad of vials and bottles standing on the dowager's bedside table and mutter, "'There are some remedies worse than the disease.' Syrus," to which her grace was heard to reply breathlessly, "Amen."

This prompted the aunt to offer her opinion of the doctor. "'Old men are only walking hospitals.' Horace," which actually brought a wavering smile to the dowager's lips, for she was in truth quite weak.

So encouraged, Aunt Lucinda added one quote too many. "'O Death the Healer, scorn those not, I pray, To come to me: of cureless ills thou art the one physician. Pain lays not its touch upon a corpse.' Aeschylus."

It was a full week later before Aunt Lucinda was brave enough to sneak back into the sickroom to offer the dowager a copy of John Heywood's 1562 *Woorkes, A Dialogue conteyning the number in effect of all the proverbs in the English tounge, compact in a matter concernynge two maner of Maryages, etc.,* a book that followed behind her in her retreat through the door some scant seconds later.

There was another ruckus belowstairs when Farnley removed the cat from the pantry, stating that everyone knew if a cat was allowed to kill a mouse when someone was sick in the house it was a sure omen of impending death. Tansy allowed that incident to blow over by itself, but put a quick halt to the valet's plans to drop deadly poisonous henbane seeds onto the hot coals in the dowager's sickroom grate so that she could "benefit" from the resulting vapors.

Farnley was a mite daunted by this setback, but the innocent devotion which Pansy showed for his higher intelligence more than made up for any slights Tansy could cast on his knowledge.

For Tansy had been correct: the guileless Pansy was thoroughly awed by Farnley's readily recited store of charms, curses, cures, and supposed clairvoyances, and hung most adoringly on his every word. Indeed, unbeknownst to Tansy (thank goodness, for Farnley's skin would have been in grave danger otherwise), the valet had even gone so far as to use his knowledge to convince Pansy of his—Farnley's—rightness as her partner (and mentor?) for life!

Early one April morning, Pansy tiptoed down the backstairs from her attic room and stole out into the misty dawn, a willow branch clenched firmly in her left hand. Making certain no one was about, she held the twig before her and ran not one, but three full circuits around the large mansion chanting, "He that's to be my good man, come and grip the end of it." Need it be mentioned that upon completion of her third circuit a pale, wraithlike hand appeared out of the mist to grasp the other end of the willow stick, and Pansy was gifted with a fleeting glimpse of Farnley's ashen face before the apparition disappeared into the haze.

Before a dazed but happy Pansy could react, Farnley was back inside the mansion and rubbing fiercely at the flour that whitened his face and one hand. He did not feel any dishonesty had occurred, for after all, the only thing he had done was to hasten Pansy into taking a step toward what, he felt sure, was their Fate.

Unfortunately for some other inhabitants of Avanoll House, Farnley's tempting of the fates had set in motion some unforseen complications. For Pansy was now all a-twitter as to how to earn some extra funds so she and Farnley could fulfill their destiny in as short a time as possible.

Comfort was much too busy nursing the dowager—and making a fine job of it, by the way—so the Lady Emily was left very much to her own devices. Her social outings had been drastically curtailed since her grace's illness.

Pansy may have made a dreadful botch of her first assignment—which had resulted in the purloined letter—but Emily was willing to give the girl another try at subterfuge. There was this simply exquisite gentleman who miraculously appeared in the Mall each morning when Pansy accompanied her on a morning stroll amid the nursemaids and their precious charges. It was child's play to lose Pansy long enough to make the gentleman's approach possible, and less than difficult to enlist the maid's aid in the passing of messages—for a slight fee, of course.

Alternating spoonsful of milk pudding with dainty forays into the box of sugarplums lying beside her on the coverlet, the dowager remarked on Emily's magnanimous acceptance of her limited social life. "The girl is hopelessly silly, but she bears watching. It isn't normal for her to be so docile. I smell something rotten—like a *man*," she told Tansy seriously.

Avanoll was also concerned. "Even with Grandmama still abed, I think, cousin, it is time you and m'sister were out and about."

Tansy agreed with them both, but it was left to Aunt Lucinda to put a seal on it. "'He who is bent on doing evil can never want occasion.' Syrus."

So, with Aunt Lucinda lending an air of respectability if not a whit of restraint, Tansy and Emily were launched on a mad round of routs, balls, theatre parties, assemblies, tea parties, dinners, luncheons, and at-homes. Emily fairly glowed as she whirled from partner to partner, and was fervently courted by no less than a half-dozen youths as brainless and flighty as she.

Tansy, on the other hand, was bored to flinders within a sen'night. She knew for certain now that she had, against all good sense, tumbled headlong into love with Avanoll.

The Duke, refusing to admit to any deep emotional entanglement, doggedly clung to the lively sense of self-preservation that had so far kept him ahead of the parson's mousetrap, and refused to dwell on his more tender feelings—making a huge show of busyness and detachment where his cousin was concerned.

The dowager, once her charges were safely back in Society, spent her convalescence teaching Horatio to beg prettily for bonbons, and telling him the story of her life as he curled up next to her on the coverlet.

Perhaps these reasons do not excuse the inability of her guardians to penetrate Emily's compliant façade. But then, who could have foreseen the latest maggot the fair woman-child had taken into her head?

Chapter Fifteen

ONE FINE NIGHT not too many days hence, the Duke was to be found spending a longed-for quiet evening by his own fireside. Tansy was attending a quiet card-party in Brook Street, which—not so surprisingly—Emily had declined, calling the game a rather insipid amusement. Assuring both her brother and her Aunt Lucinda that she was more than happy to bow this once to Tansy's preferences, and personally planning to retire early, she daubed her petal-smooth complexion with Denmark Lotion because, as everyone knew: "If but a single freckle were to appear I should absolutely *perish* from embarrassment."

And so it was that, while the dowager was tucked up snugly between the covers of her outlandish bed (her attention riveted upon the lurid marble-backed novel propped upon her bent knees, Horatio companionably warming her toes and feeling quite fatuously content), and Aunt Lucinda was busy doing whatever she usually did to keep herself occupied (which included a complicated myriad of pointless exercises too silly to enumerate), the Duke of Avanoll had just comfortably ensconced his large frame in his favorite overstuffed armchair in his private salon. His grace was armed with a pair of well-worn slippers, a decanter of fine old brandy, and a nearby silver tray upon which reposed an ample supply of thin cigarillos.

Farnley held a lighted spill to the tip of the cigar already gripped between his grace's strong white teeth, and just as the cigar—with the aid of a series of satisfying puffs—was lit, a sound from the door threatened to break the peace.

"*Psst,*" went the sound. And then, "*Psst!*" again.

Farnley cast a furtive look toward the door and allowed his small jet eyes to widen a fraction. He then swiftly shook his head in the negative, and just as swiftly assured his grace brightly—or at the least, with more animation than was usual for the valet—that he had neither heard nor seen anything to upset his grace, no sir! Not a single solitary thing.

The famed eloquent Benedict eyebrow rose slightly at this bit of gammon, but he refrained from doubting his valet outright. Obviously the man had an assignation planned with one of the housemaids and the chit was become impatient (although a picture of the spindley-shanked Farnley indulging in a round of slap and tickle was nigh impossible to envision).

The Duke decided on a bit of devilment. "Care to draw up a chair and chat a while, Farnley?" he asked in a world-weary voice. "I find my own company devilishly flat, and I'm convinced you can serve to amuse me with some farradiddle or other concerning yet another affront dealt Dame Fortune by my dear cousin's irreverent abuse of the Sacred Code of Chants and Charms, or whatever name you give to your devotions."

At any other time the valet would have been inordinately pleased at such a generous invitation (besides taking time to inform his grace of the folly of laughing at ancient customs). But at the moment he had more pressing matters on his mind—as witnessed by his nervous pulling at his neckcloth and the sly looks he kept darting toward the salon door.

Avanoll allowed himself an injured sigh. "Oh, very well, Farnley, I can see you find my company no less dull than I myself. You may be excused."

As Farnley scraped a hurried bow and fairly ran toward the door (from behind which could now be heard the sound of soft sobbing), the Duke called out, "Tch, tch, Farnley, such haste is unbecoming. It will do the girl well to cool her heels a bit. Never let them think they can have you trotting after them every time they crook their little finger," he ended with a laugh.

"Yes, yes, your grace. Whatever you say, your grace. I shall remember your words and, er, thank you kindly, your grace," Farnley blustered, and disappeared around the door, giving the Duke only a second's sight of a maid—Tansy's own hapless abigail, if he was not mistaken.

But, wait a moment. Hadn't his cousin complained to him that Farnley exercised much too much influence over this girl? Pansy, he thought her name was. Yes. Yes, indeed.

And now he could hear Farnley's voice raised in anger (for they had not removed themselves from the other side of the door by more than two feet), while the girl Pansy was sobbing in ever-crescendoing wails! Perhaps he owed his cousin a favor for all her help with the dowager. Any other consideration for his cousin he hastily denied with a pungent oath.

"*Farnley!*" Avanoll growled, whereupon the valet stuck his head round the door and asked quakingly, "You called, sir?"

"You're demmed right I *called*," Avanoll replied dampeningly. "Haul your skinny arse in here! And bring the town crier with you as well, before she shrieks the entire household into believing we have been set upon by cutthroats and murderers."

It would seem, alas, that the warning (or perhaps that same warning, which when rendered by the Duke's clear baritone, echoed throughout the first floor with remarkable clarity) had come too late. Entering his previously sacrosanct room hard on the heels of the red-faced valet and the whimpering Pansy, Avanoll was dismayed to see his aunt—flounces and lace and ruffled nightcap all billowing in the breeze she stirred as she flitted into the room—crying distractedly, "'What now if the sky were to fall.' Terence!"

"It needed only this," the Duke gritted out under his breath.

But his aunt, it seemed, was not the only person who had come on the run, for his grandmother, with Horatio tucked under one arm, was not a half-dozen steps behind Aunt Lucinda, and it was she who enquired testily, "Just what in the name of all that's decent is going on here? Cannot a woman even lie sick upon her bed undisturbed by ear-splitting shouts and those incessant—I say, Pansy, stop that caterwauling this instant—wails and gnashing of teeth?"

His grace took a last deep puff of the first cigar he had enjoyed in a very long month, sighed longingly, and dispatched it to the coals. With a minimum of fuss he settled first his irate grandparent and then his agitated aunt in wing chairs facing the fire. Then he turned his attention to the two guilty-looking servants, who were at that moment endeavoring to melt into the furnishings. As soon as he turned his eyes on Pansy, the maid responded by setting in again to sobbing loudly, her hands shredding a handkerchief into a small pile at her feet.

"Oh, good grief," Avanoll swore. "Farnley, I leave it to you to untangle this ridiculous coil. Whatever is it that has set this girl off?"

Farnley made a choppy bow, cleared his throat as if to speak, and ended by simply extending a hand in which he shakily clutched a scrap of pink, scented notepaper.

"This should, er, explain it all, your grace, I do believe," he quavered.

Avanoll grabbed the paper and walked to the candelabra near his desk to read the note that his sister Emily had penned and left pinned to her pillow (this last being supplied between sobs and hiccups by Pansy).

"*To Whom it May Concern, though I Doubt my Fate matters a whit to Any of You*," he read aloud.

> "*Life for me under this roof has become Insupportable. I, like the Simplest Bird in the Sky, must be Free to Fly where I will. Society gives married women So Much more Freedom than Ever I had With You, so I am Winging my way To Wedded Bliss with my Betrothed, a Gentleman who Understands my Sensibilities and Will not Countenance Beauty Such As Mine (his own sweet words) to be Locked Away in a Cage. I Fly now to my Beloved Rescuer.*
>
> > *Your Granddaughter, sister, cousin, niece, whatever—Emily.*"

"The dim-wit plans to elope!" the dowager cried. "*Again!*"

"'I shudder at the word.' Euripedes," Aunt Lucinda said, and then promptly did.

"Hell and damnation! Was there ever such a pernicious brat? Fly, be damned! I'll clip her little wings when I get my hands on her," Avanoll declared hotly as he crushed the note in one large hand and consigned it to the fire.

"Leave a width or two of her mischief-making hide for me to strip off her smart-aleck bottom, Ashley," the dowager put in absently as she tapped her index finger against her pursed lips.

"But first things first." She turned in her chair to face the teary-eyed maid. "All right, missy, nobody here will harm you. We all know how easily that sly-boots granddaughter of mine can wrap innocents like you around her thumb. Lady Emily hasn't been out of this house unchaperoned in a fortnight. Therefore it stands to reason her *Beloved Rescuer*," she sneered a bit over the words, "and she used you as their Cupid. Am I correct so far, dearie?" she ended kindly. "Just nod, you don't have to speak."

Pansy nodded.

Avanoll cut in, an idea having just struck him. "How long have these messages been traveling to and fro through you?"

Pansy rolled her fear-widened eyes. "Oh, laws, your worship, for an age, a fearsome age."

"'Oh, what a tangled web we weave, when first we practice to deceive.' Sir Walter Scott," was Aunt Lucinda's sage, if second-hand, observation.

The Duke gave himself a mental kick as he realized how the names Pansy and Tansy could so easily be misread for each other, but his musings were caught up short by the dowager's next question.

"Just one more little jot of information, Pansy, and you may retire. The name. Give us the name of Lady Emily's correspondent."

"Did you want *all* the names of all the notes or just the ones from the gentleman dear Lady Emily has loped off with?" Pansy asked innocently.

"If I— no!—*when* I lay hands on that girl I'll fix it so she has no choice but to eat all her meals for a month standing at the mantelpiece, her rump will be so tender!" Lady Emily's nearest blood kin and guardian vowed.

The dowager pushed on, unperturbed by this outburst. "Just the one, Pansy, please. But hurry, do, as every moment is precious if we are to put a stop to this nonsense."

Aided by a poke in the ribs from Farnley's pointed elbow, Pansy burst out, "His name be Sir Rollin Whitstone and he lives at—"

"I know where he lives, that blackguard, that underhanded, despicable cod," the Duke bit out, crossing the room to take down a dueling sword from over the mantelpiece, "and he'll rue the day he dared to trifle with *my* sister! I'll have his liver and lights before the hour is out.

"Farnley!" he called over his shoulder as he trotted hastily from the room, "I'll need your assistance with my jacket and boots. Hurry man, I have no time to waste." Farnley hastened after his master, while Pansy disappeared through the door and down to the kitchens, where she could hide in a corner scraping vegetables until her part in the affair was forgotten.

Aunt Lucinda, who the dowager had more than once commented possessed more hair than wit, clapped her dimpled hands in girlish glee and sang out, "'No sooner said than done—so acts your man of worth.' Quintus Ennius."

"Lucinda, you brainless ninnyhammer," the dowager exploded, "this is not a play performed upon the boards where Good never fails to triumph over Evil and the hero always emerges unscathed from any heated encounter. This is the real world, and both my grandchildren are in mortal danger." Aunt Lu-

130

cinda subsided into her chair, pulled her rosebud-red mouth down at the corners, and proceeded to look properly subdued.

Soon footsteps were heard to pass hurriedly by, and the banging of the front door told the women that Avanoll was off to Half Moon Street and his appointment with Destiny. The dowager looked disinterestedly about her grandson's private salon until her eye alighted on the brimful brandy decanter at her elbow. "Lucinda," she ventured, "if you could search out another snifter for yourself, we might better pass the time sharing a sip or two of my grandson's best stock."

By the time Tansy returned to Grosvenor Square some twenty minutes later—both the card party and the company having proven too dull to hold her interest—she followed the trail of voices to the Duke's salon and was quickly brought up to date on Emily's latest indiscretion.

"All that meek and innocent manner she has been parading by us these past weeks were nothing but a sham. She has made a May Game of all of us, the little monster!" Tansy exclaimed hotly when the dowager told her what was going forward. "She promised me she would behave, and like a fool I believed her."

"'A womans vows I write upon the waves.' Sophocles," Aunt Lucinda quoted with a wise nod.

"And Sir Rollin! Why, everyone with a jot of sense knows he's nothing more than a hardened seducer who eats babies like Emily for breakfast," Tansy continued as she paced furiously back and forth, her fist pounding into the palm of her other hand. All at once she stopped, took a deep breath, and yelled at the top of her lungs, "*Farnley!*" (which was really quite unnecessary, as the valet was eavesdropping just outside the door to hear whether his beloved—who was by some coincidence also the greatest admirer of his exceptional insight and knowledge—was to be sacked for her blunder).

The valet appeared at once and watched in gape-mouthed astonishment while Tansy took down the black leather case containing the Duke's favorite dueling pistols and calmly loaded the pair. Tansy hefted each piece and nodded, apparently satisfied, before slipping a pistol into each of the ample pockets in the evening cloak she had yet to discard. "All right, Farnley, I am ready. About-face, my good fellow, and let us shove off."

"Wh-where do you think you are going?" the dowager asked hollowly.

"I'm off to stop a duel, your grace," Tansy replied without a blink. "A rare bumblebath it will be if Ashley kills his man and must flee the country. Men don't think, you know. A simple horsewhipping or a sound thrashing would serve the purpose just as well, but men tend to lean toward histrionic displays whenever they believe their honor is at stake. I'd be damned if I'd get myself exiled for a silly chit like Emily: better to blacken Sir Rollin's peepers and lock Emily in her room on bread and water than spend the next five years touring India or some other outlandish spot, don't you think?"

The dowager was sure she should put a stop to Tansy's plans, but love of her grandchildren (and a goodly intake of vintage brandy) had dulled her wits just enough that she could not think of any rebuttal but to say chaperons do not carry pistols or disrupt duels.

Tansy quietly pointed out that it wouldn't matter a tinker's curse (oh, these recurrent lapses into cant language!) what her title was if Emily was ruined—because then, logically, chaperon or no, the Lady Emily would be beyond the pale, never to set foot in Society again. Therefore she, Tansy Tamerlane, was off to do her best to aid Avanoll in saving the day.

"'United we stand, divided we fall.' Aesop," Aunt Lucinda proposed, taking another large sip from her snifter.

"Indeed," the dowager echoed, drinking a toast to her companion's oratorical brilliance.

It did not require the wisdom of Solomon, or any of the other sages Aunt Lucinda was so fond of quoting, to deduce that both the dowager and Aunt Lucinda were—to put it kindly—a trifle up in the world due to the brandy they had so far ingested. But Tansy hastily decided that a tipsy dowager was better than a frail old woman lying prostrate on a bed of sorrow over her missing granddaughter and knight-errant grandson, and opted to ignore the situation.

Grabbing the bewildered Farnley by the sleeve, Tansy bundled the valet down the stairs and through the door Dunstan already held wide open, then ordered the valet to flag down the first hackney cab he saw. Once inside the shabby vehicle Farnley hired, Tansy ordered the valet to tell the driver Sir Rollin's address, which she was sure the busybody servant would know.

He did, and they were off, clip-clopping down the street behind a large conveyance that was proceeding with all the speed of a funeral procession. "Give that carriage the go-by, driver, and push that slug of yours to his limit. There's a guinea in it for you if you do," Tansy promised rashly.

For a guinea the driver would have gotten out and pulled the hackney himself if it would make it move any faster, and the next two blocks passed quickly.

The only other vehicle now on the street was a fully loaded hay-cart, just then approaching from the opposite direction, and looking very much out of place in Mayfair. "Oh, no," Farnley cried. "Was there ever worse luck? A full hay-cart, and coming right at us!"

"So?" Tansy inquired without interest, her thoughts devoted to the scene that would greet her in Half Moon Street.

"Any child knows a loaded hay-cart is only lucky if it is traveling in the same direction as you. To *pass* one means bad luck sure as check."

"Really," Tansy said absently, turning in her seat to lean out and look at the evil cart just as it disappeared around the next corner. Suddenly Farnley saw what she was about and rudely hauled her back under the canopy. "Please say you didn't look at it, Miss Tansy," he begged.

"I confess, Farnley, I did peek at the cart, but not for long, I promise, for it rounded the corner as I watched."

Farnley turned white as a sheet at her words and for a moment Tansy really suspected he might cry. "The worst luck, the very worst luck to see it turn a corner. Oh, Miss Tansy, your uncaring attitude toward proven omens has destroyed any chance at a successful rescue tonight by either the Duke or yourself. Oh, woe! Oh, woe, betide us now," he whined, rocking back and forth on the greasy leather seat like a man demented.

There were a lot of things Tansy was willing to put up with in this life, but traveling with a weeping valet through the streets of London in a hackney carriage after midnight was not one of them. Just as she was about to soundly box his ears, a lone rider out late passed by and, wonder of wonders, his handsome grey mare tossed her hind shoe just as Farnley was casting his eyes about and mumbling incantations calling for a miracle.

"Stop! Stop this hackney at once!" he screeched, as he jumped nimbly into the street and ran forward to pick up the lost horseshoe. The hackney driver sawed on the reins and he and Tansy watched in stupefaction as Farnley gazed reverently at the shoe, spit on it, made a mumbled wish, and tossed the shoe over his left shoulder before walking away from both the shoe and the hackney without looking back.

Never turning his head an inch, he called back to the driver to move up so that he could re-enter the hackney, as looking about would destroy his good luck. Once back beside Tansy, he assured her this latest bit of good luck overruled the lesser evil power of a loaded hay-cart—and that the chance for a happy ending to the night's trials was now assured.

"You cannot possibly imagine how gratified I am to hear that, Farnley," Tansy said dryly, before adding more candidly, "I would wager a pound note to a hat pin you make up these curses and counter-curses as you go along. When it comes to downright silliness and superstitious nonsense, Farnley, I vow you bear off the palm."

Before the aggrieved servant could form a rebuttal, the hackney had drawn up before a rather dusty stucco building. The driver announced his belief that he had earned his bonus, even if the odd gent had slowed them down a bit chasing horseshoes and all that.

Tipping his battered hat in thanks to the pair who had quickly scrambled onto the flagway and up the short flight of steps, he then tested the shiny guinea with his two good teeth—and turned his horse toward the nearest tavern known to supply cheap gin and convivial female companionship.

Chapter Sixteen

FARNLEY, showing a belated sense of manly courage (an emotion abetted by the fortuitous grey-mare horseshoe), jumped in front of Tansy and pounded the brass knocker mightily until a harassed-looking manservant-cum-jack-of-all trades yanked open the door with an admonition to "leave off that racket afore Oi calls the Watch down on ya."

Tansy pulled Farnley back discreetly by the hem of his coat, and stepped into the dim light shining out the door. Aping Avanoll's most supercilious expression (a masterful combination of haughtiness, pride, and utter contemptuousness), she cast her eyes up and down any creature so foolhardy as to dare to block her way—reducing the man to a quivering mass of jelly as he felt a shivering recollection of another such examination not too lately past also directed in much the same way. On that occasion, however, the examination had ended with his person being firmly deposited, rump-down, in a nearby potted plant.

Holding his hands outstretched as if an attack were imminent, and giving out with a strangled, "Oh, no ya doesn't. Not again, or me name's not Vernon Q. Cake!" the terrified man executed a former foot soldier's excellent About-Face and bolted for the bowels of the house, thereby abandoning his post and allowing the enemy to breach his lines without even a hint of resistance.

As he was to remark to one of his cronies at the neighborhood tavern the next day, he—Vernon Q. Cake, late of His Majesty's Fifth Foot and a man who had served in more than one fearful battle—would do the same again without shame if ever either of those two fire-breathing giants were to blink in his direction, "so crazy-mad and weird-like they wuz."

For as great an impression as first Avanoll and then Tansy made on manservant Cake, it was a pity that they took as little notice of him as they did. Tansy's major concern during the ride to Half Moon Street had been how to gain entrance to Sir Rollin's lodgings. The most notice she took of the man Cake was to be relieved at his seeming cooperation, and only a little chagrined that he did not stay around long enough to inform her of the Duke and Emily's presence within.

Yet, still a bit heady with this first easy victory, she lost no time in surveying her captured territory—in this case a rather shabby dark foyer—before she counted slowly to ten to compose herself and slow her racing pulse. The first door she then approached led into a masculine bedroom fitted out in ancient if rather sybaritic splendor that, Tansy thanked the gods, showed no signs of recent occupancy.

The next minuscule room she and the reluctant Farnley entered appeared to be a sort of masculine receiving room, to be used when entertaining the gentler sex. It, too, was empty. That left but one door at the end of the hall, other than the one the servant had used, which led most probably to the kitchen. Tansy pressed her ear against the thick oak panelling and heard indistinct voices, apparently raised in anger.

"This is it," she mouthed silently to Farnley, whose courage and physical presence had both retreated closer to the still-ajar front door—or bolt-hole, depending on whether the portal was thought of by Tansy or the valet. She cast him a look of utter disgust and mentally adjusted the number of her assault force from two to one before taking a steadying breath, depressing the double latches, and giving the twin panels a gigantic shove that propelled them against the walls inside the room with an explosive *Ba-Boom* that robbed the room's occupants of all powers of speech and movement and succeeded in gaining their undivided attention.

While three pairs of startled eyes goggled at this tall, black-velvet cloaked creature who had burst upon the scene so precipitously, Tansy, in her turn, surveyed the room—which appeared to be a private study—and its occupants. First to fall under her scrutiny was the figure of her recalcitrant charge, who was still buttoned into her outerwear, topped off by a ridiculously youthful looking chip-straw hat tied under her chin by means of a huge pink and white checked grosgrain ribbon. Cowering in a corner, she was standing beside a bandbox undoubtedly crammed full of the necessities of life: toothbrush and powder, a Penny Press novel, three pair of kid gloves, a locked diary, and a half-eaten box of chocolates.

Emily looked frightfully overset, woefully helpless, painfully young, and—as soon as she understood the caped figure to be her cousin Tansy—blessedly relieved. This relief was shared by Tansy, who was assured Emily's virtue, if not her reputation, was still intact.

Next, Tansy's eyes raked over the villain of the piece, a thin-lipped, dark-complected man some women found handsome but who Tansy scorned as attempting to look pseudo-sinister and succeeding only in looking as if his liver was slightly off. Yet Mrs. Radcliffe had not gained her so-large following of readers without a great love for gothic heroes who appeared to be much of a sameness with Sir Rollin, so either Tansy's taste was too particular or the followers of the Minerva Press were more romantic than the experienced (for "experienced" read "on-the-shelf spinster") Miss Tamerlane. In any event, Tansy wasted no more than a few seconds on the man.

She lastly turned her eyes to the right to see, standing with about half of the fair-sized room between himself and Sir Rollin, the person of the Duke of Avanoll. The look on *his* face defied description, being neither surprised nor indignant or even remotely condemning; in fact, if there was a glimmering of any emotion to be discerned, the Duke would have to be termed to have looked amused.

"Good evening to you, cousin," the Duke said in his normal tone at last, ending the increasingly tense silence. "I do hope you do not have your heart set on a late supper, for I fear Sir Rollin here is promised to me for the next few minutes and is unable to play the proper host," he drawled in patently unmeant apology.

"Oh, Tansy," Emily broke in, her voice fast rising to hysterical shrillness. "You must make them stop. Rollin has admitted he meant to ruin me, not marry me—the beast!—and Ashley will not rest until he has killed him. How was I to know Rollin was a liar, Tansy? He was so sweet and in all things considerate until tonight when he—he told me he was amusing himself with me!" she admitted, her china-blue eyes awash with a fresh batch of enormous tears.

Tansy turned to her young cousin, her face showing nary a trace of sympathy, and sniffed in a most unladylike way, "What were you expecting, you bacon-brained nitwit—a romantic flight to Gretna and marriage over the anvil, followed by a leisurely honeymoon touring the Lake District? Emily, you are the most appalling idiot imaginable, and if you get out of this scrape with your skin intact you would be wise to stick to me like a barnacle until such time as you acquire a little sense."

Tansy shook her head bemusedly. "Girl, never before in my checkered existence have I come across anyone so capable of giving me such a bellyache, and believe me, you had to go some to reach the top of a long list of morons, dolts, ninnies, and downright jackasses to do it. But outstrip them all you did, and by a long chalk!"

This outburst was gaped at by Sir Rollin, and softly applauded by Avanoll, while Emily went off into a depressingly predictable temper tantrum and Tansy expected at any moment the girl would fling herself prone upon the floor and drum her heels like the spoiled brat who was her charge in Sussex—and whom she was constrained to punish for tucking up three goldfish in her crayon box, saying she could use their bright color on her next drawing.

A pretty picture, an impetuous elopement, the reasons may have varied but the spur behind the acts were alike: both girls had been spoiled beyond all thought for any but their own desires. For a moment Tansy's palm itched to make stinging contact with Emily's round bottom, the urge so strong she nearly forgot she was still a long way from solving the most pressing problem of how to get Emily and the Duke home and the whole affair buried beyond any hope of discovery by Society.

So, as Emily's fit of weeping reduced her to a quaking bundle of blue, velvet-trimmed pelisse reposing conveniently out of harm's way in the far corner of the room, Tansy directed her energies to making a swift end to the affair. The most dangerous situation now was the very visible intent of the two men again glaring balefully at each other from across the room.

First, the rug had been rolled back and all the furniture pushed to one side. Secondly, both men had shed their coats, cravats, and Hessians, and were standing up only in their stocking feet, breeches, and rolled-up shirtsleeves. Each already held equally wicked-looking blades, making their intentions impossible to misconstrue by even the most dull-witted of fellows (like Farnley, who had by now ventured so far as to stick his head round the corner of the arch for a look-see).

"Now isn't this just all too jolly," Tansy observed silkily, as her nimble mind raced madly in search of a convincing argument. "And what do you intend to prove by *this* feat of derring-do, Ashley?" she asked, willing to divert his anger onto herself. "I swear, cousin, for a man who decries impetuosity in others—namely myself—you are a sorry example of deliberate, well-thought-out action. Not only did you attempt rescue on the North Road mounted only on horseback, you now intend to duel down a man with complete disregard for the *Code of Honor* not to mention the resulting notoriety news of such an engagement will bring down upon the shoulders of Emily, who regrettably has earned every bit of censure, and also your grandmother, who doesn't deserve such shabby treatment."

Avanoll and the until now curiously silent Whitstone either didn't hear or refused to heed Tansy's words and, exchanging nods, went on their guards as if they had never been disturbed. They made to touch sword tips in salute before commencing a fight that would end with one or both of them spilling their claret all over the bare boards of the room.

At least that was the most usual ending to a duel between two disagreeing gentlemen, but then normally duels are witnessed by seconds and a benevolent surgeon—not a vaporish young miss and an eccentric, unflappable, over-aged hoyden bent on putting a halt to such dangerous nonsense.

The swords clinked as they met in salute, and the men held their weapons pointed directly upwards. The hilts pressed against their chins in a final theatrical gesture (the moves all dictated by some masculine sense of peculiar etiquette sanctioning cold-bloodedly setting out to dispatch each other by means of pricks, stabs, and slashes inflicted by razor-sharp weapons).

Next on the agenda came the duel itself, but this was destined never to take place, for at that moment two shots rang out loudly in the quiet room, the reports following one upon the other in rapid succession (drowning out Emily's three-octave spanning scream) and the tips of the two rapiers were somehow severed and sent winging into the air, rendering the swords a good half-foot shorter and the two combatants as incapable of movement as the molded figures at a wax museum.

When the Duke recovered his voice, he turned his head stiffly and spoke to the woman holding his silver-inlaid pistols, her head wreathed in a cloud of blue-grey smoke. "You, madam, are beyond a shred of doubt the most incorrigible nuisance this side of Hades," he observed calmly, with the resigned demeanor of a man who has found the Fates against him at every turn. "I can recall your saying you were taught at your father's knee, but you didn't bother to inform me he taught you to shoot as well as speak like a man," he remarked in a slightly aggrieved tone.

"It can only be a kindness if you would present me with a full written accounting of your, er, *talents* in the morning. I do so abhor surprises, you know," he ended, still maintaining a remarkable control over his temper, as well as still clutching the shattered remains of his once-favorite sword. He lowered the blade, then favored his cousin with a mock salute. "I cannot speak for Whitstone here, but I for one know when I am bested."

Tansy gave a slight bow of her own head in humble acknowledgement of Avanoll's concession, hiding as she did so her twinkling brown eyes and self-satisfied smirk. "I accept your surrender, cousin, and believe we should now discuss the terms of peace."

At last Sir Rollin found his voice and added his mite to this bizarre conversation. "You are to be pitied, Avanoll, if these two are any example of your relation. A melodramatic infant and a pistol-toting Antidote! Egad, no wonder you forced a duel on me. You were looking for a quick and relatively painless way of ending it all without having to pull the plug on your life by some means less grisly than hanging yourself with your smoking-jacket sash, or splashing your brains all over the walls with a pistol shot. Much as I have never cared for you, old fellow, I am sorry to have added to your headache," Whitstone ended with uncharacteristic sympathy.

Tansy ignored the degrading description of herself as an Antidote and spoke only to inform his grace that one of his pistols was fading a hair to the left and was he aware of this imperfection? When her cousin refrained from replying, she merely shrugged and handed the spent pistols to Farnley—who eyed them in genuine horror and held them most gingerly at arm's-length, as if they might explode at any time. His horror was not confined to the firearms alone, as it included a newborn respect for Miss Tansy and a profound hope that he never nudged such a deadly shot as she into anger sufficient as to compel her to use his protuberant ears for target practice.

It seemed the melodrama was nearly over for the evening as Avanoll—his usual good judgement at last overcoming his brotherly thirst for vengeance (as well as his inborn masculine pride, which had been badly bruised by Whitstone's arrogant dismissal of his grace's ability to protect his own against such a rake-shame no-good as he). Though still rather put-out over the episode, he suddenly realized himself to be quite honestly fatigued, and curtly summoned his sister to his side in preparation for departing Sir Rollin's abode before Tansy took it upon herself to preach Whitstone a homily on morals. There was still a decidedly militant glint in her eyes. Too, his sister might yet swoon in a dead faint and have to be hauled to his carriage, slung over his shoulder like a sack of meal.

In the midst of ushering his charges out ahead of him, he turned once more to the thwarted despoiler of young womanhood and issued a warning very thinly dressed up as friendly advice. "I would not brute about the events of this evening, Whitstone, or we will both find ourselves become a laughing-stock among the tattlemongers. If you will but promise to keep mum and take yourself out of my sight until at least the end of the Season, I shall deign to consider us quits. If you do not, however," he intoned with an awful smile, "I shall be forced to return and give you the drubbing you deserve."

Whitstone made one last arrogant (and ill-judged) remark, suggesting insolently, "You know, Avanoll, you were just lucky to have arrived in time to save your beloved sister. Another few moments and I'd have had her convinced I merely wished to anticipate our honeymoon by a few hours. If ever I saw a wench bent on a tumble it is she, and," he added with a smirk, "if Boodle's Betting Book doesn't soon sport a wager on the day and time she is found flat on her back with her skirts above her head in some hostess' back garden, I vow it won't be because the lady refuses to yield. She may be *Lady* Emily in name, but in nature she's no better than the little opera-dancer I keep in Kensington. Yes, indeed, your chaste little innocent has all the makings of a first class wh—"

That's all the further Sir Rollin got (and it was only due to the distractions of finding the fainting Emily a chair and holding back a cousin bent on physical violence that the inevitable was for so long delayed) before Avanoll's large fist put an end to the flow of verbal filth by the simple expedient of crashing into the speaker's jaw with all the force—and much of the finesse—of the great Gentleman Jackson himself. Tansy's "Well done, Ashley, give him another!" accompanied by some enthusiastic shadow-punching of her own, went unheeded by the Duke as he stood, fists at the ready, watching Sir Rollin stagger for a moment before launching a retaliation.

His punch was thrown wild and missed, but Avanoll's wicked uppercut connected solidly, propelling his opponent backwards across the floor to bang against the Shearer fire-screen and slide down against it before coming to rest with his legs sprawled on the bare floor. The screen, a rather lovely piece of work, was equipped with a convenient fold-down writing table that the impact of Whitstone's body served to release. The tabletop, while not designed for such abuse, was sturdily made of solid oak, and it descended to land with some force on Whitstone's skull—thump-thumping his Brutus Crop-adorned noggin a total of three punishing times before coming to rest. All but the first bump were not felt, more's the pity, for Sir Rollin was already "fast asleep."

Tansy was elated and made no bones about it. "That was a neat bit of cross and jostle work, Ashley, and that muzzler sure put a crimp in Whitstone's style. If his bone-box isn't broken it's bruised enough to have him on milk gruel for a sen'night or more." She patted her cousin on the back amicably and pretended to pout. "And you said I kept secrets from you, while all along you were a talented amateur of the Fancy—as I could see by your form—and the possessor of as fine a pair of fives as Maddox or The Black or even Belcher, I wager. I cannot begin to tell you how proud I am of you, Ashley," she ended, beaming up at him.

Avanoll covered the hand Tansy had in her excitement put on his arm with one of his "pair of fives" and smiled down at her to observe, "You do have the most charming way of expressing yourself, my dear, although I shudder to think where you gained such first hand knowledge of fisticuffs."

"Papa—" she began, only to have the Duke admonish her by using a bit of cant language himself. "Put a muzzle on it, Tansy," he admonished kindly, and then—overcome by the pleasure of feeling such great affinity with the outrageous female who dared convention to protect her charge (and himself, he had a slight suspicion)—he threw all caution to the winds, hauled her into a tight embrace, and kissed her quite ruthlessly.

A groan from Emily, slowly rousing from her swoon, caused the pair to separate hurriedly, placing several feet of floor space between them before Emily could fully open her eyes and Farnley could re-enter the house to inform his master that his carriage, which had been waiting discreetly around the corner, was out front and awaiting their convenience.

"What about Sir Rollin?" Emily quailed as she was led to the street. "If he speaks, I am forever destroyed." Her brother informed her of his assurance that Whitstone had learned a valuable lesson in discretion and could not be of any further concern to them—unable to restrain himself from adding a few choice words about her part in the mess and warning of further elaboration on her expected conduct in the future on the morrow.

"I have been dreadfully silly, haven't I, Ashley?"

"Let's just say, brat, that if the wits beneath your golden hair were any dimmer you would be not a female, but a dandelion," her brother told her ruthlessly.

"You've been an inconsiderate, impulsive, selfish and none-too-bright little minx who needs a hiding," Tansy added, in a last burst of temper before relenting a bit and allowing Emily to hide her tear-swollen face against her shoulder until the carriage arrived in Grosvenor Square.

Dunstan swung the door open before they had mounted the portico, while upstairs a curtain moved as Aunt Lucinda peered out into the Square. "'Throw fear to the wind.' Aristophanes," she heralded, just as footsteps were heard on the stairs.

A few seconds later the returning adventurers straggled wearily into Avanoll's salon, to be greeted by the sight of their aunt swaying slightly on her feet in the middle of the room and holding a nearly depleted brandy snifter in her raised hand. "'Veni, vide, vici.' Plutarch," she slurred in salute.

Tansy, seeing Emily's bewildered expression, translated "It is Latin for, 'I came, I saw, I conquered.'"

"Oh," Emily whispered vaguely.

"Precisely," Avanoll replied, frowning, his eyes scanning his cherished domain to see the furniture awash with bits of feminine draperies, one empty brandy decanter on the silver tray with another already at half mast, a wet, spreading stain and an overturned snifter on the rug beside his favorite chair, and a fine porcelain bowl (that had lately resided on a side table) now somehow come into the possession of that usurping mongrel—who was avidly lapping at its contents, which looked suspiciously like yet more of his choicest brandy.

"Far be it from me to intrude on your little party, Grandmama," he said, bowing toward the elderly woman who at that moment was trying to present a posture of dignity in a chair so cavernous it did not even allow her feet to touch the floor, while attempting to close her gaping dressing robe and straighten her tilted nightcap—all with little or no success. "But it may interest you to know that all is well, and that no scandal should arise from this night's adventures."

The dowager opened her mouth to make some congratulatory remark, found her tongue to be quite dry, and availed herself of a sip of brandy. It was a rather large sip that burned her throat and set off a fit of coughing.

"'To blow and swallow at the same time is not easy.' Plautus," Aunt Lucinda advised, wagging her finger at the sputtering woman.

Tansy whispered to Avanoll, "It would appear our elders chose to blunt the edge of their concern with a bit of your private stock, cousin."

"That, cousin, is an understatement," he returned.

Emily picked that moment to scamper across the room and drop to her knees beside her grandmother. "Forgive me, Grandmama, please do, for I am prodigiously sorry!" she cajoled in her most theatrical accents.

Aunt Lucinda, using obvious concentration to wend a reasonably straight line to her niece's side, poked Emily sharply in the middle of her back and warned, "'You have put your head inside a wolf's mouth and taken it out again in safety. That ought to be reward enough for you.' Aesop."

"Oh, Lucinda, my dear, that was so intelligent of you. I could not have said it better myself," the dowager complimented the woman.

"The Duchess actually commending your aunt for one of her quotes? Oh, Ashley, I fear you are right: the pair of them are absolutely bosky!" Tansy giggled.

The dowager heard this and protested. "Slightly up in the world, perhaps, maybe even a trifle disguised, but never bosky, Tansy. Gentlewomen cannot be bosky."

"'I call a fig a fig, a spade a spade.' Menander," Aunt Lucinda said, admitting at least her castaway condition before tottering to a chair and dropping into it heavily (with no sign of caring that she now lay sprawled like a rag doll dropped by a careless child), and recited sing-song, "'O to be a frog, my lads, and live aloof from care.' Theocritus."

The dowager roused herself to ask fuzzily, "Theocritus? Is that the Greek fellow who used to stuff his mouth with stones and try to outshout the ocean waves?"

She was destined not to be answered, due to Horatio's deduction that it was time all good puppies were abed, and all eyes—at least all the ones not yet seeing double—watched in astonishment as the animal traced a meandering course in the general direction of the hall, his four appendages somehow suddenly supplied with an overabundance of joints so that his legs bent and bowed most alarmingly and refused to move in any semblance of simple coordination.

Within mere yards of his goal, these uncooperative limbs collapsed entirely and Horatio rolled onto his side, flung his head upon the carpet, closed his glassy eyes (but was unable to retract his lolling tongue or shut his slack jaw), and, after his tail had given a final spasmodic jerk, commenced sleeping off a prime snootful of brandy.

"He'll have a rare bruiser of a hangover in the morning," the Duke observed dispassionately, ignoring Tansy and Emily and their *oohs* and *aahs* of compassion. As the dowager emitted a sad moan he added imperturbably, "And so, too, my so-proper grandparent and genteel aunt."

"They were better off indulging in a little relaxing brandy than pacing the floor in a turmoil all the while we were gone," Tansy pointed out. By now the two thoroughly relaxed ladies were endeavoring to rouse themselves sufficiently to retire to their own chambers, and Emily was already long gone— deciding the less she was seen the less reminders of her indiscretion would strike her relatives, resulting in more tiresome lectures. (Now that she was home safe and dry, Emily's recollections of any fear for her virtue or her narrow escape from a "fate worse than death" were rapidly being reduced to a mild scrape soon righted and, once in her bed, sleep came quickly and untroubled by nasty dreams.)

Avanoll believed it pointless to attempt rousing the drunkenly snoring Horatio, and merely stepped over him to call Farnley to help in putting the ladies to bed.

Aunt Lucinda had partially submerged herself in a hazy fog of contentment and was loath to be disturbed. "'Shut, shut the door, good John! fatigued, I said: Tie up the knocker! say I'm sick, I'm dead.' Pope," she implored Farnley, as he poked tentatively at her shoulder.

"The name is Farnley, ma'am," he corrected, with little hope of being understood before leading the woman to the stairway. Halfway up the flight Aunt Lucinda turned to utter her exit line with a sweep of her arm. "'So ends the bloody business of the day.' Homer," she decreed, hiccupped, and disappeared from sight.

Avanoll and Tansy personally escorted the dowager to her chamber, assuring her that Emily's honor was indeed still intact, and promising a full report in the morning—with which she had to be satisfied since her dratted eyelids refused to remain open any longer.

The Duke walked with his cousin along the hall to Tansy's door where they stopped, faced each other for a long moment, and then dissolved into paroxysms of hilarity that left them wiping their eyes and clutching their sides. "You know, of course, that only persons of a very odd sense of humor could find anything amusing in the debacle we just survived," Avanoll imparted with a grin—if a Duke can be described so frivolously—that bordered on the impish.

Tansy could only smile and nod, so complete was their accord that she wished to do nothing to shatter the mood. Avanoll stood looking benignly at his cousin a moment longer before— just as if he, too, felt their rapport, and was disconcerted by it— his expression became shuttered and he abruptly moved off toward his own chamber.

"And a good-night to you too, your grace," Tansy murmured beneath her breath, opened her door, and hugging her arms about herself (the better to retain the lovely warm glow that still radiated through her body), she drifted across her room to the window. She stood there gazing out at the stars, weaving fantasies that had little to do with the probable future of one very ordinary, very vulnerable, Miss Tansy Tamerlane.

Chapter Seventeen

THE NEXT MORNING Tansy found herself alone at the breakfast table, the Duke having left the house at an unfashionably early hour without breaking his fast, and the rest of the ladies either hiding (Lady Emily) or recuperating (the dowager and Aunt Lucinda) in their chambers. It wasn't until she returned from a fruitless expedition to Bond Street, in an attempt to secure ribbon to match a gown of a particularly odd shade of yellow, with a red-eyed and still-sniffling Pansy in tow, that voices coming from the first floor sitting room (which the dowager had commandeered as her own) alerted Tansy that at least two of the ladies were up and about. She quickly shed her bonnet and pelisse, shushed the curious maid, and tiptoed to the slightly-ajar door to shamelessly eavesdrop on a conversation she had an idea would prove most entertaining. She was not disappointed.

The first words Tansy heard were from Aunt Lucinda, who groaned piteously, "'I pray thee let me and my fellow have a haire of the dog that bit us last night.' Heywood."

"Stuff and nonsense, Lucinda, you bird-witted creature," the dowager's voice returned, a bit feebly. "Such a cure is only for seasoned drinkers, which by our joint performance last night is a title we cannot and certainly *should* not covet. Farnley is bringing us some camphorated spirits of lavender that he swore on his hopes of Heaven will ease our discomfort, for I must own to feeling as miserable as you do physically. Which is not to mention suffering from emotional agonies of remorse and humiliation that have so overset my nerves."

"'It is a consolation to the wretched to have companions in misery.' Syrus," Aunt Lucinda admitted with a sigh.

At this the dowager gave a snort of bitter amusement. "Just do not make the mistake of counting Horatio as one of our company. The only reason I dragged myself from my bed was to render aid and comfort to what I thought was a poor innocent puppy fallen afoul of our debauchery. And what did I find? A hound prostrate on the floor too enfeebled to lift his little head? I did not! The dratted mutt was down in the kitchens gulping down some horrid slop of meat and gravy and looking to be in fine high fettle. I tell you, Lucinda," she confessed crossly, "if I weren't so fond of that scrap of fur I would have choked him on the spot. You would have thought he was weaned on brandy," she trailed off in wonder.

While Tansy hastily stuffed a glove in her mouth to keep from giggling aloud, Aunt Lucinda observed, "'Perhaps some day it will be pleasant to remember these things.' Virgil."

There was a pregnant pause before the dowager could find voice enough to answer this ridiculousness. "Lucinda," she finally returned most cordially, "if I were to be marooned on a desert island for the remainder of my days and must needs choose between your company and that of an organ-grinder's flea-bitten monkey, I should not hesitate a moment before opting for the latter. If I could not be assured of intelligent conversation, at least I would not be subjected to your aping recitations that ceaselessly roam between the boundaries of the Land of Idiots and the Kingdom of Twits. Besides," she added glibly, "if pressed, at least I could eat the monkey."

Tansy stumbled away from the room, her face a flaming red and her eyes streaming with the effort to keep a leash on an inevitable explosion of hilarity that thankfully held off until she was out of earshot.

She was supporting herself against the newel post when Emily descended the stairs cautiously, looking about for any person or persons liable to feel bound to deliver her a lecture on her latest lapse from propriety. Just as her slippered foot reached the landing, Aunt Lucinda erupted from the sitting room like a gale in full force, her draperies clutched convulsively about her pudgy frame and looking to be in a raging temper. As she swept past the two girls she charged in an injured tone, "'I would not have borne this in my flaming youth when Plancus was consul.' Horace."

Emily was bewildered. "Plancus? Not her late husband's name, I don't think. Is this Plancus another relative, do you suppose? I do hope not, for it is such an odd name, to be sure," she concluded, a puzzled frown marring her marble brow as she directed her query to Tansy. Lady Emily was destined not to be answered, however, as Tansy had given up all pretext of ladylike behavior, plopping herself on the bottom stair to rock back and forth, howling with unalloyed glee.

Time has a way of dulling the edges of anger and fading unpleasant memories, as was the case with this latest upheaval to hit Avanoll House. Two weeks went by and the grateful dowager's gift to Tansy for her help in protecting her grandchildren from scandal arrived on a splendidly fine day, to the delight of everyone—except, perhaps, the Duke, who manfully withheld the majority of his objections.

"I do not wish to question your judgement, and I certainly am not dull-witted enough to doubt your skill with the ribbons, but if my Grandmama wished to present you with your own transportation for the Promenade I am convinced a conventional ladies equipage would have been more, er, fitting," he did say, this slight censure having been impossible to suppress.

His cousin, who had been staring at her high-perch phaeton and superb pair of Welsh-bred bays and had only been listening to her cousin's attempt at tactful criticism with half an ear, replied to this homily vaguely and then repeated her thanks to Avanoll for his kind gesture of personally selecting her horses for her at Tattersall's.

This diverted the Duke into reiterating the features of the horses. "They are a prime bang-up pair of blood and bone at that," he preened, "with grand hocks and their forelegs well before them. Your choice of tan and black for the phaeton makes for a natty turnout to astound the populace privileged to see it this afternoon in the Park. But I still say a perch phaeton is too dangerous for a—"

He was cut off by Aunt Lucinda's cheerful cry of, "'Steep thyself in a bowl of summertime.' Virgil," as she stepped onto the flagway and with twinkling eyes implored the Duke to hand her up into the phaeton.

Tansy hastily preceded her, unaided, and as the older lady *ooh-ed* and rolled her eyes in fright at the great elevation of her seat, Emily scrambled up to make a completed, if somewhat overcrowded, party.

"You are too many for this vehicle," Avanoll pointed out. "Why crowd yourselves like that when you can take the carriage?"

"'An agreeable companion on a journey is as good as a carriage.' Syrus," his aunt told him with a childlike grin. Ever since her disastrous descent into drunkenness, Aunt Lucinda had taken on a devil-may-care air that confounded and astonished her family, who were at a loss to explain this change in personality. When questioned, she merely smiled and cooed, "'When the sunne shineth, make hay.' Heywood."

And so the Duke had to console himself with the knowledge that his own groom was standing up behind the ladies on the perch provided for a tiger, and could only warn, "Leo, take care of the ladies," in a tone that hinted of dire consequences should one hair of their heads be put out of place. Avanoll had decided Tansy would consider it an insult to her ability if he were to shadow her around the park, so he moved off down the flagway to meet some friends at Brook's. As he turned for one last peep, Tansy snaked out her whip, handily caught up the thong, and moved out into traffic with admirable finesse.

The Park being quite well attended on this pleasant day, Tansy and her party were much looked at and commented upon, while she was hard pressed to move more than a few feet without someone hailing them to talk.

Emily was almost purring, such was her delight in her popularity, when she spied a lone horseman fast approaching them. "Oh, Lud," Emily hissed none too softly, "It's that gawky infant, Digby Eagleton. Can't you get past him, Tansy? He'll embarrass me by staring at me like a love-sick puppy, his tongue clove to the roof of his mouth, and behaving for all the world like a turnip-headed bumpkin," she complained nastily. "If he were the least bit presentable I would be flattered, but there is no consequence in being the object of adoration if the adorer is a piddling nobody like Digby."

Aunt Lucinda, glimpsing from underneath her drooping bonnet the crestfallen expression on Mr. Eagleton's face and knowing he had heard at least a part of Emily's nasty tirade, rounded on her and said, "'I only wish I may see your head stroked down with a slipper.' Terence."

Tansy only had time to warn from between clenched teeth, "I am heartily sick of your behavior, missy," before pinning a bright smile on her face and endeavoring to put Mr. Eagleton at his ease with some inane reference to the fine weather. She succeeded to some small extent, but Emily—wretched child that she was—refused to do more than bestow a frigid nod in her erstwhile swain's general direction before waving excitedly to a gloriously uniformed Hussar who raced at once to her side.

"Isn't Lady Emily in high good looks today, Miss Tamerlane?" Mr. Eagleton asked in a choked voice before lapsing into a muddled clarification of his statement, hoping it not to be thought that estimable young lady was not *always* to appear as a diamond of the first water.

Aunt Lucinda sniffed. "'She looked as if butter would not melt in her mouth.' Heywood," she offered facetiously.

Tansy was at last able to grasp a moment—when Emily was deep in conversation with the small multitude of bucks, dandies, and military gentlemen now surrounding the phaeton—to crook her finger at Mr. Eagleton and draw him down to hear her conspiratorial whisper. "If you were to call in Grosvenor Square tomorrow at half past the hour of ten, Lady Emily will be out of the house and we can discuss one or two matters of mutual interest in private."

Mr. Eagleton looked slightly taken aback, but a concurring nod from Aunt Lucinda convinced him he could be no worse off than he now was and had nothing to lose by listening to whatever Miss Tamerlane had to say.

The next morning, just after Emily left for a day-long picnic outside London, Mr. Eagleton was ushered into the second withdrawing room and settled into a comfortable chair facing the two ladies who had desired his attendance.

In the silence that fell while Tansy poured tea and Aunt Lucinda meticulously arranged her ruffled skirts, Digby ran a trembling index finger around the inside of his neckcloth and cleared his dry throat half-a-dozen times. When Tansy held out a brimming teacup, he clutched at it gratefully and took a huge gulp of the liquid without regarding its temperature before sputtering as the tea scalded his tongue. A sprinkling of tea-colored spots quickly appeared on his disheveled neckcloth, prompting Tansy to exclaim, "Mr. Eagleton, it would simplify matters if I could address you as Digby. You may call me Tansy. *Whatever* are we going to do with you?"

"I—I beg your pardon, ma'am, er, I mean Tansy?" Digby questioned while scrubbing at his stains with the napkin Aunt Lucinda had helpfully supplied.

Tansy took a deep breath and, as was her nature, baldly laid her cards on the table. "I am assured that you genuinely care for my loose-screw cousin Emily, though I cannot for the life of me see why, and as the dowager agrees that you are a very well set-up young man, we—Aunt Lucinda and I—have decided to help you to press your suit if we can."

Digby first blushed, then grinned, and at last stammered his thanks. "But I fear it is a hopeless cause, dear ladies, as Lady

Emily is completely out of charity with me, not that I can blame her. I am nothing out of the ordinary way and do not command either her respect or admiration, but inspire in her only cold indifference and at times, her rather heated condemnation." Delivering himself of this self-deprecating speech, Digby lapsed into silence.

Tansy would not be satisfied that Digby was as nondescript as he painted himself, and proceeded in the next minutes to turn him inside out like a sack with questions about his home, family, upbringing, interests, talents, and prospects for the future. These were all found to be quite unexceptional, indeed. The only real stumbling block in his make-up appeared to be his inherent shyness and, as Tansy rather indelicately put it, his "wishy-washiness."

"But, ma'am, I mean Tansy, I was never so—as you say— *wishy-washy* before. It is only in the presence of exalted persons such as I have met since coming to Town, and when within sight and sound of dear Lady Emily, that my wits seem to desert me," Digby said as he tried to justify himself. "Then all at once my brains seem entirely to let and my foolish mouth spouts only the most mundane, silly, and mawkish platitudes, until I make a complete cake of myself."

Aunt Lucinda deposited her teacup on its saucer with a slight rattle. "'There is no greater bane to friendship than adulation, fawning, and flattery.' Cicero."

Digby was momentarily diverted by this pronouncement. "Does she always speak in that way?" he asked Tansy innocently. "It sounds real educated-like, if a bit hard to follow sometimes."

Tansy, her eyes twinkling, informed him that, yes, famous— and not so famous—quotes were Aunt Lucinda's solitary method of communication.

"Well, to each his own, I say," Digby allowed generously. "We had a great uncle who nurtured a wish to trod the stage, and he always ran on and on like Kean or somebody performing in Drury Lane, talking from somewhere deep in his stomach and shaking the chandeliers with his boomings. I remember he rumbled off words like *rath*er and *real*ly like they was shot from a cannon." He paused a moment and then could not resist asking, "Ain't never opened her mouth just to talk, huh? I mean, to say 'good morning' or 'shut up' or 'I'm hungry'?"

Tansy shook her head. "*Perish the thought!*" she intoned with mock effrontery.

The young gentleman was amazed. "I say!" he said, casting a look of great awe at Aunt Lucinda. "If that don't beat the Dutch, and m'uncle, for that matter."

Oh, my, thought Tansy, this boy is still so painfully young. No wonder Emily cannot see him for dust. "Digby," she queried cautiously, prizing his attention from the preening Aunt Lucinda, "are you at all at home in Society, or do you think you still need some town bronzing before Emily finds you up to snuff?"

Digby thought for a minute, chewing on his bottom lip to aid his concentration, then supplied, "Can't say as I am that comfortable in town as yet, except with my own fellows. Once away from them it seems I'm forever landing in the basket because I am still rather green. Just last week," he went on in explanation, "my Club, a dandy place, was closed down for repairs. One of our parties had got a bit out of hand, and what with the broken windows in the dining room and the smoke and dirt from the fire one of the fellows decided to light in the middle of the card room floor—he had complained of a chill, you see— the rooms had to be vacated for a space. Anyway, as I understand is the custom, we were invited to use the facilities at another Club farther along on St. James's. Now you must understand, ladies, at my Club it is all very informal. If someone wishes to gain another's attention he has only to aim a bit of roll or something at his head."

He paused a moment to allow Tansy to chuckle a bit, then went on with his story. "Well let me tell you, this other establishment was as far from my Club as chalk from cheese. None of the members could have been less than three score and ten, and a duller set of dogs you'll never find. One old boy propped up in a wing chair near the fire appeared dead, but I didn't venture close enough to find out. Instead I sat in a rather uncomfortable chair near the door—or at least I did until a member of the Club advised me that it was reserved for another member and I was trespassing, so to speak. As nicely as I could I told the man I would be more than pleased to remove myself when the man in question wished to seat himself. That's when, stiff and seemingly highly insulted, the member told me that the reserved chair was for a member who had been dead and put to bed with a shovel some five years past. Well, I sprung up quickly then, you can be sure, and bolted from the Club as fast as might be, promising myself to never go there again, no matter what the inducement."

"Now that was a highly amusing tale, Digby," Tansy informed him. "If you could but relate the thing half so amusingly to Emily, she would be forced to realize you have the makings of a tolerable wit. As for feeling uncomfortable with the elder, more staid of our Society, you are not alone in your feelings. No, I would say our main concern is to somehow show yourself to a better advantage where Emily is concerned. The question remains, though, as to how."

Silence reigned for a while, and then Aunt Lucinda's voice started out low, only to gain volume and confidence as it went on. "'I know the disposition of women: when you will, they won't, when you won't, they set their hearts upon you of their own inclination.' Terence."

"Aunt!" Tansy said, a look of astonishment and dawning knowledge on her face. "Are you suggesting we deliberately set out to trick Emily into seeing Digby in a different light?"

With a grin that could only be termed malicious, Aunt Lucinda replied almost defiantly, "'I know, indeed, the evil of that I purpose; but my inclination gets the better of my judgement.' Euripides."

Digby was totally at sea and admitted it, so Tansy explained patiently, "What my aunt has so cleverly suggested is that you drop your pursuit of Emily, turning to her a cold shoulder even, and instead pursue some other female. If Emily harbors any feelings for you at all, she will become mightily chagrined and discover where her heart truly stands in the matter."

"Isn't that a bit underhanded?" the upright young gentleman asked in a quavering voice.

"'Crime is honest for a good cause.' Syrus," Aunt Lucinda shot back incontrovertibly.

Tansy pooh-poohed any further objections and turned to her aunt. "That leaves us with but one problem," she pointed out.

Her aunt nodded sagely. "'Who is to bell the cat? It is easy to propose impossible remedies.' Aesop!"

"Huh?" Digby mumbled.

"Yes, most assuredly, aunt," Tansy agreed. "Who? Who can we enlist to play the recipient of swain Digby's romantic overtures?"

At last the light dawned on Digby and he understood the ladies' scheme. "Oh, I really don't believe such a plan possible . . ." he began timidly, only to be cut off by Aunt Lucinda's sharp, "'Though a man be wise it is no shame for him to live and learn.' Sophocles."

"I agree with my aunt, Digby. After all, we have nothing to lose by such an experiment, do we? And I, I have decided, am the best person to be the new object of your affections. Living in the same house, cheek-by-jowl so to speak with Emily, has its advantages—added to the elimination of the sad complication of any young miss chosen at random being heartbroken when you withdraw your attentions."

After a few more feeble protests from Digby, the matter was considered settled. Tansy's new suitor was given a detailed list of the duties required of him, and sent off in a slightly bewildered state to ponder the bizarre direction his life had taken.

Aunt Lucinda retired to her rooms, highly satisfied with the morning's events. After all, she had suffered much from Emily's selfishness in the past and could be excused if she was hoping to get back a little of her own.

If Tansy had any second thoughts or misgivings about her role of love interest to an immature, naive swain, she kept them to herself. And if there were apt to be any undesirable repercussions, these too she chose to disregard as risks necessary to the success of the plan. After all, she had already decided to let the dowager in on the scheme, and Emily—the object of the whole charade—could only benefit from a bit of comeuppance.

But Tansy neglected to consider the possible incorrect conclusions that could be arrived at by another member of the household, the usually astute Duke, and the fine muddle these conclusions could create.

Chapter Eighteen

IT ALL BEGAN simply enough. Tansy and Aunt Lucinda let the dowager in on their little plan, gaining her full approval and not a few eminently helpful suggestions aimed at teaching "that tiresome chit" a well-deserved lesson.

Digby stopped by in the mornings to escort Tansy on her errands around town. More often than not he was then invited to luncheon at Avanoll House, and most afternoons either rode with Tansy in the Park or could be seen up beside her in the high-perch phaeton, a seat of honor envied by more than a few. In the evenings it was invariably Digby Eagleton who squired the Avanoll ladies to the amusement of their choice.

By the end of the first week, Digby's near-constant presence in Grosvenor Square was beginning to grate mightily on Lady Emily's nerves. Not only was the nodcock always underfoot like a scrap of tarred paper stuck to her dainty slipper, but he had consistently made the object of his presence in the house more than sufficiently clear. At first she had assumed—quite naturally, considering Digby's past track record of faithful adoration—that *she* was the target of his concerted assault. But slowly it dawned on her that Tansy, her long-in-the-tooth and penniless cousin, was the bait around which Digby was dangling.

A reasonable person would have been thankful her unwanted suitor had taken the hint and cried off, but Emily was never known for her reasonableness. Instead, she reacted in typical Emily fashion.

At first she treated the entire situation as one huge joke. "How too, too embarrassing for you, dear cousin, to have that die-away Digby Eagleton always about, haunting the house and harassing you with his love-sick stares," she commiserated companionably. "It really is too bad of him, but then I did warn you he was a bit of a leech. You are kind to have become a martyr in my cause, diverting his schoolboy romantic attentions upon yourself, but I am so sorry he is so thick he does not take the hint and just go away."

"My dear child," Tansy replied, with—she hoped—an incredulous intake of breath, "whatever can you mean? Dear Digby only visits with my permission. I find him of all things agreeable and a pleasant, intelligent, and quite amusing companion."

This answer, so contrary to what she had expected, took Emily aback a moment, but she rallied by offering with a touch of hauteur. "To each his own, I imagine. Very well, cousin, I offered him to you once before and fair's fair. You may have him."

Tansy looked at Emily very levelly and answered with maddening calm, "Why, thank you, *cousin,* but I was not aware he was yours to give." With her smile frozen on her slightly white face, Emily stood like a vision chiseled in marble while Tansy swept past her and went off to inform her co-conspirators of the first bit of reaction to come from their "Digby Plan."

"'Pride, when puffed up, vainly, with many things unseasonable unfitting; mounts the wall, only to hurry to that fatal fall.' Sophocles," Aunt Lucinda quoted passionately.

"We have set the pigeon amongst the hawks for sure," the dowager laughed in high good humor. "If there's anything bound to nudge Emily into making a direct set at poor Digby, it is the idea that *he* and not *she* put an end to their little romance—one sided though it may have been."

That same night Digby was to escort the ladies to a ball at Lady Sefton's, and upon his arrival at Avanoll House he presented Tansy with a small bouquet of flowers in a gold filigree *bouquetière* and only vaguely inquired as to Lady Emily's health before turning his attention back to Tansy, thereby rudely cutting off Emily's flustered reply in mid-sentence.

The following afternoon Tansy and Digby were closeted in the small salon (with Aunt Lucinda's softly snoring form ensconced in a far-away cushioned chair in order to observe the conventions), enjoying a lively discussion of Mrs. Godwin's pamphlet, "Vindication of the Rights of Women," that lasted through tea-time. Tansy was much relieved to find that Digby had a good mind and was more than just a pretty face.

Emily, however, was noticeably annoyed by this further

impolite snubbing of her company; and the Duke, painfully aware of Digby's constant presence under his roof and more than a little agitated at the conclusions he had drawn from it, was more than half willing to join forces with his sister that evening when the subject of a certain young man's irritating invasion of their home was broached by her at the dinner table.

"Last night at Lady Sefton's I was asked, quite maliciously I assure you, if I was aware of a Situation between my chaperon and Digby Eagleton," Emily began baldly. "It quite set my teeth on edge, let me tell you, and when it was suggested Tansy had taken the *inner track* on a fine young man with nice expectations and how did *I feel* now that my cousin had stolen Digby from me, I knew for certain that this ridiculous circumstance could not be allowed to continue without my becoming a common laughingstock—not that my affections were ever engaged in the first place. It is simply the principle of the thing, you know," she ended lamely.

"I never thought I should see the day when I was forced to agree with m'sister, but I agree this Digby fellow constantly haunting the house has set some tongues to wagging in my ear also. And I don't much care for the remarks I am forced to endure."

The dowager tried lamely to pooh-pooh the gossip as the vulgar tattling of a bunch of mischief-making old tabbies, and too piddling to acknowledge, but her grandson was having none of it. He informed her that he had no stomach to face the gossips and their mindless conjectures on the goings-on in Grosvenor Square. One acquaintance even had the audacity to ask, he told his assembled family (and Dunstan, so that it might be safely said the entire household knew the whole of it within the hour), whether Emily and Tansy had thrown dice with the winner getting all rights to Digby. Again, he warned, he refused to be so unjustly beleaguered by such nonsense.

Aunt Lucinda took advantage of a slight pause in the conversation caused by Dunstan's faultlessly executed removal of the soup dishes to declare, "'Guilty consciences always make people cowards.' Pilpay," a pronouncement that nearly caused Emily's half-eaten *consommé* to be dumped down her exposed back by the astonished butler. Imagine the affrontery, all but calling the Duke a white-feather to his face!

Tansy stepped bravely into the breach before the vilified Duke could mouth a crushing set-down and disclaimed, "But this is all such a big to-do about nothing. Digby," and she winced a bit at Avanoll's piercing look when she spoke of the young Mr. Eagleton so familiarly, "is merely a very good friend. I find his company much to my liking, as I think he finds mine, but to say we are harboring some grand passion is ludicrous."

The dowager, after giving Aunt Lucinda a meaningful look, suggested, "Perhaps young Digby is nursing a—as you said, my dear— *grand passion* for you, just as, if memory serves, he once believed himself in love with my silly granddaughter here. Emily's protests earlier lead me to believe she is not wholly overjoyed by his defection, and perhaps your friendship with the young man should be discouraged so that two innocent people," here she bestowed a rare indulgent smile on her granddaughter, "should not be harmed."

Aunt Lucinda picked up her cue admirably and scolded Tansy by waving a fork—with which she had just speared a small boiled potato—at her and cited, "'Never thrust your own sickle into another's corn.' Syrus."

Things were not going along quite the way Emily had predicted. She did not want Digby back because Tansy had retired from the field, she wanted him to come begging forgiveness for his treasonable change of loyalty after he had dropped her usurping cousin flat. "I never said I wanted Digby back!" she cried hotly. "I just think it is wrong for Tansy to have him."

Her brother's snort told her she had just lost her lone ally with her impetuous outburst, but it was left to her aunt to put the resulting censure into words. "'Would you both eat your cake and have your cake?' Heywood."

"Cake?" Emily babbled desperately. "Who is speaking of cake? I declare, I feel as if this entire room has been somehow lifted up and transported to Bedlam. First Digby, then cakes, and both subjects too sickeningly sweet to contemplate. I wish the entire subject *dropped,* if you please."

"Oh, no, you don't, young lady," the dowager demanded in a rallying tone. "You are nothing but a dog in the manger, young lady. You do not want Digby for yourself, but you cannot stomach anyone else having him. Now it becomes clear. You wish to remove Tansy from the field, call Digby to heel like an obedient puppy, and then turn the tables and dismiss him as he has dismissed you. Well, perhaps your tame pet has slipped his lead and will acknowledge your summons only by showing you a clean pair of heels as he scampers off in the opposite direction."

"But I don't *want* him!" Emily shrieked. "Digby Eagleton's attentions are the last thing I want!"

"'Hence these tears.' Terence," Aunt Lucinda purred, rather maliciously.

"Oh!" Emily gasped. And again, " *Oh!*" before she jumped up from the table and, whirling about blindly, sent a large silver tray loaded with stuffed pigeon breasts Dunstan was just then carrying into the room crashing to the floor, where the pigeons exploded in an avalanche of rice and vegetables and the tray and silver plates spun round and round like tops—slowly clang-clanging to a stop long after Emily had made good her escape.

In the tense silence that seemed so ear-splittingly loud after the cymbal-like crashing of the plates, Avanoll carefully wiped his lips, refolded his napkin with meticulous care, reinserted it in his napkin ring, rose carefully, and bowed to the ladies.

"I will take my leave of you ladies now, secure in the knowledge that you have each contrived to accomplish whatever obscure objectives you set out to achieve this evening. No, no," he said, and held up his hands to ward off their denials, "do not try to cozen me with proclamations of innocence. Something smoky is going on here, and I believe it necessary to my grip on sanity to remain in blissful ignorance of it all." With a final bow he quit the room and the house, hoping against hope the atmosphere would be calmer upon his return.

The dowager, after calmly instructing Dunstan to have the footman dispose of the pigeon carcasses and bring on the next course (minus two servings), observed that if it had been anyone other than her confirmed bachelor grandson, she would swear he was overreacting to Digby's attentions to Tansy because of simple human jealousy. "Perhaps there is a second, more personal benefit to be derived from our project, Tansy, my sweet?" she teased.

The following morning found Digby once more in attendance, regaling Tansy and the old ladies with a tale about the suicide of one Mr. Boothby, who had left behind a note saying he could "no longer endure the *ennui* of buttoning and unbuttoning."

"Keeping up appearances in town can be very trying on any gentleman of taste, I suppose," the dowager chuckled. "I have heard tales of you dandies, tulips, and corinthians dressing and undressing from the skin out up to five times a day and taking hours achieving just the proper crease to a neckcloth. A criminal waste of time if you ask me, and I do not blame your Mr. Boothby a bit for sticking his spoon in the wall."

"Well, no," Digby hurried to correct the dowager, "I believe he blew his brains out, actually," a statement that sent Tansy into peals of laughter.

Emily chose that moment to enter the room and stood a moment just inside the door, assuming a pose that combined innocence and allure most effectively (just as she had practiced it in front of her mirror all the morning long), before advancing daintily upon Digby and holding out one soft, white hand to be kissed. "Lawks, Digby, it is above all things delightful to see you again today. You have become such a fixture in our household that if you were to absent yourself for above a day I should surely pine horribly and go into a decline. I should miss your companionship that sorely."

Tansy ground the pointed heel of her slipper warningly into Digby's instep and manfully he refrained from falling to the floor to hug Emily tightly about the knees and swear his undying love. Merely did he clasp Emily's hand in a friendly handshake and, though becoming quite white about the eyes and lips, he carelessly thanked Lady Emily for her condescension before dropping his hand from hers almost abruptly and directing his attention once more to the woman seated beside him on the love seat.

Emily's rosy-red bottom lip trembled poignantly but she marshalled her pride sufficiently to remove herself to a nearby chair just as Avanoll strolled into the room with studied nonchalance and took up a position propping up the mantel-piece.

After a moment Digby searched in his coat pocket and brought out a fragile, hand-painted fan that he offered to Tansy to replace the one which had unfortunately come to grief recently in a carelessly-closed coach door. Neither Tansy nor Digby mentioned whose masculine hand had sent that door crashing down on the fan Tansy had treasured ever since the Duke had so off-handedly bestowed it upon her quite early in their acquaintance.

While Avanoll was eyeing with distaste the uncalled-for, lengthy hand-holding Digby employed as he begged Tansy to accept his small gift, Emily's control was slipping rapidly until all at once it disappeared completely and she burst into noisy tears and ran from the room with her hand pressed to her mouth. Her brother followed close on her heels, disgusted with the lot of them.

Digby sprang at once to his feet, only to drop back down onto the love seat by means of Tansy's violent tug on his coat-tails and her fiercely whispered, "Don't bungle it all now by crumbling just when things are progressing so nicely. Show some touch of spunk, Digby, or she'll lead you by the nose your whole life long."

The dowager agreed with Tansy. "I am heartily sick of Emily's floods and torrents of tears every time she is thwarted. You can't knuckle under now, dear boy, or you'll be expected to pander to her every whim at the drop of a tear."

"'Do not turn back when you are just at the goal.' Syrus," Aunt Lucinda added encouragingly.

"But, she was reduced to *tears* by our underhanded plotting!" Digby challenged his cohorts. "She will condemn me as the greatest beast in Nature!"

Tansy rolled her expressive brown eyes, as if to say Digby had more in common with Emily than first met the eye—especially when it came to melodramatic exaggerations.

The dowager put an end to the whole affair by declaring repressively that Emily was being foolish beyond permission. If she wished to indulge in one of her hysterical takings she for one saw no reason to deny her the pleasure, and Emily could stay sulking in her room until she grew roots for all her grandmother would lift a finger to gainsay her.

"Just allow yourself to be guided by older and wiser heads and we'll have the entire matter neatly tied up within a fortnight—and Emily content to ride in your hip pocket for life," she promised Digby solemnly.

After Digby had taken his leave, still undecided as to the questionable honor of his part in the deception, and the older ladies had retired to their chambers to rest before their regular Wednesday evening sortie among the other dowagers at Almack's, the Duke sought out Tansy—counting silver in the butler's pantry—and demanded a moment of her time.

The fan Digby had given her was lying on the table beside her, and Avanoll directed a long dispassionate stare at it before boldly asking if it was really necessary for young Digby to be forever fondling her hand. "He'd try to take it home with him if you gave the twit half a chance," he informed her tightly. But Tansy only laughed.

"You're too old for him you know," he returned, undeterred.

"We are much of an age, Ashley," Tansy responded calmly.

"You haven't been his age since you were in your pram," the Duke countered with a sneer.

Tansy accepted this sharp dig with a smile and politely asked if there was anything else her cousin wished to discuss—or did he think he had spread enough good will to consider himself able to push off and find someone else to insult.

The Duke, with one last frigid glance at the offensive fan, stomped from the room, turning at the door to announce almost belligerently that he was off to change for a dinner engagement—an invitation he had invented on the spot and foolishly blurted out a second before he realized his lie had condemned him to Wednesday night's boiled poultry at Crockford's and a thin company too insipid to be borne. Drat Almack's and its depressing impact on Society for one day of every week of the Season.

Chapter Nineteen

ALMACK'S was no excursion into delight for Emily that night either when Digby—acting on orders but with his heart not in his work—barely nodded at her in passing and stood up for three dances with Tansy before retiring to the card room, only to reappear in time to accompany Tansy home. Melancholy and more than a few glasses of burgundy had combined to sink Digby into the glooms, and he sulked in a corner of the coach all the way to Grosvenor Square, alternately sighing and moaning and hiccupping while elsewhere in an equally dark corner of her grandmother's coach, Emily alternately sighed and sniffed and whimpered.

It required no great flight of the imagination to see that things were soon to come to a head when Emily lost control completely the next morning at breakfast and tearfully declared that she had been the greatest fool in creation for not recognizing sooner that Digby was the only man on earth with the power to move her heart.

After Comfort was summoned to lead a weeping Emily away to lie down in her chamber and have her temples patted with *eau de cologne,* the dowager happily declared the Digby Plan a resounding success.

"And I shall soon be free to get on with my life, unhampered by a certain histrionic debutante and her sweet but somewhat wearing on the nerves beloved," Tansy pointed out, smiling bravely into the unknown future, her eyes deliberately directed slightly to the left and above her companions' heads. Thus, although a certain emotion-sparked brilliance in her eyes was apparent to them, their conspiratorial winks at each other went unnoticed by this unsuspecting object of yet another minor intrigue the two ladies were plotting in their fertile minds.

Tansy repaired to the sun-lit morning room to compose a

letter to Digby, telling him that Emily was ripe for the taking but if he were smart he would stay completely away from the house for a full week, disappearing from sight socially as well. Meanwhile Tansy would drop hints that he had been mistaken in his feelings for her, and friendship was their only bond. Perhaps, she would suggest, he was ill, or depressed. By the time he made his triumphant arrival in Grosvenor Square a week hence, Emily would be too overcome to do more than fall on his neck with relief and joy that he was still willing to have her. Remember, Tansy cautioned him, he must not break down, he must remain strong until Emily was completely at his mercy. Then he should demand—repeat, *demand*—she marry him at once and put an end to this foolishness. He must be strong-willed, masterful even, and Emily would melt as surely as a snowflake in June.

Sighing in relief that all would soon be settled, Tansy made an error in judgement and entrusted Pansy with the task of giving the note to a footman for delivery. Pansy promptly turned the note over to Farnley, who beat a hurried path to his grace's chambers and waved the envelope under Avanoll's nose with an I-told-you-so flair that was almost nauseating in its smugness.

To the Duke the envelope showed all the signs of a *billet-doux*. So that was how the land laid, was it? he thought with the single-minded blindness of the emotionally involved. He ordered Farnley to make sure the message was delivered immediately, and just as immediately decided to accept his friends' invitation to visit Newmarket for Race Week, leaving as soon as Farnley could pack bags for them both.

He tracked down Tansy, sitting alone in the now dusk-dimmed conservatory, where she was bravely trying to envision a future devoid of a certain arrogant Duke, but where he supposed she had escaped to weave dreams of her wedded life with that peach-fuzz faced infant Digby.

He crept up behind her stealthily, turned her about by the simple method of propelling her with his hands on her shoulders, and crushed her startled, half-open mouth beneath his own in a long, hard kiss that threatened to loosen her front teeth. After an endless time, with Tansy's body all the while remaining ram-rod stiff beneath his merciless grasp, Avanoll allowed the kiss to soften, his lips moving caressingly along hers until she began to respond. His fingers slackened in their grip as his arms lowered to encircle her back in an embrace she returned with a fervor she was too honest to conceal. But as always,

Tansy was to be suddenly thrust away while just on the brink, she was sure, of some earthshaking discovery.

"There!" Ashley crowed triumphantly as he grinned into Tansy's bemused face. "Compare that with that halfling Digby's idea of grand passion, if you dare."

"Are you saying you are harboring a grand passion for me, your grace?" Tansy asked quietly.

"I'm *saying,* my dear woman, I don't need you scurrying back here a year from now with a snuffling infant clinging to your skirts, disillusioned with a marriage between two people having about as much in common as Beau Brummell and a chimney sweep, and expecting me to take you in. The kiss was merely a reminder of one of the major differences between a mature man and a callow boy."

Tansy began to see the Duke through a haze of angry red. "I see, your grace, and I thank you. I really do. Until now I had believed the major disparities to be those dealing with maturity, experience, and responsible behavior. Now I see my error. The only difference is in the accumulation of the monstrous quantities of insufferable arrogance and illusions of omnipotence a male begins to amass from the moment he is out of short coats. It is depressing to realize that Digby will one day, if your example serves as any guide, equal you in these regrettable acquisitions. Perhaps, if I can be by his side during these next important years, I can help avert this disintegration of decent behavior and modesty so apparent in your grace. In other words," she ended firmly as the Duke's complexion darkened to a dull crimson, "I'd rather be leg-shackled to a well-meaning, honest youth than bracketed to a devious, insufferably overbearing dictator like you."

"That is fortunate, then," the Duke sneered, his pride much affected, "for I wouldn't touch you with a barge pole."

"You didn't seem so adverse a few minutes ago, your grace," Tansy retaliated, heedless of an inner voice that told her she was only making matters worse.

"*That* was a mistake," Avanoll growled, "and one you can rest assured I will not make again."

"On that head at least, dear cousin, I believe we are in agreement. And I must tell you I will consider any further advances by you upon my person that bring you to within a distance less than that of the length of *two* barge poles as provocation sufficient to warrant a retaliation directed at increasing the number of bumps on your high and mighty Benedict nose by at least one," she ended threateningly.

The Duke was suddenly moved to recognize the absurdity of this conversation, and allowed a small smile to curve one side of his aristocratic face. "Am I to consider that as a threat or a challenge, dear cousin?" he queried silkily.

Tansy drew herself up to her full height, refusing to acknowledge Ashley's exasperating talent for making her always to appear, at the least, in the wrong, or at the most, ludicrous, when it was invariably he who instigated their quarrels in the first place. She had no illusions in her realistic mind of sharing anything but the same impersonal roof with the Duke, with that small solace coming to an end with Emily's marriage, and her heart was already more involved than she cared to admit. No, if a final break must come, and she was sure it would, it would be better to begin working toward that break now.

Therefore, the reluctant smile the Duke had been covertly searching for did not appear, and the haunting sight of a pair of deep brown eyes deliberately devoid of any expression and the sound of the bitten out words, "You are to consider it a *promise*, your grace," traveled with him on his trip to Newmarket as surely as if Farnley had tucked them up in the luggage alongside his master's clean shirts and changes of linen.

The only thoughts that surfaced more frequently were the memory of that last, impulsive kiss—and the gnawing fear that something rare and wonderful was inexorably slipping from his grasp, some nebulous stirring of his emotions that he had so far been unable to categorize or relate to any other experience in his lifetime.

After a fine, if simple, dinner of rabbit smothered in onions, he tried to frame a mental listing of words describing his cousin: exasperating, infuriating, obstinate, strong-willed, stubborn (he made an imaginary erasure and substituted the word tenacious for that last adjective), nosy, independent, and unladylike came swiftly into his mind almost without conscious thought. These were followed swiftly by the words sympathetic, generous, loyal, courageous, inventive, intelligent, witty, versatile, and trust-worthy.

But then, after he had cracked his second bottle in the solitude of his room in Newmarket, words like vulnerable, soft, graceful, alluring, sweet-smelling, lovely, and, at long last, *lovable,* wrote themselves at the top of his imaginary list. His glass of fine, aged

167

burgundy became destined to remain in his suddenly stilled, half-raised hand, until he at long last remembered its existence and placed it carefully back on the table—untouched—before rising to cross to the window to stare unseeingly at the darkening countryside.

Superimposed over the scene before him came a clear-as-day picture of a radiant Tansy standing in the stately St. George Church in Hanover Square, her ivory satin gown and floor-length tulle veil combining to make her look almost ethereal. Her hand was resting on the Duke's black-clad forearm, and as they proceeded slowly past the assembled crowd of happy onlookers her face melted into a smile that proclaimed that this was a woman who was both loved and in love.

The Duke felt his heart begin to swell at the "rightness" of this obvious marriage ceremony, but that same heart suddenly plummeted to the tips of his leather encased toes when he realized that he and Tansy had not been walking out of the church as man and wife, but were moving *up* the aisle toward the altar and Tansy's eagerly waiting bridegroom, Digby Eagleton. Young Eagleton's immaculately tailored wedding suit looked a bit odd, as it was spanned by juvenile leading-strings looped about his waist and topped with a lace-trimmed baby bonnet tied under his chin in a small bow.

"Damn!" the Duke shouted into the empty room, and the hideous vision before him exploded into a million jagged pieces and disappeared. "Damn, damn, and blast! The devil a bit if they think I'll play stand-in for father of the bride—or foot the bill for the wedding and all the fripperies either. What a fool I have been. What a stupid, asinine, blind, dumb fool!" he berated himself, pounding his clenched fists against his forehead.

"I love her," he enunciated aloud slowly, as if he had to hear the words before he could truly believe them. He threw his body into a cavernous wing-chair near the small fire, in an attitude of utter despair usually shown only by volatile youths in the throes of their first calf-love.

"I love her," he whispered softly this time, dropping his head onto his chest. "Just when I had resigned myself to a life unlikely to be blessed with love, I am presented with the one woman who holds the key to my heart. And jackass that I am, I do my best to make her hate me. Now, she's besotted with that knock-in-the-cradle Digby Eagleton, and I've lost my only chance at happiness. Grandmama is right: I am a hopeless case."

Slowly, Avanoll's hand reached out and grasped the fireside-warmed glass of burgundy, which he drained to the dregs in one long swallow before dashing one of his landlord's finest crystal goblets to the hearth in an uncommon display of pique.

For the rest of that long night the Duke drank directly from the decanter, and as the sky began to lighten he staggered to his bed with a mind at last dulled to a degree sufficient to allowing him to fall into a fitful, dream-laden sleep. If his Aunt Lucinda had somehow been able to observe her nephew these last few hours, no doubt she would have had an extensive retinue of applicable quotes with which to scold him and point out the errors of his ways. But it was probably a great kindness to the Duke—and a life-saving grace to his aunt—that she had not.

Meanwhile, back in Grosvenor Square, the servants were in a dither trying to manage a group of ladies who all seemed to be outdoing themselves in acting as queer as Dick's hatband.

Lady Emily was prone to indulge in raucous bouts of weeping, interrupted only by high flights of good humor—when she would write copious lists of possible wedding-guests or make dozens of sketches of gowns she would need for her trousseau—before descending once more into the glooms while she vowed her heart was broken in a million pieces and she was the most wretched creature in the world.

Miss Tansy, on the other hand, was being so determinedly cheerful and full of energy that her devoted servants were becoming completely fagged with trying to keep up with her in endless rounds of housecleaning—for all the world as if she was getting the house in order for a new owner.

The old tabbies, as the dowager and Aunt Lucinda were known belowstairs, were carrying on like a pair of confirmed lunatics as they huddled for endless hours, whispering and giggling and generally disrupting the staff with their unorthodox behavior.

The servants could only thank their lucky stars the Duke (who had been growling about the house these weeks past as if his skin didn't fit) and Farnley (who would cast them all in the glooms with predictions of evil spirits and omens of bad luck suitable to each individual eccentric act of the masters) were not in residence.

Dunstan knew more than he was letting on, of course. He walked about nowadays with a slight, secret smile always lurking about his placid face, a smile that broadened to a grin the day he instructed Leo to ride posthaste to Newmarket with a note from the dowager that was to be placed in the Duke's hands personally.

The missal read:

> *My dearest grandson,*
> *You will be as pleased as I to hear that there is soon to be a notice in the Times concerning the imminent nuptials of a loved one close to all of us. Your presence in Grosvenor Square at this time would be appreciated if you could but tear yourself away from the diversions in Newmarket in time to participate in the happy announcement.*
>
>

Yours in affection,
Yr. Grandmother.

Farnley was very put out with the ridiculously short notice he was given to pack up and be ready to leave Newmarket for London. With three good days of racing still to go, and with Farnley's extremely reliable tip about a sure winner in tomorrow's second race cast to the winds, the Duke's party started back to London at breakneck speed. Taking the shortcut that bypassed Cambridge entirely, they stopped only to rest the horses and take some quick refreshment at Bishop, Stortford, before heading out again, with Avanoll and Farnley in the curricle and Leo riding along on horseback.

Farnley's death-grip on the brass bench-rail was by necessity reduced to a one-handed acrobatic maneuver as his right hand was almost constantly engaged in worrying an infuriating itching on the end of his pointed nose.

"I'm that worried, your grace," he shouted to the Duke over the din of the galloping horses. "When a nose itches like mine it can only mean I will be kissed, cursed, vexed, run against a gate post, or I will shake hands with a fool. If you would please to slow down, I should fear less the idea of meeting up with a gate post."

"There's no need to slow the pace, Farnley, you gudgeon. Just shake my hand and your nose will cease its itching at once," Avanoll shouted back.

The curricle, its occupants dust-stained and exhausted, turned into the mews behind Avanoll House just as abruptly as it had left just days earlier. Avanoll wearily dragged himself toward the small salon where Dunstan would soon provide him with a cold supper and a colder bottle, and opened the door slowly, fatigue seeping from every pore. He was met by the sight of his baby sister being thoroughly kissed by one Digby Eagleton.

"*You despicable, two-timing ingrate!*" he bellowed, every muscle coiling in his readiness to pounce. As Emily and Digby turned questioning eyes toward the disheveled figure in the doorway, their arms still around each other in total unselfconsciousness, Avanoll advanced on them with violence his clear intent. Emily stepped protectively in front of Digby and warned her brother to keep his distance as things were not as they seemed.

The Duke lifted her out of his way without breaking stride, and a moment later Digby was nursing a bloody nose from his prone position on the hearth rug. "*You stupid fool!*" Emily accused her brother before dropping to her knees to croon to her fallen hero. Within seconds the room was crowded to bursting with servants, Tansy, the dowager, and her shadow Aunt Lucinda; Digby groaning all the while and Emily screaming invectives at her brother.

At that moment—when Avanoll froze as if poleaxed to stand mute in the midst of the chaos he had created—Farnley's nose, which had been plaguing him near to distraction since Newmarket, miraculously ceased to itch.

Chapter Twenty

"WHAT in the name of all that's wonderful is going on here?" the dowager shouted above the din that showed no signs of abating, especially since Horatio had joined their number, and thinking all the hub-bub to be a great new game, was now capering about the room on his hind legs and howling for all he was worth. "Anyone would think there has just been a murder in the house," she added in a lower voice once order was raggedly restored and the many speakers clamoring to be heard at last "put a mummer on it," as Tansy was harried enough to have demanded in a clear voice.

Aunt Lucinda took advantage of this lull in the storm to totter to a nearby chair and proclaim in the tones of a true tragedy-queen, "'The very hair on my head stands up for dread.' Sophocles."

"And so it should," Emily, Avanoll House's other aspirant to the ranks of such immortal actresses as Sarah Siddons pronounced in awful tones from her position on the floor, the figure of outraged innocence as she cradled Digby's head on her lap. "To think that my own brother, blood of my blood, would stoop to brute animal force and bludgeon my poor innocent darling Digby down without a shred of warning, attacking my dear beloved like a wild thing, with murder in his eyes."

"Oh, twaddle," Tansy cut in just as Emily was catching her breath by striking a tragic pose with the back of one trembling hand pressed to her forehead. "If Ashley had truly wanted Digby's liver and lights the young looby wouldn't be lying in your lap right now with that ridiculously inane grin on his face and milking every drop of enjoyment from his comfortable, if outrageous, position that he can. Oh no, you gullible widgeon. He would be toes cocked up and stone cold by now sure as check if your brother's intentions were any more than to throttle your swain and perhaps," she paused a moment to look at the Duke who was still standing ramrod stiff in the center of the room, hands bundled into fists at his sides, "if I am correct, to right what he feels has been a wrong done, heaven bless us, to yours truly herself. Am I right, Ashley?" she asked directly.

"'We have made you for a time out of marble,' Virgil," Aunt Lucinda said as she scrutinized the Duke from her vantage point.

At last Avanoll found his voice. "I will thank you, Aunt, to refrain from any more of your pithy observations as to my person. I received a note from my grandmother telling of a wedding announcement soon to be made from this household. This young cub," he jerked his head toward the still recumbent Digby, "has been dangling after Tansy these weeks past, the two of them peacocking about in Society together, and I assumed, now I can see quite wrongly, that they had decided at last to make a match of it. So when I came upon Eagleton and m'sister close as two turtledoves in here, I acted as a man enraged at a cad of a perfidy so evil as to allow himself to become engaged to one member of my family while maintaining a clandestine romance with another. It is as simple as that," he ended in a valiant try at bravado that fooled nobody. The Duke was in disgrace and everyone in the room, which even with most of the servants now gone, was a considerable number, knew it.

Aunt Lucinda fidgeted in her chair and then could resist no longer. "'Look ere you leape,' Heywood," she muttered in a loud stage whisper that was heard by all.

"It is all my fault, your grace," Digby gulped bravely as he strove to disentangle himself from Emily's clutching arms and rise to face the man who must agree to give her to him in marriage. "You see, there was this idea. . . ."

"'Wise men say nothing in dangerous times,' John Seldon," Aunt Lucinda interjected hurriedly with a nod toward the unknowing Emily and the dowager quickly stepped in front of the would be confessed conspirator and cajoled, "Now, now, poor Ashley has had more than enough confusion for one evening. Anyone can see he's tired." She aimed her next words at her grandson, "You look like a death's head on a mop-stick actually," she observed not unkindly before addressing the whole room again. "I can see no need to setting him off again, so to speak, don't you all agree?"

Since anyone with eyes in his head could see that Avanoll truly was looking more than a little fagged as well as sorely confused and miserably embarrassed, the room cleared most rapidly. Aunt Lucinda went off to ponder the evening's events, Tansy escaped to her room to sift through Ashley's uncharacteristic volatile behavior and try to make some sense of it, the servants escaped to share this latest bit of domestic gossip with their less daring fellows who did not have the backbone to remain on the scene, and Emily, the wounded Digby leaning heavily on her arm, marched off with the remains of her righteous indignation slowly fading before the more pressing concerns of bathing up Digby's bruised nose and praying Comfort knew how to get those horrid blood stains out of her favorite blue cambric gown.

That left the dowager with the task of informing Avanoll that Digby and Emily had at last agreed to acknowledge a mutual passion that could only end happily in a trip to St. George's, Hanover Square, before the *ton* removed to Bath the end of July. Tansy's heart, she insisted, had not been in the least bruised as she considered Digby, an assertion she had already made to Avanoll, merely a very good friend. And that, no matter how hard her grandson questioned, was all she would say.

Much later, after washing away the grime of travel and filling his protesting stomach with some cold meat and cheese, the Duke sat slumped in his favorite chair in his private study and tried to make some sense of all that had happened.

Horatio, who just happened to be passing by the Duke's opened door and who could be counted on only for his unpredictability, padded into the chamber, sat himself down in front of Avanoll's chair and proceeded to attack an annoying itch on his shoulder with some energy.

The Duke directed a long, dispassionate stare at his uninvited guest and then said with remarkable *sang-froid,* "If you can recall George Brummell, Horatio, the man who assisted in your—er—rescue, I would like to tell you that he is a man whose word is considered law as pertains to personal grooming. Beau advocates regular bathing, indeed, he is most adamant about it. You might do well to profit from his wisdom and at the same time rid your ungrateful hide of some of its more irritating inhabitants."

Horatio chose not to be insulted but merely cocked his head to one side and returned the Duke's gaze with canine candor until once again itch came to scratch and he gave in to the impulse.

Avanoll sighed in exasperation. "You disturb my peace, you encroaching hound."

Aunt Lucinda was just then returning down the corridor

from a fruitless search for her needlework, heard this last exchange, and peeked in to coo, so Avanoll thought, quite sickeningly, "'His faithful dog shall bear him company.' Pope."

"Stuff and nonsense!" the Duke retorted. "He is only here to gloat over my disgrace." As Aunt Lucinda wisely retreated, Horatio yawned a wide doggie yawn, stretched himself out full length and rested his toad-eating head on his master's slippered feet as if to proclaim he was both totally at his ease and prepared to spend the rest of his evening giving aid and comfort to his former adversary.

"Oh, good grief!" Avanoll exclaimed and reached for the brandy decanter.

It really was a pity the Duke could not have been left to enjoy his solitude and have sufficient time to ponder the events that had brought him so low as to have only a hound, and not even his *own* hound, for company. For in time, experience of the Duke's ability to see himself in an honest light taken into account, he would have been able to laugh at himself. But life was not being particularly kind to Avanoll that night, for it wasn't too many minutes since his aunt's departure (only enough time, in fact, for Horatio to have set up a raucous snore or two), before Tansy, in search for her missing pet, entered the study.

Avanoll looked up at his cousin who was dressed head to toe in an unflattering pea-green robe from her governess days with her bare feet sticking out from the skirt and her long brown hair done up in a single plait down her back, and thought she was the most beautiful thing he had ever seen. Tansy, on the other hand, was thoroughly dismayed at having been caught out in such shabby garments and would have given everything she owned (not all that much, but important to her) to have been swallowed up then and there by a large hole that came supplied with a lid for shutting over herself.

As Tansy stuttered and mumbled something about Horatio, the Duke rose from his chair, tripped over the still dozing dog, and said curtly, "Wait, cousin. I had thought to put this off until the morning but there is no time like the present, I guess. Please come in for a moment for there is something I wish to say to you."

Here it comes, thought Tansy, I'm to be sacked. Fired, set off without a reference. Her courage faltered for a moment but she stifled her impulse to flee and took refuge in cold civility. "Very well, your grace. As upon another occasion you will insist on an interview when I am at a decided disadvantage. The first time I was cold, tired, and dowdy. Since tonight I am only tired and dowdy, I can see no reason to postpone what I am sure will be another uncomfortable interrogation." She crossed to the cavernous arm chair facing his and plunked herself down (unlike the dowager, Tansy's bare feet did touch the floor and she quickly raised them to hide her toes under the hem of her gown on the cushioned seat). "Proceed, cousin," she invited wearily.

"Er—perhaps you are right, my dear, the morning will suit just as well," Avanoll relented, but at the sound of that so-loved "my dear" Tansy lost all desire to cut the interview short and begged him to go on.

And so, as if the gods had specially designed this day for disaster, Avanoll went on. He had rehearsed his speech over and over on the mad dash from Newmarket, but the words deserted him now that he had need of them. Instead, he launched into a bracing pep talk on how Digby was too much of a green boy for her anyway and she should not be too overset by his defection.

"I never cared a rap for that child and you know it, Ashley. Do get to the point." In retrospect, Tansy was beginning to believe her first impulse had been the right one and she should have fled while she could.

"Uh—um, er, yes. *Yes,* of course your heart was not involved," he corrected himself hastily before blurting, "Have you thought at all of your future now that Emily is to be taken so neatly off our hands?"

So it had come at last, the dismissal. Well, if she were to go down, she would go down fighting. "I am sorry to say I have been so busy settling your sister I have not really devoted much time to my own future. What do you suggest, cousin, should I try to bag a husband of my own in the short time left in this Season or go directly back to governessing? As I have no dowry, I believe suitors for my hand will be rather thin on the ground, so I guess governessing it is."

"Damn you, madame, you are not so sorely straitened!" the Duke rallied. He came over to her chair, leaned down to put one hand on each upholstered armrest and peered deeply into her eyes. "You are bright, reasonably pretty, a good housekeeper, a tolerable hostess, and possess a clever, if outspoken, wit. Any man would be glad to have you."

Tansy looked up at the Duke's flushed face and an imp of

perversion invaded her tongue. "Any man, your grace?" she teased with a twinkle in her eyes. "Even *you*, Ashley?"

Avanoll straightened abruptly. "Yes, dammit all, even me! Why not? Why not me? My nose bother you?" he asked, immediately on his high ropes.

Tansy giggled. "Indeed not, the Benedict nose is highly distinguishing. Clearly my father's best feature. But you are not serious, Ashley, you couldn't be."

"I am deadly serious, Tansy. I am only five and thirty, so I am not too old or too young for you, don't you agree?"

"Certainly, sir," Tansy answered, tongue still in cheek. "I would say, upon reflection, your age seems to be just right."

Avanoll stopped his pacing and looked down at her from his great height. "Well, then? Just think of the advantages to such a match. You will no longer have to worry about your future, for one thing. There would be no need to concern yourself over your welcome into the family as you already have my entire relation at your knees and the servants of the house positively drooling over you. As for myself, I have grown rather used to having you about the house. We don't fight above once or twice a fortnight, and you don't hang on a man, spoil his life with demands for amusement and the like," he argued reasonably.

The twinkle in Tansy's eyes had all but disappeared. "Yes, I suppose we could rub along quite tolerably, your grace," she agreed dully.

Then Avanoll supplied the *coup de grâce:* "One final compensation we cannot overlook is the desirability of being called Tansy Benedict rather than Tansy Tamerlane. I should think you would be grateful to shed that sing-song handle." Tansy's head jerked up at this last statement and Avanoll took the motion for assent. "Then it's settled," he sighed. Really, proposing wasn't at all the mind-shaking, heart-stopping trial his cronies had talked it up to be. He relaxed visibly. "We'll be married next week, before Emily can say we have thrown a damper on her moment of glory."

"No."

Now Avanoll's head jerked. "What did you say?" he rasped incredulously.

"I said, *no*," Tansy replied with some spirit, twin flags of color waving in the cheeks of her otherwise ashen face. "No. Negative. On the contrary. Out of the question. I decline," she added sarcastically. "Cognizant of the great honor, your condescension, etc, but *no!*" And while the Duke was still striving to raise his lower jaw from its half-mast position, she quit the room, Horatio hard on her heels.

Chapter Twenty-one

THE SUN was well up when the Duke rose the next morning, his head cleared of drink this time, but groggy none the less due to the fact that it was almost dawn before he got to bed at all. As he stood glowering into the mirror above his dressing table, Farnley was pushed to remark that a face such as that was apt to crack the glass, bringing on seven years of sure bad luck.

"Six years, nine months, and three or four days, Farnley," his grace corrected.

The valet was confused, for he had never heard of this particular omen. "Sir?" he questioned.

Avanoll sighed. "Miss Tamerlane arrived in March. It is now late June. I do not believe any further explanation is necessary."

Farnley bobbed his head in enthusiastic agreement, then wisely handed the duke his cravat in silence. Suddenly the door to his dressing room, that most private of sanctums a gentleman can hope to have, was thrown open and Aunt Lucinda, draperies at full mast, came sailing in to exclaim, "'It was not for nothing that the raven was just now croaking on my left hand.' Plautus."

"What idiocy is this?" Avanoll bellowed in confused rage.

In answer his aunt stuck a piece of folded foolscap in his face, nearly taking the tip off his Benedict nose. "'I have found it!' Archimedes," she pronounced in tones of high drama.

Avanoll grabbed at the paper, more in self-defense than anything else, warning dryly, "Don't carry on so, Aunt, you'll do yourself an injury." He then retired to the window, where the light was better, and unfolded the crumpled note—for he could tell it was a note—and began to read. Seeing at once that it was addressed to him, he shot his aunt a quick look, knowing full well she had already read it.

179

Dear Ashley the note began quite simply, and then went on to thank him, in the most formal of terms, for his gracious extension of aid when *she* (by now he was sure the note was from Tansy) was sorely in need of it.

She asked only that he look kindly on a match between Emily and Digby and put himself out to be nice to the servants—pointing out that it would be only polite to learn their names as a start. In the same paragraph she begged that, since it would be impossible to take him along, could Horatio remain under Avanoll's roof ("he adores marrow-bones, but insists upon burying them under your Grandmama's bed, so please try to discourage him"). The note ended with her assurances that she would soon find a suitable post, along with denials of any need for any of them to worry a jot about her in the future. This last bit of heroic sacrifice fell short of the mark, however, when the Duke detected what looked suspiciously like dried tear stains on the paper.

"Hell and damnation!" he shouted, crumpling the note into an untidy ball and flinging it in the general direction of the fire. Hair still uncombed and untied cravat flying, he set off down the hall for the dowager's room, with Aunt Lucinda in hot pursuit. Farnley headed in the opposite direction, quickly ascertained that his beloved Pansy was also among the missing, and boldly joined his master in the Duchess's chambers just in time to hear Aunt Lucinda say sulkily, "'There are some who bear a grudge even to those that do them good.' Pilpay."

"Do me *good?* Oh, that fairly ties it, doesn't it? You, Aunt, and you, me dear, *frail* old grandmother, have between the two of you with your machinations bungled my *entire life,*" he said, glaring at them both with venom and—at last, at least verbally—showing some resemblance to his sister Emily.

Obviously the story of the plot was "out," and just as clearly Avanoll did not like being moved about by his female relatives like a pawn in a perverted chess game. He turned to his aunt in astonishment.

"Only a complete ninnyhammer such as you could believe for one moment that my current position has even a mote of 'goodness' about it."

The dowager, whose day so far had been one simply crammed full of joyous plotting and scheming, took a moment to inform her grandson that they—she and his aunt—had between themselves succeeded in bringing to a head a situation that he, being a lowly and somewhat *slow* mere male, would have allowed to drag on for heaven only knew how long.

"Within the span of a few weeks we have settled Emily and forced you to admit to a feeling for Tansy that is more than cousinly. I have no doubt you all will soon be quite comfortably leg-shackled, and I will be free to retire to my estates to wait in peace for the arrival of my first great-grandchildren," she observed smugly.

Avanoll ran his hand through his already disheveled crop of curls and said tightly, "Emily and her moonling calf may be all right and tight, I grant you, but with Tansy gone to ground, God only knows where, and me about to go to the gallows for the cold-blooded murder of my aunt and grandmother, I fail to see why you should look so pleased with yourselves."

"I knew it would come to this," wailed a distraught Farnley.

"'I would rather be ignorant than wise in the foreboding of evil.' Aeschylus," Aunt Lucinda gritted.

"Beggin' your pardon, ma'am, but I can only calls 'em as I sees 'em, so they say," Farnley retorted, quite overset by the defection of his lady-love. "Besides," he added, with commendable if self-serving foresight, "I'm just trying to serve my master, poor demon-ridden soul that he is."

"'There is also a sure reward for faithful silence.' Horace," his tormentor quipped acidly, and the valet retired from the field in defeat.

There was silence in the room for a few moments while the Duke paced, the servant moped, the aunt preened herself, and the dowager sat back and enjoyed the show. Finally she broke the uneasy peace by asking if Avanoll knew *why* Tansy had taken flight so precipitously.

He hung his head. "I believe it was something I said, but for the life of me I didn't know the thought of marriage to me was so repugnant she would rather run away than face it."

The dowager smiled. It was a wickedly satisfied smile that lit her eyes and curled the corners of her mouth with unholy glee. "It was not the marriage Tansy flew from, but the proposal. If memory serves, and I must admit understanding little of Tansy's hysterical mouthings this morning, I believe your declaration lacked for something in romance, Ashley."

The Duke flushed an angry red and retorted, "Well, what would you have me do, Grandmama? Say I love her and take the chance she would turn me down anyway? I would have confessed more than a companionable affection immediately if she had only given me some sign she returned my feelings."

"'The cat would eate fish, and would not wet her feete.' Heywood," his aunt purred archly.

The Duke ignored this remark and zeroed in on his grandparent's hints. "Tansy came to you? *Ah, ha!* Then you know where she has gone." He loped over to leer down at the old woman and warned, "Tell me her direction you crafty old crone, or I'll cut off your sugarplums for a month."

The dowager stalled for time, arranging her shawl about her thin shoulders before saying, "She and that ninny Pansy are in my closed coach, heading north to Olivia Rockingham's. You know where she is situated, don't you? I sent them off with some farradiddle about companioning Olivia, who needs a keeper far more than she needs a dogsbody, secure in the knowledge that you would have the pair of them back safe in Avanoll House before the day is out. That is, if you don't bungle it again, grandson."

"And you think that simply by saying 'I love you,' Tansy will fall on my neck and agree to become my wife?" Ashley asked doubtfully.

"'Love conquers all.' Virgil," his aunt suggested.

The Duke of Avanoll, that mature man about town, that notable whip, excellent sportsman, and admired statesman, stood like a gawking schoolboy and blushed to the roots of his hair.

His aunt sighed. "'I loved thee, Atthis, once—long, long ago; long long ago—the memory still is clear.' Sappho."

Enough was enough, and too much was definitely too much. Avanoll quit the room, with Farnley close behind saying he would ready his grace's traveling clothes and order the racing curricle. Left behind in the dowager's chamber, two old ladies clung to each other and chortled with a depth of humor denied them for many a long day until tears of joy ran down their cheeks.

While the Duke was springing nimbly up behind his spirited team of four (only a nonpareil such as he or a man deeply in love would dare drive a curricle with four in hand), the dowager's coach—with a deliberately plodding Leo at the reins—was rumbling along the North Road with its two dispirited occupants.

Tansy's mind was full of conflicting thoughts as she remembered she had yet to see the Elgin Marbles, or take in the theatre on a night when the great Kean was to trod the boards. Oh, well, she could put paid to excursions like that now and forevermore. Perhaps she had been hasty—maybe even guilty of looking a gift horse in the mouth—in turning down Avanoll's cut and dried offer. But, no. She could not endure a one-sided love any more than she could a completely loveless marriage.

If only Pansy would cease her sobbing that had only just moments ago finally diminished from a loud caterwauling that had nearly driven Tansy to distraction for the entire passage across Hampstead Heath!

In time the coach was pulled into a small wayside inn—none too soon for Tansy, who was experiencing an almost overpowering need to put some space between herself and her watering-pot abigail. Since assurances that she would be returned from Mrs. Rockingham's with Leo had not stifled her tears, and threats to box her ears had met with similar failure, physical separation for a few temper-cooling minutes was the only avenue left open.

While Pansy, sniffling and gulping, dragged herself off behind Leo, who was giving orders to have the horses seen to and a private parlor laid with luncheon, Tansy took off in the opposite direction at a bracing pace that ended abruptly when she turned a corner and literally barged into a well-dressed gentleman just approaching from the side of the stables.

"Why, stap me if it ain't Lady Emily's rescuer!" a voice cried out, and Tansy lifted her head to see the grinning face of Godfrey Harlow looking down at her. Since he had grasped her by both elbows to halt her possible spill to the ground, Tansy was unable for the moment to do more than remain still and return his greeting.

"I appreciate your saying you're happy to see me, miss, though I doubt I'm as welcome as the flowers in spring, but I must admit I have thought of you more than once since that fateful day in March. Thanks to you I took myself off to Ireland and, would you believe it, I am now on my honeymoon with a grand, grand girl. Rich as Golden Ball she is, and with no smell of the shop," he went on, still not relinquishing his hold.

Tansy looked him up and down, taking note of his rather foppish finery, and summoned up a weak smile, "I am happy one of us has come about so nicely."

Another man would have realized his joy was one-sided, but not Mr. Harlow. Carried along by the mood of the moment he went on amicably, "And I owe all my present happiness to *you*, dear lady!"

With that he swooped down to deliver an exuberant smacking kiss right on Tansy's startled lips, a kiss that ended abruptly when a hand of iron pulled Mr. Harlow about before a fist of similar strength caused his body to take up an acquaintance with the dirt pathway.

Tansy put a hand to her head and leaned weakly against the stable wall. "Oh, Ashley, you've done it *again!*" she groaned.

"I say," came a voice from the ground, "who the devil are you?"

"Emily's brother," Tansy supplied gently.

"Oh," Godfrey Harlow said hollowly. "Isn't it a bit late for revenge?"

At Avanoll's quelling look, Godfrey prudently skittered back a few feet on his haunches while Tansy, now quite beside herself with rage, performed the introductions and explained that Mr. Harlow was just thanking her for a service she had performed for him some months past.

Just then a Junoesque creature with flaming red hair came down upon them with a wrathful look on her freckled face and demanded to know "jist what the divil is goin' on here?"

Avanoll tried to speak, but had trouble locating his voice. This mattered little to the woman, who had already single-handedly hoisted her slight husband to his feet and was dusting him off with a vigorous hand and dusting him down with an equally vigorous tongue.

"I can't leave you alone for a minute, can I now, Godfrey, me love? Come off with Kathleen now and I'll be hearin' the whole of it over a nice cup of tea."

Harlow made a hasty bow and went off with the love of his life, his hands flapping wildly as he endeavored to talk himself back into her good graces.

Avanoll looked after the pair, well and truly puzzled, while Tansy held on to the stable wall, convulsed as she was with laughter. "Poor besotted fool, he'll not have an easy life with that one, I wager," she chortled.

Seeing his quarry in good humor, the Duke dismissed Harlow and his outrageous wife and concentrated on making it up with Tansy. He held out his hand—the same hand that had milled down two innocent men in less than four and twenty hours—and pleaded, "Please, dear, stop all this nonsense and come home with me. I know you love me."

So the dowager had betrayed her! "*How dare you!*" Tansy shrieked, and bolted for the road. Avanoll caught up with her just as she reached the highway and stopped any further recriminations with a sound kiss. When he at last lifted his head, Tansy opened her mouth to tell him a thing or two but he cut her off by claiming her lips yet again, so gently and with such vast feeling in his embrace that her arms had no choice but to curl up and around his neck.

When he was sure he had at last robbed her of the strength to spurn him he lifted his lips slightly and blazed a path of kisses and gentle nips along her cheek to her ear. Once there he whispered, "I love you, too, you know. Quite desperately, in fact."

Instead of answering in kind, Tansy dredged up enough spirit to return a bit of his deviltry. "You took your sweet time letting me in on the secret, your grace," she suggested insolently.

"Oh, and when did you know *you* cared for *me?*" Avanoll retorted with a nasty grin.

Tansy blushed, then recovered and said with complete candor, "From the time I sat behind a nag named Horace and first looked up into those horrid, mocking eyes of yours peering out at me from behind the Benedict nose. I was immediately resigned to donning my caps and living the rest of my life as a female ape-leader, my charges all agog at my secret sighs and silent tears, knowing me an unlucky victim of unrequited love. It was very romantic, but hardly practical.

"That's why I fell in with your inane suggestion to chaperon Emily so readily. I had hoped familiarity would either cure me of my affliction or—wonder of wonders—allow you time to notice all my sterling qualities as I made myself, as you so meanly guessed, indispensable to you." So much honesty nearly over-whelmed Tansy, and she buried her head against his broad shoulder.

Avanoll chuckled wryly. "As for your charms, my pet, I noticed them all right. Me and half of London. I never much cared for crowds. I think I counted on your good sense, seeing through all those fops and halflings surrounding you morning 'til night like barnacles on a hull. Then, at the end of the Season, when we retired to my house in the country I would have pleaded my case.

"Of course," he admitted truthfully, "I didn't *know* this was my plan until I was wearing the willow at Newmarket, but when I was finally honest with myself I realized I was lost from the moment you alluded that I was a blundering idiot—which is the same as saying from the moment we met."

"You were—acting like an idiot, that is. You were also arrogant, overbearing, disgustingly objectionable, and irritatingly . . ."

"Drat you, woman. Will you always be so brutally honest?"

"Yes, my dear," she replied, gaining confidence by his declaration of affection, "I shall. Even now, I am afraid. It seems debutantes of six and twenty are very practical types. I feel bound to point out that at the moment my shoes are soaking through in this muddy road, I am hungry, tired, and nearly overwhelmed with happiness all at the same time. Still, my discomfort is winning out.

"Is it possible for us to climb upon your curricle that I see back there in the inn-yard, and leave Leo and Pansy to make their way back themselves?"

"Leo, Pansy, and Farnley," the Duke corrected. "You cannot know what I have been through with that carrion crow riding beside me all the way from Grosvenor Square, not to mention the sound tongue-lashing I had to take from Dunny—I mean *Dunstan*—before ever I was allowed to leave at all," he told her, kissing the tip of her nose.

"But first things first. Grandmama informed me it was my lack of form that sent you fleeing in the first place. Therefore, before we go another step, I must ask formally for your hand."

So saying, the staid member of Parliament pulled out his snowy linen handkerchief and proceeded to, with a fine flourish, spread it on the muddy roadway. Before Tansy could stop him, he was kneeling in broad daylight on the fringe of the heavily-traveled Great North Road.

"My dearest Tansy," he began solemnly, "for a long time now I have regarded you with deep respect and admiration—admiration that has deepened to devotion. I pray you to consider my petition and agree to become my Duchess, making me the luckiest and happiest of men."

"Oh, Ashley, get up, do," Tansy giggled. "There is a rider approaching."

"Hang the man. I'll not move until I get my answer."

"Good God, here comes a sporting curricle. We'll be run down! Let loose my hand, Ashley, and get up."

The Duke remained where he had knelt. "My answer first, if you please, madam."

Tansy looked about with no little agitation and finally sputtered, "Oh, confound it all, *yes*."

"What? I'm afraid I was not attending. The mud is penetrating to my knee and my attention wandered," Avanoll excused himself. "Would you please to repeat that last part?"

"I said, yes, you lovable loose-screw. Yes, yes, *yes!* A thousand times yes. Only move or I'll be a widow before I can ever become a wife!"

In one motion Avanoll rose, lifted her high in his arms, and walked to the curricle where Leo, his face beet-red and nearly choking from the effort of trying to hide his laughter, was barely holding the four matched bays in check.

"Turn your back, Leo. You've enough sport for one day." The groom turned obediently. "Madam," Avanoll said, "I claim my betrothal kiss."

Leo, sneaking a quick look over his shoulder, grinned broadly at the sight of his master thoroughly kissing the nice young Miss Tansy. He then turned to direct a stony stare at the farmer who had stopped dead in his tracks, completely forgetting he had to get his only horse to the blacksmith or there'd be no plowing tomorrow, and another at the young gentleman in the smart black-and-yellow curricle who was holding onto his reins with both hands—a gold rimmed quizzing glass stuck to his eye.

"Beggin' yer grace's pardon, but we seem to be, er, puttin' on a bit of a show, like," Leo whispered hoarsely.

Avanoll raised his head and looked rather dazedly at his audience. "Bladesham, y'r servant sir," he said as calmly as if he were just passing the Viscount on Bond Street. "Like to introduce you to my affianced wife, Miss Tansy Tamerlane."

"Ch-Ch-Charmed, I'm sure, ma'am," stammered his lordship, his horses dancing as he released one hand to tip his curly-brimmed beaver. "Wish you happy." Then he seemed to comprehend the import of the situation. By Gadfrey, he'd be the center of it all at White's tonight with this story, hang that visit to his Uncle Chester anyway.

"You there," he called to the farmer. "Shove yourself off, I've need of some room to turn my pair." The farmer looked glad for any excuse to quit the scene and its balmy gentry. Kicking his poor horse in its skinny flanks, he bounced off down the road, never once looking back.

"Where to, Bladesham? Have you forgotten something in London?" Avanoll inquired innocently.

"No. *Yes!*" answered the Viscount. "Recall an engagement. Bad *ton* to neglect my fellows when they wish to gather. No fourth at cards, you know. Must fly now," he ended desperately before adding, "Felicitations again, old fellow." With a turn that spoke more of haste than whipmanship, his lordship was off.

Avanoll threw back his head and roared. "That turn won't get him any votes for the Four Horse Club, I can tell you. Ah, you're good for me Tansy. I feel young and gay and quite deliriously happy. And you can't back out now, my love. By the time we get to Grosvenor Square, half of London will have already had the whole of it from Bladesham."

"Nor can you withdraw, your grace," Tansy pointed out, "for I am thoroughly compromised, besides being able to sue for breach of promise. You claimed me as *fiancée* before witnesses. Isn't that right, Leo?"

"Me? I haven't heard a word if you don't wish, your grace," Leo avowed fervently. "Though I think it downright balmy to pass up a right 'un like the miss, your grace, if I may be so bold."

Avanoll laughed again as Tansy calmly thanked Leo and told him she thought he was a right 'un too, "a real prince of a fellow," before the Duke sent him off to the inn to drive Pansy and Farnley back to town while he and Tansy followed in the curricle.

Once Leo was out of sight, Avanoll hoisted Tansy up to the seat and joined her, but another kiss seemed in order before they set out on their journey. As the two new lovers blissfully indulged in what seemed a very edifying pastime, the South Bound Mail Coach pelted by them, loaded to the rails with outside passengers.

"Coo," one passenger called, relinquishing part of his two-handed hold on the coach roof to point out something to a fellow traveler. "Now there's somethin' you don't see everyday, Chumford: two gentry morts a-kissin' and huggin' out in the open for all to see, just like regular folk. *Give her another one, sport!*" the man had time to yell before the coach rounded the next bend.

Over Tansy's embarrassed protests, Avanoll proceeded to do just that.

By just a little past nine of that same day, the dowager and Aunt Lucinda stood in the foyer of Avanoll House while behind two closed doors two separate sets of lovers were allowed a few short moments alone. Hand to heart, a sign of deep emotional involvement, Aunt Lucinda at last gushed, "'Love looks not with the eyes, but with the mind, and therefore is wing'd Cupid painted blind.' Shakespeare."

The dowager answered this observation with her usual vague,

"Yes, yes, Lucinda," before suddenly jerking up her head—an expression of horror on her face. "Shakespeare? *Sh-Shakespeare!* Oh, no Lucinda, say it isn't so! You haven't been dipping into my private library?"

Aunt Lucinda smiled serenely, so sure her little surprise had gladdened the dowager's heart—Shakespeare being the lady's favorite poet, and nodded her head in a gesture of farewell before turning to mount the stairs.

The dowager took a step toward her and ordered, "Lucinda, you just march yourself back over here and we'll have this thing out right now and for all time. I will *house you* once Ashley is wed, I will *clothe you,* I will *feed you,* I will even *allow you* use of my library in your asinine and never-ending search for quotes. But I will not, I repeat, *will not* countenance the wanton bantering about of Shakespeare's immortal words whenever you wish to remark on such subjects as cinch bugs on my roses or the proper time to turn sheets. Do you hear me, Lucinda?" The offended woman nodded sadly. "Good," said the satisfied Duchess. "It's late. You may now retire."

Aunt Lucinda again made to mount the stairs, this time crooning softly, "'To sleep: perchance to . . .'" She cut off the end of the Hamlet quote as the dowager began to make noises like an angry bear and improvised quickly as she hastened her ascent, "'To err is human, to forgive divine.' Pope."

"What a maddening loose-screw; sixty and two and with all the brains of a chamber pot and twice the brass," lamented the dowager before lifting her skirts and striding toward the drawing room, determination lending speed to her stiff limbs.

"Ashley," she called out as she burst open the doors and stepped inside. "Grandson, if you will but leave off pawing that poor child a moment I have a proposition to put to you both. I will turn over to your first-born those cozy estates in Hampshire as well as the coal mines your grandfather won so long ago at Faro, which are now producing greater profits every year, if you will but agree to making Lucinda a part of your household."

Tansy giggled. "What is she up to this time, your grace?"

"What is she up to?" the dowager parroted distractedly. "I'll tell you what that feather-wit is up to: she has set her pointed little teeth at chewing up and spitting back her own interpretations of the Bard himself. It's sacrilege, I tell you. And if you condemn me to a lifetime of listening to her, you will have murdered me as surely as if you had stuck a knife in my heart.

I'm not a young woman anymore, Tansy," she pleaded, falling back on the excuse of her advanced years. "Have pity on me, please. I'll toss in my ruby pendant to sweeten the pot. You can have it made into a ring if your first is a boy."

Tansy stood on tiptoe and whispered into her beloved's ear. He smiled and turned to address the older woman.

"Tansy, the dear darling, may have a better suggestion for you, Grandmama. Keep your pendant and your coal mines and all but one of your Hampshire estates to dispose of later on as you wish. Simply turn over one of the smaller homes—retaining control of the land, of course—to Aunt Lucinda, and promise to provide her with a generous allowance for the rest of her life on the condition she never darken your door again. It should suit her to feel more independent as mistress of her own household once more, besides giving her a room in which to place her horrid chairs."

The Duchess grinned and clapped her gnarled hands in glee. "Why didn't I think of that? Not that I shouldn't have presently if I were not so overset. You are quite capital, Tansy; you too, Ashley. I shall talk to my man of business first thing in the morning and order him to have all in train by the end of the week. She can return for the weddings; never let it be said I was not magnanimous. I shall also have him sign over those mines to you both as a wedding present.

"Tut, tut," she warned as they made to protest. "You've earned it. You may go back to what you were doing now. Goodnight, my dears, for you have made me a very happy old lady." She left then, pausing only once at the door to shake her head in seeming amazement. "Getting that dratted woman to do justice to dear Will's pearls of wisdom would be about as possible as teaching Horatio to sing Italian opera," she said to no one in particular.

Ashley and Tansy shared a smile, content that every last loose end had now been neatly tied up—at least for a while—and obediently returned to their earlier occupation. With bodies softly pressing together and arms firmly entwined, their lips alternately advanced and engaged or retreated to whisper inane love words—quite expected murmurings when spoken by the very young (like the two lovebirds in the small salon), but uncommonly touching when uttered by two people who have had to wait so long to share the heady giddiness of true love.

If Aunt Lucinda were there, and it must be noted her presence was not missed, she quite possibly might have said, "'All's well that ends well.' Heywood."

And she would have been quite right.